To
Laurie
Happy Trails
Chuck
_____

JACK MONTANA

A NOVEL BY CHUCK MORRIS

JACK MONTANA

Tate Publishing & Enterprises

Published by Tate Publishing & Enterprises, LLC
127 E. Trade Center Terrace | Mustang, Oklahoma 73064 USA
1.888.361.9473 | www.tatepublishing.com

Tate Publishing is committed to excellence in the publishing industry. The company reflects the philosophy established by the founders, based on Psalm 68:11,
"The Lord gave the word and great was the company of those who published it."

Published in the United States of America

ISBN: 978-1-61663-754-5
Fiction: Westerns
10.07.19

DEDICATION

I dedicate this book to my family.

My brother Raymond, who loved to read about the west.

My sisters—Mae, Mary and Betty.

And my lovely wife, Debra.

CHAPTER 1

The year was 1862. The end of the Civil War was still fresh in most people's thoughts and speech. On this chilly spring morning, Dan Walker was standing on the large, wooden front porch of his Montana home, enjoying a hot cup of coffee and drinking in the beautiful scenery of his vast empire, as he did every morning after breakfast. Within the next forty-five minutes, he and his crew of ranch hands would begin their busy day. Martha, his wife of thirty years, came out of the house to enjoy a few minutes with him before she began her busy day. She stood beside her husband, and they lingered there in silence for some time.

"Martha," he said suddenly. His deep voice cut through the stillness like a knife, startling her momentarily.

"Yes, Dan?"

"What is that small speck of a shape way out there in the distance?"

"Why, I don't know," she said as she strained her eyes, looking out in the direction that he was pointing. "It's so small I can hardly even see it at all. Maybe it's a clump of grass or something like that."

"No," he said. "Whatever it is, it's moving and seems to be getting bigger. It must be heading this way."

"Maybe it's a cow or a horse."

"No. It isn't that either. I don't see any dust blowing up behind whatever it is, so it must be somethin' small and moving very slowly."

Martha shrugged her shoulders and turned to go inside. "Well, I better get back inside and get busy if I want to get anything done today."

About that time, Hank Shaw, Dan's right-hand man and foreman, came out of the bunkhouse and joined him on the porch.

"Morning, chief. You got any special orders for today, or do you want me and the boys to finish branding that small herd of cows that we brought in yesterday?"

Deep in thought, Dan didn't answer right away, so Hank looked out in the same direction as Dan to see what he was staring at.

"Can you see what it is? Oh. Morning, Hank."

"Can't tell exactly, chief. It's too far away for me to see."

Finally, Dan turned away abruptly. "Well, guess we'll find out what it is sooner or later if it keeps coming in our direction. Meanwhile, we'd best get busy branding those cows."

"Okay, chief. I'll go roust out the boys and get started."

As Hank stepped off the porch and started for the bunkhouse, Dan turned to take a last look out in the distance. "Beginning to look like a person," he said aloud. After another minute, Dan left the porch and walked over to the corral, where Hank and the crew were heating up the branding iron.

Rusty Warren, a young boy of fourteen whom Dan had taken in and hired a year earlier, had roped a calf and was dragging it to the fire so they could brand it. Dan was sitting on the top rail of the corral gate and was ready to jump down and help out with the branding when he heard Martha's voice and turned to see what she wanted.

"Dan," she said. "This young man wants to see the ramrod of this outfit. He says he needs a job real bad."

Dan almost fell off the fence at what he saw. Martha was standing there with tears in her eyes, and beside her was a little boy. He was dirty and ragged and looked half starved to death. His hair was bright red, long and shaggy, his face was so freckled that you couldn't have touched it anywhere without hitting a target. The boy had a rumpled, old, felt hat that he held in front of him with both hands.

Dan jumped down from the fence. "Is that right, cowboy? You lookin' for a job?

"Yes, sir," the boy replied. "I'd be mighty beholden to ya. I ain't ate a lick in two, three days."

Dan looked at his wife. "Martha, take the boy inside and give him some breakfast."

Almost sobbing, she said, "I told him to come in the house and I'd fix him something to eat, but he insisted on 'talking to the boss of this outfit first.' He doesn't want charity."

Dan just about broke into tears himself. He called to the men in the corral, "Go on with your work, boys. I got more important business to take care of." Turning back to the boy, he said, "I'm the ramrod of this outfit, and I'm about starved to death. Come on in the house. After we eat and have our coffee, we'll talk."

The boy smiled real big. "Yes, sir!"

Inside, Martha got a plate and heaped it up with beans, cornbread, and gravy. Then she set a big glass of milk beside it. At the other end of the table, she set a cup of coffee for Dan. "Come and get it, men," she said.

The boy sat down and began to eat. They could tell by the way he dove into that big plate of food that it had indeed been awhile since he'd had any sort of nourishment. He became so involved in the food before him that he wasn't aware of anything going on around him. At that point in time, he was in his own little world.

Dan and Martha watched in amazement.

"What do you think?" Martha asked.

"I don't know. I guess we'll have to play it by ear and see what we can find out about him."

Dan sat down at the other end of the table and began sipping his coffee as he watched the boy eat. Martha stood and watched the boy and her husband. She knew her husband inside and out, and by watching the expression on his face, she knew what he was thinking about.

They only had one child, a little girl, eight years old: Cindy. She was away at this time, visiting one of her aunts. They planned to send her back east to attend one of the all-girl schools that was highly recommended when she finished elementary school. It was a school that taught higher grades with the option of continuing one's education through another four years of finishing school. Dan and Martha both loved living in Billings, Montana, and they especially liked their ranch here. However, Montana was not very populated, and they wanted their daughter to have the best education possible. Soon after Cindy was born, they found that they couldn't have any more children. Dan was just about brokenhearted over that, and being the kind of man that he is, he tried hiding it because he didn't want Martha to feel bad about not giving him a son.

Now, watching her husband as he looked longingly at this little boy, she knew exactly what his heart was aching for. He was just about the right age to be Dan's son, if they could've had one. Thinking to herself, Martha figured the boy to be about eight years old, the same age as their Cindy.

Finally wiping his mouth with a napkin, the boy said, "Wow, ma'am. That's the best chow I've ever ate. Thanks."

Now Dan took charge. "What's your name, son?"

The boy made no effort to answer the question or show that he even heard the question.

Again, Dan asked, "What is your name, son?"

Seeing that he was being pressed to answer, he said, "I don't really know, sir. I've lived with different families all my life. Each person

I lived with called me by a different name. I didn't like any of the people or the names they called me by."

After a pause, Dan asked, "What are some of the names they gave you?"

Without flinching or batting an eye, the boy answered. "Sonofabitch, turdhead, bastard, shi—"

"That's enough." Dan interrupted and held up his hand to stop the boy from repeating any more names. Despite the tragedy of the boy's dilemma, Martha could hardly keep from laughing. However, Dan was furious.

"Well, you won't be called any of those names while you're under my roof," he promised. Softening, Dan could see that the boy was very tired. "Martha," he said, "will you fix a bath for our guest? Then take him to Cindy's room. She won't mind him using it while she's gone."

"Of course," she said. Then, to the boy, she offered, "Come with me, son. We'll get you fixed up." It felt odd to hear herself say "son," but it felt good. She led the boy to the tub in the chamber room and asked if he needed help. She felt that his first impulse was to say yes, but then he said, "No, ma'am. Thank you." He wouldn't get undressed 'till she left the room.

She waited outside a few minutes to give him time to get into the tub and then stepped back inside to get his clothes so she could wash them. She had gotten one of Dan's shirts so he could sleep in it, and when she picked up his clothes, she said, "After you get out of the tub, you can wear this nightshirt of Dan's until your clothes are washed and dried."

As she walked behind him, she caught a glimpse of his back and was shocked to tears. There were large welts and bruises all over his sides and back. Instantly, she wanted to grab him up and comfort him, but she knew he wouldn't stand for that. He wouldn't like being pampered or pitied. She left the room and prepared to wash his clothes. First, she searched his pockets to make sure they were empty. Again, she was stunned at what she found. There were pictures of three men on a wanted poster—all horrible, evil-looking men. The boy had evidently been carrying the poster around for a long time because it was all faded and worn from being folded inside his pocket. After looking at the poster of the three men for a few minutes, she knew that the law was after them. *Oh my,* she thought. *What a terrible life this poor boy has had to live.*

After putting the boy's dirty clothes in a washtub of hot, soapy water to soak, she took the poster into the kitchen and showed it to Dan. She told him about the bruises, welts, and scars that she had seen on his back and sides. "What do you make of all this?" she asked.

"Darned if I know. I just hope these men aren't any blood kin to the boy."

When the boy's clothes were dry, Martha put the poster back in his pocket where she found it. "The poor boy's so worn out that he probably won't even think about us seeing the picture of those three men," she mentioned to Dan.

"Just as well," Dan agreed. "We'll have to take it real slow with him or he might just take off. The Lord only knows what would happen to him then."

They didn't have to discuss what to do about the boy. They both felt that God had placed him in their care. They were willing to be patient with the boy, and if he would allow it, they would raise him up in their Christian home and see that he was well educated and had all the love and family that he needed. They wouldn't allow themselves to even think that this venture might turn out to be a nightmare, that the boy might turn out to be a killer like those men in the poster that he carried around with him all the time. What they saw was a skinny little boy with flaming red hair and freckles—so many that you couldn't count them—and he desperately needed help.

After the boy got out of the tub, he put on Dan's shirt that Martha gave him to wear while his clothes were drying. It was growing late in the evening, and he was very tired, so he went into Cindy's room and lay on the bed and fell fast asleep.

Tired as he had been, the boy was up the next morning at the break of day and seated at the breakfast table. He bowed his head while Dan gave thanks to God for their food and good fortune.

After a hearty breakfast, he asked, "Sir, when can we talk about that job?"

"No need to be in a hurry," Dan said. "First we have to go into town and get you some decent clothes. Then we got to figure out what job you can handle. Meantime, you can just be our guest. Okay?"

"I guess so, but," the boy added determinedly, "I always pay my way by doing my share. I don't take no handouts."

Dan looked the boy right in the eyes. "I knew you'd say that, partner, and that's the kind of man I like. You're all right in my book."

Dan hooked the team up to the buckboard, helped the boy climb up on the seat, and they were off. Neither of the two spoke all the way to town, but they both did a whole lot of thinking.

No real record of the boy's past was ever found, but after piecing together what he told them, they had a pretty good idea of what his life had been like. He was born somewhere back east. His mother, probably a woman of the street going by what he could remember of her, took care of him until he was weaned from her breast. She then abandoned him on the doorstep of a stranger's house. From there, he was abused and traded from one family to another. That was the way his life went. Finally, he wound up somewhere in Montana. One night, he was taken into a saloon by an outlaw he was staying with, after beating him within an inch of his life, the man got drunk and told him, "Get out of my sight. I'm sick and tired of looking at ya." The boy ran out of the saloon in fear of his life. No one was paying any attention to him, so when he saw some horses outside tied to the hitch rail, he climbed up on one of them and rode out of town.

The boy didn't have any idea of where he was or where to go, so he just held onto the saddle horn to keep from falling off. He let the horse have his head and go any direction he wanted to go. Eventually, after a couple of days of no food or water, he became so tired and weary that he passed out and fell off the horse. After a while, he came to and saw that the horse was gone, so he started walking. He was tired and very weary, but he kept stumbling along until he wandered onto Dan and Martha's ranch.

Dan and the boy drove the buckboard down the dirt street of Billings. They tied up at the hitch rail in front of Jerry Reeves's general store. When they went inside, Jerry was busy with a customer. Dan noticed that Jerry and the man he was waiting on were the only two people in the building. The man was a hard-looking case and was arguing with Jerry over the price of the merchandise he was buying. Dan was a good judge of character and had seen a lot of mean people in his lifetime. This man gave every appearance of an outlaw the way he looked and acted. Dan figured that the man's intention had been to take the merchandise and leave without paying for it. He walked over and stood beside the man.

"Hello, Jerry," he said while looking the man in the eyes. "How's business?"

The man shifted his eyes away from Dan's stare.

Jerry gave Dan a grateful glance. "Pretty good, Dan. I'll be with you in a minute."

The man took some money from his pocket and paid for the merchandise. As he turned to leave, he saw the boy. Looking at Dan, he demanded, "Whose kid is that?"

Stepping between the man and the boy, Dan said, "That's my boy. Who wants to know?"

The man shifted his eyes away from Dan. "Jist thought I'd seen him somewhere before," he said. Then the man turned and walked out the door.

"What was that all about?" Jerry asked.

"I have no idea, Jerry. What was going on before we came in?"

"Well, the man came in and picked out what he wanted. Then when he brought it to the counter, he started saying how outrageous the prices were. When I told him he was welcome to go somewhere else, he got mad and started arguing with me. I sure was glad to see you come walking in because I think he was going to leave without paying for his supplies."

"That's what I was thinking. That's why I broke up the argument."

Jerry looked at the boy and then at Dan. He knew that he and Martha only had one child. "If you don't mind me asking, whose boy is he?"

Knowing the boy was sensitive, Dan said, "This here is my new ranch hand. We just came into town to get some new working clothes."

Jerry took the hint and, looking at the boy, said, "Howdy. Glad to meet you. You guys look around and pick out whatever you want."

Dan and the boy looked around the store and picked out a pair of boots, a couple pairs of jeans, and some shirts that the boy liked.

After they had finished shopping and were on the way back home, Dan questioned the boy. "That man back there, do you know him?"

"No, sir."

"Have you ever seen him before?"

"No, sir."

Dan didn't want to ask the boy too many questions, so they rode the rest of the way home in silence. Later at the ranch and while trying on his new clothes, he acted like any other little boy who had just gotten new duds. Ultimately, tiredness and the events of the day caught up with him, and he fell asleep. Dan gently picked him up and put him to bed.

Dan told Martha all had happened while they were gone, and they discussed the boy at length.

Martha became very concerned when she heard about the man in Jerry's store. "Mark my words," she warned. "That man will bring trouble to us and the boy."

In the days that followed the confrontation with the stranger in Jerry's store, the boy seemed to look at Dan in a new light. He had thought of Dan as a friend right from the start because Dan took him in and treated him well. Since the confrontation, however, he seemed to think of Dan as his hero. Later, Dan learned that the stranger knew someone who was inquiring about the boy. As far as he knew, no one except himself was interested in the boy's welfare, so he figured that maybe they meant to harm the boy for taking off with the horse.

CHAPTER 2

Even as tired as the boy had been yesterday, this morning, he was up and at the breakfast table, ready to eat. As soon as breakfast was over, he again stated that he wanted to talk about that job.

"Well," Dan said, "we do need someone to help Martha out in the kitchen. And we need someone to help with the chores around the house. Is that okay?"

The boy squirmed around in his chair a bit. "I guess that's okay, but I can do other things besides chores and work in the kitchen. Ain't you got any *man's* work I can do?"

Dan studied that question for a minute. "Well, you know, we've hired several young men to do the chores and things around here, but none of them seemed to be tough enough to stick with it. Do you think you could handle it?"

That seemed to lighten the situation some, but the boy still didn't seem to be completely satisfied.

"I can do lots of things besides chores."

"Hmm," Dan said. "What other things can you do?"

"Well, sir, I didn't always get to eat with the people I was staying with. Sometimes I had to go without food for a couple days, so I got real good at killing rabbits and squirrels. Then I would cook them myself and eat them."

"I see. And how do you kill the animals? Do you shoot them or trap them?"

"Naw. I can shoot real good, but they never let me have a gun, and I don't know how to build traps."

"Well then how do you kill the rabbits?"

The boy seemed to be waiting for that question to be asked. "If you give me some rawhide, I'll show you."

Amused, Dan got up from his chair. "Come to the barn with me. I believe we have whatever you need in there."

The boy followed Dan to the barn, with Martha trailing close behind. She wasn't about to miss out on this. Once inside the barn, Dan showed him where the tack room was, and the boy went straight to the worktable. He took a piece of cured rawhide, a sharp knife, and a leather punch.

Next, he trimmed a piece of rawhide down to an oval shape. With the leather tool, he punched a hole in both ends of the oval-shaped piece of leather. He quickly cut two long strips of rawhide into equal lengths. Both strips were just a little thicker than a shoestring, only about two feet long. Then he tied knots at one end of the two strips of rawhide and threaded the leather strips through the holes of the oval-shaped piece of leather. Holding it up, he said, "There. That's my weapon."

"Why, it's a sling!" Martha exclaimed. "Just like the one that King David killed Goliath with in the Bible."

"Yep," the boy said. "That's where I got the idea from. I practiced and practiced until I could knock down a running rabbit."

Dan was clearly impressed. "That's mighty good. I'd like to see you in action. "Sure," the boy said as he turned and went outside. There, he stooped and picked up a rock a little bigger than a marble. He looked around for a target and pointed at the metal weathervane on the roof of the house. A westerly breeze was blowing, so the weathervane was spinning at a pretty good clip. "There. I'll hit that weathervane."

With Dan and Martha looking on, the boy carefully put the rock in the sling and began twirling it around over his head faster and faster. Suddenly, he let go of one of the leather strips and immediately the rock was propelled like a bullet as it shot out of the leather sling and struck the weathervane with such a force that it sounded like gunfire. The weather vane stopped turning for a second. In that second of immobility, they could see a huge dent in the metal. Then the wind caught the weather vane again, and it slowly began to spin around. The boy folded the sling up real nice and neatlike and, with pride in his smile, said, "Can I keep the sling? I lost my other one somewhere."

Martha was so impressed that she couldn't speak. Dan shook his head and returned the boy's prideful smile. "You bet you can keep it. Now I see what you meant when you said you could knock down a running rabbit."

Martha began to clap. "My. How amazing. And I do have a man-sized job for you. The rabbits have been eating my garden as fast as I can plant it. Could you get rid of them for me?"

Beaming all over, the boy said, "I'll start my new job first thing in the morning. That's when the critters like to come out for food."

Sure enough, the next morning, around seven o'clock, there were six dead rabbits on the front porch. Four of them were jackrabbits. Dan and Martha came out of the house and were amazed. Hank, Rusty, and some of the other ranch hands came over to see what all the hoopla was about.

The boy was proud as punch as he said, "There you go. The jack's are a bigger target, but they're the hardest to hit because they can run a lot faster and they zigzag back and forth a lot quicker."

"Wow," Hank said. "Now everyone can call you dead-eye Jack."

The boy wrinkled up his brow. "Well, that's better than the names people used to call me, but I do like the name Jack."

So the name Jack stuck. Later, they added the name Montana. Then he was known as Jack Montana.

"Then it's settled" Dan said. "That's what we will call you: Jack Montana."

That night, the boy lay in bed, excited about what all had happened that day. He had not only proven himself worthy of his keep, he had also earned a real name. Though beginning to get drowsy, he said his name over, time and again. "Jack, Jack Montana." The last thought he had was, *I must bring honor to my new name so that I can always be proud of it. And so Dan and Martha will be proud of me.*

The weeks and months flew by fast for Jack. He was ten years old, and he had learned and done a lot. Dan and the ranch hands had taught him to rope and to brand cattle. He also was shaping up to be a top-notch bronc rider. Whatever he did, he did well. The life that he had lived in the past probably had a lot to do with it; however, he never let the past enter his future. He sometimes thought about his past, but he didn't dwell on it. In the two years that he had spent on the ranch with Dan and Martha, he made friends with all the ranch hands.

Hank was like an older brother to him, and Jack got along well with all the other cowhands. He actually got along too well with the young man they called Rusty. Martha continually tried to discourage Jack from hanging around with him. They had taken Rusty in when he was a youngster too, but he always seemed kind of shifty. He would seldom look her in the eye when she was talking to him. On account of that, Martha said she didn't trust him. Rusty Warren was about six years older than Jack.

All the cowboys wore six-guns. Most of them only packed iron on account of snakes or coyotes or other vermin, but some men lived by the gun. Some of them were good men, and some were bad. Rusty was neither good nor bad, but he bought a gun with the first money he got from working on the ranch, and he practiced with it day and night. Now he had Jack learning to use a six-gun. Every chance the two boys got, they would ride out to the woods and shoot at targets and practice at quick draw.

"See," Martha would say. "Rusty's got Jack following in his footsteps. You mark my words. One of these days, that boy will get in with the wrong crowd. Then, before you know it, the law will be after him. And if he has his way, Jack will be running right alongside of him."

At her prompting, Dan would go and speak with the boys. However, it never made any difference. The boys kept right on with their practice.

On one instance, when Dan and Hank went out to where the boys were shooting bottles and cans, Dan asked, "Practicing huh? How do you practice quick draw?"

The two boys looked at Dan, and Rusty said, "Let's show him."

Jack said, "Okay."

Rusty looked at Hank. "Will you help us demonstrate?"

"Sure," Hank said. "I've seen you boys do this before."

He stood facing Rusty with both hands held out directly in front of him, both hands about a foot apart, with palms turned inward. Rusty then stood with arms hanging down at his sides. The idea was for Hank to clap his hands together before Rusty could draw. Suddenly, Hank attempted to clap his hands together, but before his hands were closed, Rusty's .45 was up and pointed at his belt buckle. Hank's hands closed on the cold steel barrel of the .45.

"Wow!" Dan exclaimed. "I don't think I've ever seen anything that fast." Then he asked Jack, "Are you that fast?"

"Just watch," Jack said proudly.

Hank volunteered again, and he and Jack went through the same motions—only this time Hank held out his hands while Jack demonstrated his swiftness with his .45. The end results were the same as with Hank and Rusty. When Hank's hands came together, they closed on the barrel of Jack's .45.

Hank shook his head. "You guys are too damn fast for me. How do you know when a man's going to draw down on you? What gives you the edge, if there is such a thing as an edge?"

Jack answered, "If you've practiced enough, you'll know. Your opponent will nervously bat an eye or flinch or drop a shoulder as he starts to draw. If you're fast enough, that's all the edge you'll need and you'll beat him to the draw."

Dan was amazed at the demonstration. "That was some demonstration, boys. I'm impressed. But how would you know which one of you is the fastest?"

"Good question," Rusty said. "I'm the fastest, and I can prove it." Swaggering away, he said, "Come on, Jack. Let's give them another demonstration."

Rusty and Jack led the way to where they had two fence posts set in the ground about fifteen feet apart. Rusty stood beside one of the posts, and Jack stood on the opposite side of the other post. Rusty then tossed Dan a coin.

"Here. Hold this coin about waist high, and whenever you're ready, drop it in the dirt."

Dan paused only long enough for the boys to get ready, and then he dropped the coin. As soon as the coin hit the dirt, both boys flew into action. Dan could hardly see the hands move, and he couldn't tell which .45 went off first. All he heard was one loud roar. They examined the posts. Both had bullet holes clean through the middle, just about chest high.

"Well," Rusty asked, "what do you think? Who is the fastest?"

"Damned if I know," Dan answered honestly. "I ... I think it was a tie."

Rusty shook his head. "Nope. I'm faster. I cleared leather first!"

Dan looked at Jack. "Is that right? Did he beat you to the draw?"

Jack, not being a bragger, simply said, "I don't think so."

Hank agreed with Dan. "It looked like a tie to me too, so you still don't know who was the faster."

Rusty turned around, and, looking dead serious, he said, "Well, there's one way to tell for sure."

Plainly irritated, Jack said, "It just might come to that someday. However, until then I guess we'll just keep practicing."

Later that day, Hank and Dan was discussing the incident between the two boys.

"I don't know, Hank. I'm afraid for Jack. He's only ten years old while Rusty's sixteen. Martha is always telling me that someday Rusty is going to get them both into a lot of trouble. Up until now, I haven't really paid much attention to what she was saying. But after seeing that demonstration, I just don't know what to make of it. Think about it. Jack's only ten years old, and he can handle a six-shooter like that. He's faster now than most gunslingers are."

"Dan, I wouldn't worry about Jack. He has a lot of respect for you and Martha. I don't think he would do anything to hurt you. You're right though. He's damn fast, especially for a ten-year-old boy. That's for sure."

Dan had to chuckle in spite of the seriousness of it. "Yeah. I think he had Rusty beat. But you know, Hank, sometimes I think Rusty's a little crazy."

About a month after that incident, Jack heard Dan and Martha talking about their daughter, Cindy, coming home in a few days. He didn't know what to think about that. He remembered them telling him that they had a daughter named Cindy and that she was about the same age as he. He was still just a little shy, so he never asked about her, and sure enough, one day Dan asked him if he wanted to go to town with them to pick Cindy up. She would be on the next stagecoach. He declined by saying that he had some things he had to do.

When they left, he stood and watched them drive off. Because it was Sunday, the ranch was almost deserted, and suddenly, he felt very lonely. For want of something to do, he climbed into the hayloft and sat there, watching for them to return.

As he sat there waiting, he suddenly thought of the wanted poster that he'd carried around every since he could remember—not that he could ever forget the three men who were pictured on the poster, but he kept it with him just in case. He climbed down from the hayloft, went in the house, and got the poster. He was gone but a few minutes, and then he was back in the loft, looking at the poster. "One of these days," he said aloud, "I'll run into you, Tom O'Leary! And you, Willis! And you too, Gilbert!"

Even though the three men had beaten and taunted him and sometimes made him go without food for several days, he could only vaguely remember them. "That's why I'm going to keep this poster with your pictures on it," he said, still talking to the poster as if the three men could actually hear him. Finally, while studying the faces of the three men, he drifted off to sleep.

Suddenly, he heard a sound that startled him. He sat up and rubbed his eyes, and there before him, big as life, were all three men. Tom O'Leary was always the worst one. He had a shock of bright red hair, and that always made Jack wonder if Tom was his father. He hated the thought that he could be the son of a man like that. If it was true, how could he treat his own son like he did?

Tom grinned menacingly at Jack. "There you are, you little bastard. You'll never get away from me again cause I'm gonna kill you right now."

As Jack frantically thrashed around in the hay to get away from Tom, he woke up with a start. He had been dreaming.

"Oh, thank God," he said aloud.

When he was younger, he often dreamt that Tom was trying to kill him. This was the first time he'd had that dream since he came to the Walker ranch. Quickly, he folded the poster, put it in his pocket, and again sat down in the loft.

He was still sitting there, waiting and watching, when the Walkers finally returned. He saw them from afar, and he could see a girl sitting between them, as the seat of the wagon was pretty high. Suddenly, he felt a twinge of jealousy, but just as quickly, he shook it off. He decided that he wouldn't allow jealousy to come between himself and the people who had done so much for him. He watched from the loft as they got down from the wagon. Hank Shaw and two of the boys, Lucas Duran and Leon Hatfield, came out from the bunkhouse to greet Cindy and to take care of the team and wagon. He kept watching the house, and soon, he saw Dan come out on the porch. Then he heard his name being called. After a while, Dan went back into the house and Jack again felt a loneliness. Since his stay with the Walkers, he had hadn't felt alone. Now it came back and reminded him what that feeling was like.

Pretty soon, he summoned up enough nerve to climb down from the barn and go into the house. Dan and Martha and Cindy were sitting on the couch, talking. They all looked up when he walked in.

He took off his hat and said, "Hi, Cindy. I'm Jack."

It was an awkward moment for the two of them, but they made it through the evening.

Finally, in discussing the sleeping quarters, Jack said, "I've been sleeping in your room. I hope you don't mind."

"No. Not at all," she replied.

Looking at Dan and Martha, he said, "I'll sleep in the bunkhouse with the other men so Cindy can have her room back."

"Thanks, Jack," Cindy said. "That's nice of you."

"No," Dan said. "I'll not have no boy of mine …" Then, realizing what he was saying, he corrected, "I mean, I'll not have Jack sleeping out in the bunkhouse. He is our guest."

Martha agreed with Dan and quickly got some blankets and made him a bed on the parlor sofa.

After the first day and night, the two began to get along just fine. They talked a lot and sometimes went riding together. Cindy even helped Jack with some of the chores. One day, while out in the back chopping wood for the kitchen stove, Jack had his shirt off, and Cindy came out to bring him some water. He heard her walking up behind him when suddenly he heard, "Oh my God!"

He quickly lowered the ax and turned around. "Cindy!" he said excitedly. "What's wrong?"

She handed him the glass of water and said, "I'm sorry. I didn't mean to startle you, but when I saw those scars on your back, I...how? I mean..."

Embarrassed, Jack grabbed his shirt and quickly put it on. "I'm sorry you had to see that. I'd rather not talk about it."

"Okay," she readily agreed.

He drank the water and handed her the empty glass. "Thanks for the water, Cindy."

She had intended on staying outside with him, but now she too was embarrassed. She took the glass and said, "You're welcome," and hurried back inside the house.

Neither of them spoke of the matter again until much later. Meanwhile, their friendship grew. She continued doing things for him so she could be near him. Jack continued being very protective of her whenever they left the ranch. They both dreaded the arrival of the school year because this was the last year that Cindy would be going to school in Montana. Her parents had arranged for her to start school the next year at a finishing school for girls in Boston. She and Jack talked about her leaving, and neither wanted her to go away, but the arrangement had already been made and she would have to go. They made the best of this last year though. Jack was like her big brother, and they were together nearly all the time.

Finally, summer break was over. A new school year was beginning, and the time came for Cindy to leave. Cindy said she didn't want to go because she would miss her school friends, and her big brother. That made Jack's face turn red, and the few freckles that he had left stood out as if they were about to fall off. However, when the time came,

Dan and Jack harnessed a horse to the wagon and drove Cindy to town to catch the stagecoach. After they helped her get on the coach, they stood in the street, watching the big concord coach carry her farther and farther away until she was out of sight. Jack noticed a tear in Dan's eye, and he had a big lump in his own throat.

Jack never knew until years later that Cindy had cried almost all the way to Boston. It just about broke her heart to see him standing there in the road, waving, until she was so far away that they couldn't see each other any longer.

Jack was ten years old then, and now he was fourteen. He had grown into a big, strong man, as Martha kept reminding him and everyone else. In these four years, he had become a topnotch all-around ranch hand, and he was outworking every cowboy on the ranch, including Rusty. He was good at everything he did. Martha said, "He is still spending too much time with Rusty. They are always together. They are still practicing with their six-shooters. And," she said, "Rusty's polite and respectful and all that. However, he's much too proud of himself. And you know what the Bible says about pride? Pride goes before a fall." Then she got after Dan to go lay the law down on the two boys. "They're wearing their sidearms all the time now."

"Aw. Don't worry about them. They're just young boys showing off. They'll be okay."

"I'm not so sure about that. I hear that the two of them are hanging out at the saloons now, playing cards and drinking."

"Okay," Dan promised. "I'll have a talk with them."

CHAPTER 3

The Montana winds and snow were breaking records. The past summer had been very good, and Dan's ranch had prospered greatly, but winter came early, and they still had several head of cattle out on the range. Dan's crew had just spent four days out in severe snowstorms. They reported that there were still some cattle out there that they couldn't round up. If they had stayed any longer, they wouldn't have been able to get back and would have had to stay in a line shack until the snowstorm broke, and that might have taken weeks.

That morning at breakfast, Dan and Jack were discussing what, if anything, could be done about those cows. "They will be dead within the next day or two if we don't do something."

Martha joined the conversation at that point. She normally didn't voice her opinion when it came to the cattle or anything beyond her garden. Inside the house was her domain, but she wanted to quickly discourage any talk about Jack and her husband going out in a blizzard searching a few cows.

"They're just cows," she said, "and not many at that, according to what the men said."

"We're not going out there blindly searching for cows," Dan said. "It's just that surely there's something that we can do. I haven't worked for all these years building this ranch up to what it is now to just sit by and watch the elements kill off my prize stock."

"Well," Jack said, "couldn't we just take a wagonload of hay out there and unload it where we figure the cows would likely be? We could wait until the snow lets up some and then take it out there and dump it, and then head right back home. If the cows find the hay, they would at least have some nourishment. That'd generate body heat, so just maybe they would have a chance to survive."

"I was kind of thinking about that myself, Jack. I remember one time a few years ago I had to do that, and it worked too."

They both looked to Martha for her support of their idea, but she wasn't giving it. She turned around and went back to her work at the kitchen stove. "Men," she said, "you're all so thickheaded."

"Okay Jack," Dan said almost in a whisper. "You go out and start loading the hay in the wagon. I'll be out to help you in a minute."

"You got it," Jack said. After he downed the last swallow from his coffee cup, he got up from the table, slipped into his mackinaw, and went outside. He knew that Dan wanted to talk to Martha alone.

An hour and a half later, they had the wagon loaded up and were waiting for the storm to let up. When the break came, they headed for the open range. Within a half hour, the storm grew worse again. Dan shivered and pulled the heavy mackinaw up tighter around his neck and slapped the team with the reins, yelling at them above the wind.

"Come on. Let's get a move on."

The team lunged forward in the traces, and the snow and ice crunched under the weight of the wagon. Twenty minutes later, the blizzard hit with such force that if possible, hell would have frozen over. Dan looked over at Jack, and they both were thinking the same thing. *We should have listened to Martha and not taken on this task.*

Should we turn around and head back, or should we stick it out and finish the job? Both being as thickheaded as Martha claimed, they kept on going. They had already dropped off half of the load of hay. Now Dan shouted as loud as he could so that Jack could hear him above the din of the blizzard.

"Another few hundred yards, and we'll drop the rest of the hay and turn back. I'm about to freeze to death."

The wind and snow were blowing so hard that they could barely see the horses, so Jack didn't bother to try and answer. He just nodded his head. A few minutes later, the horses stopped on their own accord and wouldn't go any farther. After squinting their eyes and peering ahead of the team, they could barely make out a dark, looming shape just ahead of them.

Dan shouted, "It's one of the line shacks. I think we'd best put the team up in the lean-to and get inside the shack and build a fire before we freeze to death."

Again, Jack nodded in agreement, and they both got down from the wagon and unhooked the team and led them inside the lean-to. After that, they hurried inside the line shack.

This shack was one of the better ones. It had everything a person could want. Besides a huge stone fireplace, it was well stocked with food and water. Within minutes, Jack had a roaring fire going and Dan had a steaming pot of coffee ready.

"Well," Jack said as he poured the two of them a cup of the hot black liquid, "this ain't so bad."

A shiver ran through Dan as he took a sip of the hot coffee. "You're right about that. We're lucky the horses stopped at this line shack instead of going around it. I hate to think of the outcome if they *had* gone around it."

"When this blizzard let's up, are we going to go a little farther and drop off the rest of the hay, or are we going to head for the ranch?"

Dan thought about that for a minute. "I don't know. We'll have to wait and see. I don't mind telling you, Jack. This storm has got me worried some."

"Yeah," Jack agreed. "This is the worst storm that I've ever been in."

Dan shook his head. "I reckon it is, Jack. I've lived in Montana all my life, and this is just about the worst I've ever seen. Sometimes these blizzards come up real fast, with almost no warning at all. I recall a rancher just north of here who got caught by one of these sudden storms one time while out in the barn. He tried to make it to his house. They found him the next day, buried in the snow just fifteen feet from his doorstep. I know another fellow who got caught out one time and got frozen so bad that they had to amputate both legs." After pausing for a moment, he shrugged his shoulders. "But I guess it ain't going to do us any good by talking about all that stuff at a time like this."

The blizzard continued to blow all day long, only letting up a few minutes at a time. Finally, they lit the lamps and cooked up some beans and hardtack and more hot coffee. After eating, Dan shrugged himself into his heavy mackinaw and stepped outside to check on the horses again. He forked some more hay into the manger for them, and on his way out of the lean-to, he gave both horses a pat.

"You guys stay warm. Hopefully we'll be going home in the morning."

Back inside the line shack, he stood in front of the fireplace, warming his hands. "Horses are doing fine, but as I stepped out of the lean-to, I noticed how the snow is piling up on the roof. I hope it holds up under the weight."

"How about the roof on this line shack?"

"I wasn't going to mention that. Truth is I'm not too sure about this roof either. The lean-to and this building are just about buried in snow."

After finishing their coffee, Dan said, "I guess we might as well turn in for the night. We can't help matters by sitting up all night, talking about it."

Jack agreed to that. "Yeah. We might need all the rest we can get after tonight." He didn't feel tired and didn't think he would be able to go to sleep, but he knew that Dan was worried and didn't want to talk about how bad things were.

After putting a couple extra logs on the fire and blowing out the lamps, they went to the bunks. There were two bunks attached to a wall on either side of the fireplace. Dan chose the bottom bunk on one side of the fireplace, and Jack took the bottom bunk on the other side of the fireplace. He lay there, listening to Dan tossing and turning, for about five minutes and then drifted off to sleep.

The next day, at about ten o'clock, it happened. Suddenly, there was a loud cracking sound. At first they thought that the roof of the line shack was giving away, but then they realized that it was the lean-to.

"Quick!" Dan shouted. "We need those horses. Let's get them out of there and bring them into the house!"

Not bothering to grab their mackinaws, they ran outside and into the lean-to. Some of the rafters in the roof were broken and sagging in the middle from the weight of the heavy snow but were still holding together by a few splinters. They could see snow falling down into the lean-to through the cracks in the roof. The horses were getting very nervous and were starting to snort and paw at the ground with their hooves.

"Good!" Dan yelled. "The roof hasn't completely fallen in yet. Let's get the horses untied and out of here."

The lean-to wasn't very big, so they had to crowd their way in between the horses to get to the manger where they were tied. Just as they got the horses untied, they heard another loud cracking sound, and the roof started to come down on top of them. The horses were frightened into a fury and started rearing and pawing the air. Dan got struck on the shoulder by a flying hoof and, slipping in the snow, fell down underneath the rearing horses. Jack heard Dan yelling out in pain and then heard the soft thudding sound as the horses trampled on him while trying to turn around in the small area. Jack didn't think about the horses. He just wanted to get to Dan to see if he could help him. Dan was out cold and was bleeding from his head. Jack could see Dan's shirt and pants turning red with blood from the places where the horses had trampled on him.

Somehow, Jack managed to get Dan inside the line shack, where he carefully undressed him and cleaned and bandaged his wounds. Then he covered Dan up with blankets. Dan stirred a little and opened his eyes. "Where ... where are the horses, Jack?"

"They got away, Dan. I'm sorry."

Dan managed a smile. "Don't worry about it, Jack. We'll be okay. How bad ... am ... I hur ... ?" At that point, Dan blacked out.

Jack had never been in a situation like this. First of all, if this had happened to one of the people that he had been forced to live with before, he wouldn't have cared about that person. He would have just run away. This, however, was Dan Walker, a man who had taken him in and raised him. Then he thought of Martha. *If Dan was to die out here, would she blame me? What would she do? Of course, I would stay and help her run the ranch. What if she told me to leave?* He shook his head, trying to shake all those thoughts away.

He knew what he had to do if they were going to survive, so he went to work. He took some of the sheets off the other bunks, washed them in some clean, melted snow, and hung them to dry by the fireplace. As soon as they were dry enough, he cut them up and made bandages out of them. He figured that if he could keep Dan's wounds clean and bandaged, he would soon be able to sit up and eat. Hopefully, he would get well. With that accomplished, he sat down beside Dan's bunk and prayed like he'd never prayed before.

The next day, the snowstorm was still at blizzard stage. Jack made breakfast, had some hot coffee, and then changed Dan's bandages. He could see black and blue marks all over Dan's body where the horses had stomped on him. *He must have some broken bones,* Jack thought. *I sure hope there's no damage to his vital organs.*

For the next couple days, things went pretty much the same way. On the third day, Dan woke up. Jack was asleep in a chair next to his bunk. He hated to wake him up because he figured that Jack hadn't had much sleep since this happened, and he had no idea how long he'd been out. Nevertheless, he was starving and craving water.

"Jack," he whispered. "Jack."

Jack woke with a start. "Hey! You're awake! How long?"

"I just woke up. How long have I been out?"

"Three days. You've been out for three days. How do you feel?"

"Thirsty and hungry as a bear." He tried to sit up. "Ouch!" He cried out in pain. "Every bone in my body hurts."

Every time he moved, he was so overcome by pain that he would almost faint. For the next few days, Jack changed his bandages and fed him. At length, he was able to get up and hobble to the table and eat. He was gaining strength every day, but now they were running out of food. The water was no problem because the snow was clean and good to drink. Jack just took a bucket outside and scooped up some clean snow and put the bucket next to the fire. In minutes, they had water.

One day, after breakfast, Jack asked, "How far do you think we are from home?"

"Actually, we're only a few miles from home. Why?"

"I notice the storm is starting to let up. In another week, it might be over and you might be strong enough to walk out of here with my help."

Dan took a moment to answer and then shook his head. "Not a chance, Jack."

"What do you mean not a chance?"

"Just what I said. But I'm glad you brought it up. I been meaning to talk to you about it."

"What's there to talk about? When the storm lets up, we'll just walk out of here."

Dan sighed. "Look. Here's the situation. I'm in bad shape. I won't be able to walk out of here for a hell of a long time. Our food supply is just about gone, and I'm not so sure that the storm is close to being over. I've seen it completely stop and an hour or two later start up all over again."

"But we got enough food to last few more days, right?"

"We might can stretch the food a few more days, but we got another problem too."

"What's that?"

"Well, I guess you've heard the roof groaning and moaning up there, haven't you?"

"Yes."

"Well, all I'm saying is if the storm does start up again, that roof is going to come down on top of us, and with all that weight, we won't survive."

"Well then what can we do, Dan?"

"Only one thing to do, and that is for you to dress as warm as you can and strike out walking. If we're lucky, the storm will stay dormant 'till you can reach the ranch and get help and come back after me. If you're real lucky, maybe you'll run into one of the horses. That way you can get home a lot faster."

"But I can't leave you here by yourself! What if the roof does cave in? You'll be killed."

"That would be better than both of us being dead, right? Besides, you might be right about the blizzard being over. Leastwise that's what I'm hoping for."

They both were silent for a long time.

Finally, Dan said, "You know what to do, and you know that you have to do it, right?"

"Yes."

"Well, the sooner you get started, the better off we'll both be. So get going."

Jack got up from the chair, put on his heavy mackinaw, and went to the door.

"When you step outside," Dan said, "put your back flat against the door and look straight forward. Look as far out as you can. Because that's the direction you want to go. If you can see those mountains in the distance, head straight for them. Our ranch is right in line between this line shack and those mountains. No matter how hard the blizzard blows, don't lose your sense of direction. Keep heading straight for those mountains. If the blizzard does start up again and you lose your sense of direction, it can mean your death."

Dan hated to put this much responsibility on Jack, but he was eighteen years old now and had already proved himself a man. Besides, there was no other way out of this mess.

Jack opened the door, and the cold wind blew inside, almost pulling the door out of his hand. He hesitated only long enough to force a smile at Dan and say, "Don't worry. You can count on me. I'll be back." He stepped out into the bitter cold and pulled the door tightly shut behind him. He did just as Dan told him to. He stepped back 'till his shoulders touched the door, and then he looked straight ahead. Far out in the distance, he could see the mountains. He also noticed how cold and still and dead everything looked. Without further delay, he headed straight for those mountains. Jack looked back just one time after he had walked a few hundred yards. The small line shack was covered over with snow and barely visible, and for a few seconds he visualized coming back and finding Dan lying in his bunk dead. He shook off the vision and pushed on with new determination.

Jack walked at a pretty good pace for about twenty minutes, thinking, *This isn't so bad. I'll be back at the ranch by nightfall or soon after.*

However, within minutes, the wind was blowing threateningly again. Soon after that, snow flurries announced another blizzard. The wind was so strong that he could hardly keep to his feet. He kept falling down and getting up. He was quickly winded, and he lay there in the freezing snow for just a minute before struggling to his feet. "I have … to … keep going," he said over and over to himself as a mantra. He knew that if he lay down too long, he would fall asleep and never wake up. He was amazed to realize that the main reason he kept pushing himself was that he was determined to save Dan.

It was a battle of endurance. Man against blizzard. Eventually, the blizzard won, and Jack fell down for the last time—freezing, exhausted, and thinking, *I'm sorry, Dan. I just couldn't make it.* Suddenly, he heard something. He raised his head to see what it was, but the snow was coming down hard, and the wind was blowing so strong that he couldn't see or hear anything. *It's no use,* he thought. Thinking the sound was all in his imagination, he laid his head down in the snow and closed his eyes. Just before the death sleep closed in on him, he heard the sound again. This time he recognized the sound. It was a cow mooing weakly. He tried getting to his feet, but the strong wind wouldn't allow him to do so.

With sheer willpower, he began to crawl toward the sound. After going a short distance, he could see the cow, and suddenly, he knew what to do. It was as if an angel had instructed him. He reached down at his side and drew his .44. "I'm sorry," he said. He shot the cow between the eyes, and it dropped to the snow-covered ground. Taking his knife, he opened the cow's belly, and its intestines emptied out neatly and cleanly onto the snow. It was a gruesome sight, but seeing the steam rise from the hot intestines onto the cold snow gave him hope for life. With hands that were nearly frozen, he quickly shoved the intestines to one side and crawled into the cow's body cavity. By drawing his knees up, he fit inside. He reached out and pulled the cavity shut. His last thoughts were, *The warmth feels good. Please, God, don't let me die.*

Immediately after closing his eyes, he fell into a sleep born of exhaustion. It was good that he did, for five minutes later, the blizzard hit with all the forces of nature. Within another five minutes, there was neither a trace nor sign that he or the cow had ever been there. The ground was a sheer smooth blanket of snow. The blizzard lasted for a couple more hours, and just as suddenly as it began, it stopped. It was over. The sun came out, and the stillness caused Jack to awaken. At first he thought he was dead, but after a moment, he remembered praying to God that he wouldn't die. The cow's bones and hide were frozen stiff and buried in the snow, so he had a little trouble getting out and standing up. Tentatively, he managed. Once on his feet, he looked up at the sky and yelled as loud as he could, "Thank you, Jesus."

Remembering Dan, he started hurrying his way toward the ranch again. He knew there were only a couple of hours of daylight left, so he ran as best as he could in the deep snow and then walked awhile. It had stopped snowing hard—just a few snow flurries now and then landing and melting against his face. Just as he was at the point where he would have to stop and rest, here came Hank and three more men with a wagon.

Hank stopped the wagon beside him. "Hop in, Jack. Where's Dan? Is he okay?"

"He's back at the line shack over to the south and busted up some from an accident we had earlier, but I think he's okay. Boy, I'm thanking the Lord that you came along when you did." He climbed in the back of the wagon and covered up with some blankets that the men brought along. When they reached the line shack, they went inside to get Dan. Half of the roof had caved in from the weight of the snow. Luckily, Dan was in his bunk when the roof fell and the half that gave way was on the other side of the shack. Now the remaining part of the roof was starting to give away. Just as they got him out, they heard a loud cracking sound and the remaining part of the roof caved in.

"Boy, that was a close call," one of the men said.

"Yes, it was," Dan said, "and I sure thought I was a goner when I saw the first part of the roof caving in."

"Well," Hank said, "it's a good thing we ran into Jack when we did because we figured you was holed up in one of the line shacks, but we thought it would be the one further north. That's where we were headed when we saw Jack hoofing it for the ranch."

"Well," Jack said, "I guess everything I went through today wasn't all for nothing then."

Dan looked at Jack. "We got a lot to be thankful for and a lot to talk about, right?"

"We sure do, Dan."

By this time, they had Dan in the wagon and were on their way to the ranch. With the horses moving as fast as they could in the snow, they reached the house in about forty-five minutes. When they pulled up in the yard, Martha was there, anxiously waiting. With Jack's help, she had Dan in the house and in bed within fifteen minutes.

"Maybe you stubborn men will listen to me next time. Lord, I don't understand how you ever lived to be as old as you are, Daniel Walker. Don't you ever do this to me again ... " Realizing how she was carrying on, she stopped talking and started hugging and kissing him.

At that point, Jack left the room.

CHAPTER 4

One evening, when all the work for the day was finished, Jack went into Dan's room to sit and talk for a while as he usually did. Dan was recovering well but still had to spend quite a bit of time resting in bed. "Jack," Dan said, "I have something to say to you. It's something that Martha and I have been talking about for a long time now."

"Okay. Shoot. Let's hear it."

"First, go to the door and call Martha. I want her to be present when we talk about this."

Jack went to the door and called Martha, as Dan had asked. She came in and sat down on the edge of the bed and held Dan's hand.

Jack sat back down in the chair. He felt that this talk was going to be about how he was going to have to stop hanging around with Rusty and how the two of them were going to have to stop spending so much time in the saloons, so he thought he'd start the ball rolling. "Look," he said, "I know I've caused you a lot worry these past few months, but—"

"No," Martha said. "That's not what this talk is about." Then she wrinkled her brow. "But since you brought it up, you are spending too much time with Rusty, and I've heard the talk about how you and Rusty spend almost every Saturday night in town in the saloons. Do you realize that in the past six months Dan has had to bail you and Rusty out of jail five times on account of fistfights? Furthermore, sometimes there's even gunplay involved."

"Okay, okay. I've got the message. I'm sorry. I'll try to keep out of trouble."

In spite of the seriousness of this conversation, Dan had to laugh. He held up his hand. "Whoa there, you two. We can have this conversation later, but right now I want to talk about what I called you in here for."

"You're right Dan," Martha said. Then, looking at Jack, she said, "Sorry about that. Dan and I do have something we want to discuss with you."

Now really puzzled, Jack said, "Okay. I'm all ears."

Dan cleared his throat. "Jack, Martha and I have been talking for a long time now about naming you in our will as heir to the Walker ranch."

Jack's jaw dropped. "What? What did you say?"

Dan repeated the statement.

"You can't be serious," Jack said.

"Oh, but we are," Martha assured him.

There was a long pause, and Dan said, "We thought you'd be pleased."

"Well, of course I'm pleased, but that wouldn't be fair to Cindy. She is your daughter. She should be the only heir to your ranch."

Martha smiled. "We've talked to Cindy about this, and she's just as excited as we are about it. Jack, you and Cindy have been raised together since you were eight years old. You're like brother and sister."

Jack was stunned. "I don't know what to say."

"Then say yes," Dan suggested. "Look, Martha and I are getting old, and I might never completely recover from this accident, and we want to make sure that Cindy has expert help running this ranch after we are gone. And we would like it to be you."

Jack sighed. "Okay. If it's all right with all three of you. Sure I'd like to be joint heirs with Cindy."

The next morning, Jack sat talking with Martha after breakfast. He was about to take Dan's breakfast in to him before he went out to work.

"Wait a minute, Jack," she said. "I want to share something with you."

"Okay. I'm listening."

"It's like this. When Dan and I got married, we said we'd have children until we had a girl that I could dress and raise and do things with and Dan could have a boy that he could pal around with and teach the ranching business to. But after we had our first child, Cindy, we learned that I couldn't have any more children. Well, Dan was just about heartbroken. He tried to act like it didn't make any difference to him, but I knew better. He was crushed. His chance to have a son was gone. Then, one day, a little redheaded, freckle-faced boy right out of nowhere walked into his life. Jack, the day you first stepped foot on this ranch, you walked into his heart, and at last, Dan had his son. I could tell it by the look in his eyes when he first saw you." She paused for a moment before adding, "In that first moment, he adopted you in his heart, and you've been there all this time. Jack, to Dan, you *are* his son. He loves you. That's why we wanted to name you along with Cindy in our will. And I love you too, Jack. If I could have had a son, I'd want him to be just like you."

Even before she finished telling him about all this, he could see tears welling up in her eyes. She barely finished what she had to say before her voice choked up and she couldn't speak anymore.

Jack blinked the tears from his eyes and rose from his chair. He went to her and held her in his arms. "If I could choose a mother and father from all the parents in the world, I'd choose you two. Martha, I love you and Dan, and I thank you so very much."

After a long embrace, Martha said, "There now. You better take Dan his breakfast. He'll be wondering what's keeping you."

During the next several years that followed, Cindy and Jack grew quite found of each other. They spent a lot of time together when she was home on summer breaks from school. She would usually go with him, whether he was out mending fences or rounding up strays or sometimes even when he went into town to talk to some of the other ranchers and cattle barons about preparing for a cattle drive.

Jack's feelings for Cindy grew and grew until, on more than one occasion when they were alone, he almost revealed to her how he felt. Unfortunately, he always stopped short of telling her, thinking he couldn't do that because she would probably laugh at him. After all, they were like brother and sister.

Little did he know that she held the same feelings for him. Sometimes, when alone in her room, she would think about what it would be like if Jack would say, "Cindy, I love you. Will you marry me?" Frustrated, she would think, *Not much chance of that happening. He's not interested in me. I'm like a sister to him.* As fate would have it, both of them were afraid of revealing their feelings for fear of rejection.

Finally finishing her last year of school, she wrote home and said that she had a job offer and she was going to accept it. She wanted to see which she would prefer: life on the ranch, or life in the city as a working girl. She probably wouldn't be able to come home for a visit for a couple of years.

Dan and Martha were upset about her decision but allowed that they wouldn't interfere. They looked on Jack as part of the family, so they showed him the letter. For a couple of minutes after reading the letter, all Jack could say was, "A couple of years, huh? That will seem like a lifetime. It was bad enough when she was gone just during her school years."

Martha and Dan concurred. "I almost wish we hadn't sent her back east to that school," Dan said.

"Nonsense," Martha said. "I'm sure we made the right choice, and I'm just as sure that Cindy will do the same."

Dan recovered from his being trampled on by the horses out at the line shack, but it took several winters. Now, as he grew older, he was experiencing a lot of pain from the once-broken bones. The pain was sometimes just about more than he could bear. Old Doc Green said it was arthritis caused by the broken bones and kept him supplied with laudanum, and Martha did her best to comfort him. Hank was still Dan's foreman and doing a pretty good job of running the ranch but was gradually relying more and more on Jack's help. On the other hand, Jack was growing restless now that Cindy hadn't been home in a couple of years. Being away from her for that long was hard on him. He kept thinking that he should have told her how he felt. He knew she had grown into a beautiful woman now, and for all he knew, she might meet someone and get married. He tried to get her out of his mind by going into town every chance he got. He would make the rounds in and out of the saloons, playing cards and drinking. He and Rusty were always together.

Rusty was the instigator in getting Jack playing cards and drinking. He knew what was going on inside of Jack's head, so he would goad him into visiting the saloons with him. At first, Jack wasn't interested in going to town. He preferred busying himself with work at the ranch.

Rusty, however, would say, "Aw. Forget about Cindy, Jack. Let's go to town and get some real women and have some fun."

Rusty's idea of having fun was going to Murdock's Saloon and going upstairs with one of the girls. The rest of the evening was devoted to playing cards and getting drunk and maybe even picking a fight with someone. At that time, McDaniels, the barkeeper, who most people called Mac, would usually go for the sheriff, and that always put an end to that night's shenanigans.

Murdock's Saloon was a large, false-fronted building. It had an upstairs that was divided into several rooms, which Murdock rented to soiled doves. In return, the girls paid him one third of all money they made. When they weren't in their rooms, they were downstairs peddling themselves and drinks for the house.

It became a ritual every Saturday night. Rusty and Jack would ride into town and head straight for Murdock's Saloon. Rusty would pick a girl and do his best to talk Jack into picking one of the gals to take upstairs. Nevertheless, Jack would always refuse.

"Aw. Come on," Rusty would tease. "What's the matter? Are you afraid of these pretty little ladies?"

Again, Jack would refuse. "No. You go ahead."

An antagonistic bully, Rusty would get sarcastic. "Aw. Look at him, girls. He's wasting away for little Cindy."

All the teasing made Jack furious, but he managed to keep his temper under control. Then one day, a new girl came to work at Murdock's. She was a young and beautiful girl named Shannon. As soon as Jack and Rusty stepped inside of Murdock's Saloon, they spotted her standing at the bar. Jack knew that Rusty would pick her, so before Rusty could say anything to the girl, Jack crossed the room and spoke to her while Rusty stood there with his lower jaw hanging down. "Do ... do you work here?" Jack asked the new girl.

The girl smiled and answered, "Yes, I do. This is my first day here. My name is Shannon. What's yours?"

There was something about this girl that made Jack feel comfortable, while normally he was shy and uncomfortable around girls. Even Cindy brought out the bashfulness in him. "My name is Jack, Jack Montana."

Shannon hooked an arm in his. "Okay, Jack. Would you like a drink first, or would you like to go on upstairs?"

He knew that everyone was looking at them, and that made him a little nervous. "Let's just go on upstairs. Maybe we'll have a drink later." When they got upstairs, Jack said, "Shannon, can we just talk?"

She was already undressed but slipped on a robe. "Sure, Jack. We can talk first."

"No. I mean … can we just *talk*?"

Puzzled at his request, she said, "You mean to just talk, without having any sex? I didn't picture you as being … funny."

Now really embarrassed, Jack said, "No! It's not like that. It's just that I'm, well I'm … saving uh. … that for a girl I love."

"And does this special girl have a name?"

"Yes. Cindy is her name. Cindy Walker."

Shannon wrinkled her brow. "Oh," she said mockingly. "In the one day that I've been working here I've heard a lot about the Walker Ranch, you and your friend Rusty."

Impressed, Jack said, "Well, I guess you know me pretty well then."

After a moment of silence, Shannon sat down on the bed. "So you want to just … talk? We can do that, but it will have to be brief because I have to pay for every minute that I occupy this room."

"Oh. I didn't realize that. Well, I'll pay you for the time we spend in here, okay?"

"That's fair enough. What do you want to talk about?

"Well, we don't even have to talk if you don't want to. I'm just tired of my friend Rusty down there teasing me about being afraid of girls."

"Hmm. Are you afraid of girls?"

"Hell no!" Jack said. Then, with a red face, he said, "I'm sorry, Miss Shannon. I didn't mean to curse in front of a lady."

Shannon threw back her head and laughed almost uncontrollably.

Bewildered and a little hurt, Jack stood up from the bed where he had been sitting. "What's so funny?"

"I'm sorry," she said as she tried to control her laughter, "but this picture flashed through my head. Here you are, a tough, rugged cowboy, sitting on a bed with me, a naked whore, and you called me a ... lady."

Jack stood there for a second, and then both of them burst out laughing.

"You know," Jack said, "I don't feel uncomfortable around you at all."

Shannon patted a spot on the bed beside her. "Then sit down here, and let's have that talk. The time that we're in here is costing you money."

They talked for about an hour, telling each other their stories, all about how they came to be there, and what had happened to them from the beginning. Shannon had already heard the basics of Jack's story. He just filled her in on most of the other things that had happened to him.

Shannon's story equaled Jack's in tragedy. She too had been abandoned as a baby. Only instead of being left with strangers, she was taken in by an aunt and uncle who, when she was only twelve years old, locked her up in a room where men would pay to go in and force her to perform all kinds of sex acts on them. When she was fourteen, she managed to escape from her aunt and uncle. She couldn't find employment anywhere, so to keep from starving, she wound up going from saloon to saloon, where she found plenty of employment.

"So here I am." She shrugged, and after a moment, she asked, "Is Jack Montana your real name?"

"No," he said and proceeded to tell her about how he earned his name by killing jackrabbits with a homemade slingshot. "But Shannon is a beautiful name. I like it," Jack said.

"I'm glad you like it, Jack. I picked it out myself. I have no idea what my real name is."

"So how did you come to pick the name Shannon?"

"For a while, I worked in a saloon in Virginia. It was in a beautiful valley called the Shenandoah Valley. It's between the Alleghenies of West Virginia and the Blue Ridge Mountains. It even has a river running through it called the Shenandoah River. So I told everyone that Shannon was my name. That's the only good thing that's happened to me, Jack, until now. I've met you. I hate this way of life that I've been forced into. You're the only really good and decent man I've ever known."

For some time, they both just sat there in silence, thinking how alike their lives were. Then they hugged and kissed. That was the first time that Jack had ever really kissed a girl on the lips. The embrace and the kiss only lasted a few minutes, but it was genuine, and they were both grateful for each other. Then they made a pact. Every time that he and Rusty came into town, she would refuse to go upstairs with Rusty or anyone else. She would only go with Jack. From that time on, when Saturday night came, it was generally Jack who would say, "Come on, Rusty. Let's go to Murdock's!" It was a new experience for Jack, this driving Rusty crazy when they went to Murdock's. Rusty would try his best to get Shannon to go upstairs with him, but she would always refuse. "Boy, Jack," he would say. "You must be some kind of stud."

Before long, Rusty had the whole town talking about Jack and Shannon. "When Jack is in town," he would say, "Shannon is strictly Jack's whore."

Jack was ashamed for Shannon because of the talk and said he would make Rusty stop the gossip.

Shannon was pragmatic. "No, Jack. Just let him talk. He's just jealous. Besides, I like being called 'Jack's whore.' I'd prefer to be called 'Jack's woman,' but whore will do for now."

The Saturdays came and went as the two spent many hours together, just talking. Sometimes they would lie on her bed and sleep, but they never had sex.

CHAPTER 5

One Saturday night, Jack and Rusty entered Murdock's Saloon for a couple of drinks. It was crowded, but they elbowed their way to the bar and ordered whiskey. The large room was noisy with everyone talking, the piano playing, and the showgirls dancing and singing. Suddenly, a man stepped into the room, and everyone became deathly quiet.

Turning around to see what had happened, Rusty whispered, "That's Willie Dalton."

Everyone in this part of the country knew Willie Dalton. He had three brothers: Jed, Nate, and Bob. They claimed to be kin to the Dalton gang: Bob, Emmett, and Gratin. They were cousins to the Younger brothers, who rode with Frank and Jesse James.

Willie stepped up to the bar. "Give me a bottle of the strongest whiskey you got."

"Yes, sir," the barkeeper said and immediately set a bottle and a glass in front of him. Willie shoved the glass aside, turned the bottle up, and drank the whole thing in two big gulps. Wiping his mouth with the back of his hand, he said, "I want the purtiest gal in this saloon."

No one said a word.

Willie then looked around and spotted Shannon.

"You, whore come over here and lead me to your bed. We're gonna have us some fun."

All was quiet, and then Rusty started laughing.

Willie glared at him. "What's so funny, pup?"

"Why," Rusty said pointing to Jack, "I guess you're gonna have to walk through Jack here. That's his whore you're talking to."

Looking at Jack, Willie said, "Then I'll just have to kill you, pup, 'cause while I'm here, she's *my* whore."

Shannon was afraid of Willie and didn't want to go with him, but she was more afraid for Jack. "No," she said, as she walked toward him. "I'm nobody's whore now, but I'd like to be your whore, Willie."

Laughing, he grabbed her by the hair and pulled her close to him. "That's the way I like my women to talk."

No one said a word, but every eye turned toward Jack. It was his call. He was confident of his speed, but he had never drawn down on a man before—except when he and Rusty were practicing quick draw. Casting a shadow on his self-doubt was Shannon's courage. He knew that she was afraid, and yet she was willing to go with this killer to save him. Willie, by this time, was pulling Shannon toward the stairway to go up to her room.

"Willie!" Jack shouted.

Willie turned around. "Don't bother me, pup. I got me a fine looking filly here, and I'm gonna take her upstairs and ride her. If she bucks, I'll put the spurs to her."

That really infuriated Jack. "Get your hands off her, and haul your stinking carcass outta here!"

"And if I don't, what'll you do, pup?"

The challenge was out. He couldn't back down now if he wanted to. He found himself saying, "Fists or guns. It's your call now."

Willie shoved Shannon brutally away from him in order to free up his gun hand and went into the gunfighter's stance. "Fists?" he sneered. "I won't waste my time knocking the hell out of you, pup. My filly over there is just waiting for me to mount up. Get ready to die."

A whole lot of things flashed through Jack's head. One of those thoughts was, *In just a few seconds, one of us will be dead.* Conversely, the thing that gave him confidence was what he had told Hank when Hank had asked him, "How do you know when a man is going to draw? What gives you that edge?" His answer had been, "If you have practiced enough, you'll know. Your opponent will bat an eye or flinch or drop a shoulder. If you're fast enough, that's all the edge you need."

Finally, after what seemed like an eternity, Jack saw just a slight flinch in Willie Dalton's gun hand. The outlaw was fast on the draw, but he had given away the edge to Jack and Jack reeled it in. While Willie's fingers were still closed around the gun butt in its holster, Jack felt his own .44 buck in his hand. In a flash, he saw a perfectly round hole appear right between Willie Dalton's eyes. Instantly, the outlaw flew backward onto the stairway where he had pushed Shannon just seconds before. Blood and brains covered the steps where his head was.

The next thing Jack knew, there were people crowding all around him. They had taken Willie's gun out of its holster to examine it.

"Damn!" someone said. "There is nine notches on Willie's gun butt."

Now they were talking about how fast *he* was and how he must be the fastest gun alive and how he's probably faster than Billy the Kid and Jesse James.

Then he heard Rusty say, "Damn, Jack. You dropped Willie like a wet horse turd. He never even got his gun out. He never knew what hit him."

Jack never gave Rusty or anyone else a look or a word. He hurried over to check on Shannon. She looked pretty shaken up, and some of the other girls were trying to comfort her.

"Are you all right, Shannon?"

The girls made a path for Jack to get to her, and she fell into his arms. "Yes. I'm okay! Are *you* all right?" Jack assured her that he was okay, and after she composed herself, he told the other girls to take care of her. "I've got to go see the sheriff. He'll want to talk to me."

Jack left the saloon to go to the sheriff's office. Rusty stayed for hours after that, drinking and talking about the gunfight.

When Jack stepped inside the jail, he looked over at the sheriff's desk. Frank Morgan looked up from his paperwork. "Howdy, Jack. Been over at Murdock's?"

Jack sat down in the chair that was next to Frank's desk. "Yep," he said. He looked down at the floor and all around the room, all the time thinking about how as a kid not so long ago, he used to come in here and play when he and Dan came to town. Dan and Frank went a long way back. They had come to Montana via wagon train. That's how they met, and they'd been friends all this time.

Morgan was about forty years old. He was just under six feet tall, lean-waisted, and tough. He was a hellion in a fistfight or in swapping lead. It didn't make any difference to him. He always came out on top. Suddenly, Jack became aware of Frank's voice.

"I heard a single shot awhile ago. Sounded like a .44-caliber pistol. You know anything about that?"

Jack sighed and, lifting his gun from his holster, laid the .44 on the sheriff's desk. "Yeah, Frank. It was me."

"You want to tell me about it?"

Jack took a long breath and told Frank what happened.

Sheriff Morgan rose from his chair and, picking up Jack's gun, handed it back to him "Here. Holster this six-shooter. The first thing I have to do is go over to Murdock's and talk to everyone who saw the shooting and then get the body over to Otis Sherman's so he can measure it for a coffin.

When Jack stepped back into Murdock's with Sheriff Morgan on his heels, everyone was still there and still talking about the shooting. Someone had covered Willie Dalton's body with a sheet. Frank walked over and uncovered the body, looked at it, and covered it back up. "That's Willie Dalton all right. Anyone want to tell me exactly what they saw?"

It didn't take long to question everyone because they all said the same thing. "Willie Dalton came in, started abusing Shannon, and then challenged Jack to draw against him, and Jack outdrew him. Shot him one time between the eyes."

"Okay," the sheriff said. "Jack, you're clear, but come back to the office with me. I need to talk to you some more about this." With that, he chose a couple of men and asked them to take the body over to the undertaker's.

The news, in full detail (with some half-truths added), spread around the countryside like wildfire. The shooting of a gunman like Willie Dalton didn't bother Jack that much, although that was his first gunfight. It was the constant reminder of it by the people in town that bothered him. Practically everyone he met on the street or in the saloon would bring it up in the conversation. "So how does it feel to be the one who put Willie Dalton in boot hill?"

After that, he never left the ranch unless he had to go get supplies for the ranch or something else that he needed. He finally told Dan and Martha about the shootout with Willie Dalton and his talk with Sheriff Morgan and was surprised to learn that they had already heard all about it. Martha had learned about the shooting three days earlier, when she had gone into town for a dress fitting.

Dan had two concerns about the matter and said as much. "You know, Jack, in my younger days, I was pretty much like you. I too got into a few gunfights and almost wound up on the outlaw trail. However, I came to my senses and changed the direction in which I was headed. You see, what I'm afraid of is that the news of this will travel to other towns and some kin of this gunman that you killed will come after you. Then, after a while, all the gunmen who want to build themselves a reputation will come looking for you."

"I understand that," Jack said.

"And," Dan continued, "this woman, this saloon gal, that you put your life on the line for. Is she really your woman? Is she worth it?"

"Even if she is a saloon girl," Martha interjected, "she needed someone to stand up for her! I just wish it had been someone other than you, Jack."

"Yes. You're right, Martha. I'm sorry, Jack. It's just that we're worried about you."

Again Jack said, "I understand. I aim to be careful."

After a pause, Martha asked, "Are…are you two going to get married?"

"No, we're not going to get married. Shannon and I are just good friends, and that's all." He could have told them that if he weren't in love with Cindy he probably *would* ask Shannon to marry him. On the other hand, he didn't even know what they would think about his asking *Cindy* to be his wife, much less Shannon.

When he and Dan were alone, Dan was still thinking about their talk, so he brought it up again. "I'm sorry, but when we were talking about you and that woman, Shannon? I know you said that you was not going to marry her, but I just had the feeling that you wanted to say something else about it."

Jack thought about how to answer that. "You know, Dan, if it wasn't for a certain someone else, I just might ask Shannon to marry me, but…there's only one woman that I would ever marry or that I could even love."

After a moment Dan asked, "Is that woman Cindy?"

Jack couldn't look directly at Dan. He was afraid he wouldn't approve, but he had to let him know how he felt about Cindy. Finally, still looking down at the floor, he said, "Yes, it's Cindy. I think I've been in love with her since we were eight years old and I saw her that first time. I'm sorry, Dan."

"I'm sorry too, Jack," Dan said. "I'm sorry that you never told her that while she was still here."

Jack looked at Dan with surprise and relief. "You mean you'd approve of me courting Cindy?"

Dan laughed. "I sure would. In fact, I'll dance at your wedding. Furthermore, that's a promise." Dan raised his index finger to emphasize his point.

"Do you think Martha would approve too?"

"Jack, Martha and I have been praying for that to happen for years."

After that, Jack felt much better, but he was sure that he'd blown his chance of ever marrying Cindy.

About a month after the shooting, some of the tension had left Jack, and he felt the need to go and see Shannon. That Saturday night, when Rusty said, "Let's go to town, Jack. Your whore has been asking for you," Jack chuckled to himself, knowing that the sarcastic way that Rusty said it meant that Shannon still wasn't letting him in her bed.

"Okay. I'm ready. Let's go."

When they stepped through the swinging doors at Murdock's Saloon, the whole room became instantly quiet. Everyone at the bar moved to the other end without a word to Jack. "What's going on, Rusty? It's like I'm a stranger here."

Rusty grinned and patted him on the back. "It comes with the territory, pal."

"What comes with the territory?"

"Why, being a big time gunman, Jack. You're a hero. You're the man that gunned down one of the Daltons. It's called respect."

Jack didn't like all the attention that he was getting, but he didn't like being ignored either. "I don't know, Rusty. I don't like the feeling I'm getting about this."

"Aw. Jack, don't sweat these guys. They'll get used to being around a killer."

Annoyed at Rusty's actions now, Jack said, "Cut it out, Rusty. I don't like that kind of talk."

Rusty shrugged his shoulders and turned around so that his back was to the bar, which left him facing toward the center of the room. About that time, Shannon was approaching them. Rusty smirked.

"Here comes your whore."

Jack grabbed him by the arm. "Rusty, I'm warning you. Stop calling her that."

"Okay, okay, Jack. It's just that—"

Shannon was now standing beside Jack. She reached out and took his hand, saying, "Where have you been keeping yourself? I've been worried about you." As she was talking, she was pulling him away from the bar discreetly so as not to call attention to what she was doing. He knew something was up by the way she was acting, so he just followed her lead.

As they left the bar, he heard Rusty say, "Did you see that, guys? She's really got her hooks in him now. Can't you just hear the wedding bell ring?"

The sound of laughter filled the room.

Once in her room, they sat on her bed. Shannon was really upset.

"Jack, why are you still here? I thought you had left town already. Didn't Rusty tell you?"

"Whoa, girl. Slow down there. What are you talking about? Why shouldn't I still be here?"

"Oh, Jack. I've been so worried about you. I thought that if you didn't come in tonight I was going to ride out to the Walker ranch tomorrow to see if you were still around."

Finally, Jack got her calmed down. "Just what was it that Rusty was supposed to tell me?"

"Well, you know how fast news travels, especially from saloon to saloon."

"What news?"

"The news about the gunfight between you and Willie Dalton."

"Oh, that. Yes. Go on," he coaxed.

"Jack, it wasn't more than two or three days after your shoot-out with that outlaw that the news somehow got back to his brothers. Now the word is out that they're coming here to kill you." She paused to look into his eyes for his reaction. "As soon as I heard that, I told Rusty about it and told him to hurry and tell you."

"Aw. I wouldn't worry about them coming here—"

"No, Jack!" she yelled. "They could be here anytime. You've got to go away, at least for a while. I'll figure out a way to keep you posted on what's going on. Then you can come back."

"Wait," Jack said. "You told Rusty to tell me that they were coming here to kill me?"

"Yes. I told him as soon as I heard about it. He didn't tell you, did he?"

"Well, no, he didn't. He probably just figured that—"

"No, Jack. Rusty didn't tell you because he's jealous of you."

"Jealous of me?"

"Yes. He's so jealous of you that he wants to see you hurt or dead!"

"I just can't believe that of Rusty. We've been best friends since we were kids."

"You've got to believe it. I even believe that it was Rusty who got word to Willie's brothers about you." She was getting emotional again and began to sob. Unable to contain herself any longer, she threw her arms around his neck. "Jack, I love you. I couldn't bear it if something happened to you."

He held her close to comfort her and let her cry to get over the hysteria. He could feel her body trembling, and it seemed like he could even feel her heart beating. At first, it made him feel uncomfortable, but as he held her, he felt her warm tears on his cheek and neck, and he was very much aware of her breasts against his chest as she sobbed.

Suddenly, he wasn't uncomfortable anymore, and he realized that he could fall in love with her if he allowed himself to ignore his love for Cindy. Shannon truly loved him, and she was a beautiful woman. He could easily forget about her past. He was tempted to surrender to this moment of lust and make love to her, but he also felt that he would be taking advantage of her in a moment of weakness. She may be a soiled dove, but she was still a woman with feelings, and he couldn't betray her trust or her love for him.

After several moments, she pulled away but kept her grip on his hands. "I'm sorry, Jack. It's just that I love you so much."

"I'm sorry I can't tell you that I love you too, Shannon, but you know the reason why I can't, don't you?"

Wiping the tears from her eyes, she said, "Yes. I remember what you told me about your childhood sweetheart. And I wasn't trying to play on your sympathy, Jack. I just want you to know that I really love you. I've never had this feeling for anyone before, so I had to let you know."

Jack wiped a tear from her eye with his thumb and then let his fingers move gently across her cheek and just below her ear until his hand was behind her head. Her raven-black hair flowing softly between his fingers, he looked deeply into her eyes. "Shannon, the very first time I saw you I was in awe of your beauty. I desired to have you from that moment 'till now. And right now I have to admit that I am filled with lust for you. If it weren't for the present circumstances, I would ask you to marry me in a heartbeat."

They remained in that position as if suspended in time. She closed her eyes, imagining he was really asking her to marry him. After a few moments, she whispered, "And I'd marry you … in a heartbeat." Then the moment was over. She stood up and, facing him with determination, said, "We have to figure out what to do about this situation. Willie Dalton has three brothers, and one or probably all three of them are coming here to kill you. Moreover, we don't know how much time we have before they get here."

"Shannon, I know you're concerned, and I appreciate that, but I'm not running away. I'll just have to deal with the situation when and if it arrives."

She wasn't about to give in. "Well then if you won't go away for a while, will you at least just stay away from town? Will you stay out at the ranch? I'll keep you posted on the news about the Daltons until this all blows over."

Jack knew that it would be wise to consider what she said. After thinking about it for a minute, he asked, "Do you have a horse?"

"Yes, and a buggy too."

"Good. Do you know where the crossroads are?"

"Yes. About a quarter of a mile south of town."

"Okay. Coming from town just before you get to the crossroads, on the right side of the road, there's a big wooded area."

"I know where it is."

"Well, entering the woods at the crossroads, about a hundred yards in, is a little clearing. Just at the edge of that clearing, there's a huge oak tree. In that tree, there's a big hole. When I was a kid, I used to hide things there. That's how I know about it. Do you think you could find it?"

"Well, of course, silly. I can follow directions."

"Swell then. That's how we'll keep in touch. You'll have to go there at night so you won't be seen, but be real careful. I don't want you to get hurt. Don't go there unless you really have something to tell me. When or if you hear anything, write a note and put it in that tree. Meantime, I'll go there a couple of nights a week to see if there's a note there for me."

Jack paused to see if she was getting all that. She nodded her head and said, "Yes. I got it."

"Then repeat what I just said."

Shannon took a long breath and repeated it word for word.

After talking it over a few more minutes, Jack gave her a hug. "But," he added, "I'm only doing this for a couple of weeks." Before she could protest the length of time, he turned and left her room.

After he descended the stairs, he went to the bar to have a drink before leaving the saloon. Rusty was still at the bar. He looked at Jack and laughed.

"How's your whore, buddy?"

"Shannon's just fine, Rusty." Giving him a cold, hard look he said, "But don't ever call her a whore again! Her name's Shannon. Do you understand? Shannon. And that's my final warning." He then picked up Rusty's whiskey glass, downed its contents, and, still glaring at him, tightened his grip on the glass so hard that it shattered in his hand. He turned without another word and left Murdock's Saloon.

Rusty stood, amazed. In all their years together, he'd never seen Jack mad like that. "Okay, okay," he said. He followed Jack outside to where the horses were tied.

CHAPTER 6

There wasn't much conversation between Jack and Rusty during the ride back to the ranch. Both had their own thoughts. One of the thoughts that was on their minds was, *This is a kind of crossroads in our lives.* Jack was taking one road and Rusty another, and only time would tell where those separate roads would lead them.

Just before they reached the ranch, Rusty broke the silence. "Listen, Jack, and listen good. Don't ever talk to me again like you did back there in Murdock's Saloon. Shannon's a slut, a whore, and she will always be ready to take on any man who has her price."

Jack was furious to hear Rusty talk like that about Shannon, but he had to chuckle in spite of it. "Well, that ain't exactly true, Rusty. You haven't been able to score with her, so there must be something terrible wrong with you."

Another thing weighing on Jack's mind was what Shannon had said about Rusty. She was convinced that Rusty was so eaten up inside with jealousy because of him that he actually wanted him to be hurt or even killed. When he first heard Shannon say that about Rusty, he remembered thinking how ridiculous that was, and that they had been best friends since they were kids. That caused him to think back to that place in time when he first arrived at the Walker ranch. He was about eight years old, and Rusty was about fourteen. Rusty was only thirteen when *he* came to the Walker Ranch, but it was Jack who the Walkers took into their home, and he was treated like he was their own child. All this time, they had seemed to be best friends, but he remembered some of the things Rusty had done and said to him while growing up, like making wisecracks about him in front of the other men while in Murdock's Saloon, or when he first came to the ranch at eight years old, Rusty talked him into getting on one of the wild stallions that had been brought in right off the range. So maybe Shannon was right. There could be some truth in what she said about Rusty. From this point on, he would have to be watchful of him.

For the next few weeks, Jack secretly left the ranch a couple of nights each week to go check the tree for a note from Shannon. On Saturday nights, since there was no word during the week about the Daltons, he would ride into town with Rusty. They would have a couple drinks, and Rusty would go upstairs with one of the girls while Jack went up to talk with Shannon. "Maybe I was right," Jack suggested. "Maybe there's not that much love between those guys. Even though they're brothers, maybe they don't care what happens to each other."

"I hope you're right, Jack," Shannon said, "but let's not throw caution out the window yet."

They kept up the same scenario. Then, one night, there was an envelope in the tree. As he opened it, he could smell Shannon's perfume, but the night was too dark for him to read the note, so he put it back in the envelope and put it in his pocket. Back at the ranch in his room, he lit a lamp, sat down on the bed, and read the note.

Dear Jack,
There's word that the Daltons will be here within two weeks. All three brothers are coming, and they have sworn to kill you. Come see me. We need to talk.

Love, Shannon

Jack read the note several times and was surprised that he was not afraid. He just figured, *Well, I'll just have to come up with some kind of a plan.* He didn't tell anyone about the message from Shannon, especially not Rusty.

After receiving Shannon's note warning him about the Daltons coming, Jack became more suspicious about Rusty, but since he could be wrong about his suspicions of his longtime friend, he occasionally rode into town with him. When Saturday night came, he and Rusty rode into town together. As usual, Rusty went upstairs with one of the girls and Jack went up to talk with Shannon. She was really upset.

"What are we going to do Jack?"

"I really appreciate your concern for me and your help in all this. But *we* aren't going to do anything. I don't want you involved anymore. I don't want you hurt." Then, pausing to make sure she knew that he meant it, he continued. "I don't know what I'll do yet. But I can tell you what I ain't going to do. I ain't going to run away."

Shannon coaxed and cajoled, but Jack wouldn't budge an inch on running away or, as she put it, just leaving town for a while. "Well, we need to do something, and quick, too," she pleaded.

Jack noticed she said we again, but he figured he'd just ignore that for the time being. "I guess I'll talk to Frank Morgan and see if we can work something out."

"What do you think the sheriff can do for you? What if *he* tells you to leave town?"

Thinking on that for a moment, he shrugged his shoulders. "Hell, I didn't even think of that. That's a good question, Shannon, but it's just another bridge I'll have to cross when it comes between me and the finish line."

After talking a while longer, Jack left Shannon's room. His intention was to go down to the bar and have a drink and decide when he should go to talk to Sheriff Morgan. As he was coming down the stairs, he glanced around the room. The saloon was pretty well filled. Taking another quick look around, he didn't see Rusty anywhere. *Maybe he's out back in the privy.* That was okay with him. He'd rather be alone to think.

He elbowed in at a place at the bar. Jack had never cared much for hard liquor, which was the one good thing he had learned as a little kid. All those years he had stayed with those awful people had shown him what drinking hard liquor would do to you.

The barkeeper finally made it over to him, and he ordered a bottle and a glass. After pouring his glass full, he tipped it up and downed it in one swallow. He was just about to pour another one when Rusty edged in beside him. "You're not going to drink that whole bottle without sharing it with me, are you?"

Jack turned to Rusty and was about to tell him to go to hell when he felt a tap on the back and heard a familiar voice.

"We need to talk, Jack."

He knew before he looked around that it was Morgan. He nodded to the sheriff. Then he told the barkeeper, "Give us two clean glasses."

The barkeeper nodded and slid two glasses down the bar to him. He grabbed the bottle and glasses and walked to a table over in one corner at the back of the room. Frank followed him over to the table, and they sat down. Jack poured two glasses of whiskey and shoved one over in front of the sheriff. Frank looked at Jack and then at the glass. "I never drink while I'm on duty. You know that, Jack."

"Sorry, Frank. I didn't think." He picked up one glass and was about to take a drink.

Frank gave him a narrow-eyed look. "You never used to drink anything except soda water. What happed, Jack?"

Jack paused in midair, studying the whiskey sloshing around in the glass. Suddenly, the smell and the sight of it was pungent to his senses. He set the glass down and pushed it aside. "I don't know. I've had a lot of things on my mind lately. I guess I figured I needed it. Now what's on your mind, Frank?"

Frank sighed. "It's about them Daltons, son. You know they're going to come after you, don't you?"

"Yep."

"Yep? Is that all you got to say? Damn, man! What are you going to do?"

"Don't really know yet."

"Well you'd better think of something, and pretty darn quick too. All three of Willie's brothers could be here anytime now."

Jack shrugged his shoulders. "That's what Shannon keeps telling me. But according to the latest word, it will be about two weeks."

That surprised the sheriff. "Shannon knows about this? Why did you go and tell—"

Jack held up his hand. "Hold on, Frank. I didn't tell her. She's the one who told me."

"How does she know so much about it?"

"Think about it Frank; she works in the most popular saloon in town. She's going to know what all the latest news is."

"Guess you're right about that," Frank agreed. Then a thought crossed his mind, and he chuckled. "Maybe I should deputize *her* and keep her as an informer." Then he noticed that Jack wasn't laughing. "I'm sorry. I didn't really mean it."

For a minute, it seemed as if Jack didn't even hear what he said. Then, with a forced smile, he answered, "That's okay, Frank. What do you think about all this?"

"I don't know what we should do, but I'm thinking plenty on something else right now."

"Oh? Like what?"

"Well, if the Daltons think this thing out before they come chargin' in here to get you, they just might think that some of the townspeople will oppose them. If they think about that, then they just might bring some extra guns with them."

"I never thought about that," Jack acknowledged. "They claim to be related to the Dalton outlaw gang. If that's true, they could bring in a lot of professional gunmen and tree this town, like a blue tick hound trees a coon. A lot of people could get hurt or killed."

"That's what I was meanin,'" Frank said.

"Well, Shannon's been after me to leave town. Maybe that's what I should do. What do you think?"

Frank rubbed his chin with a leathery hand. "That was my first thought, and it might come to that if there's no other way. However, since you are willing to go away for a while, we'll just leave that open as an option. For now though, I say let's try to find some other way."

"Thanks for that, Frank. But what do you propose we do?"

"The ideal thing would be that if and when the Daltons come into town, they'd come alone, just the three of them. Then maybe, and I said maybe, we could talk them into having a real trial in court. That way we might be able to show them that it was in self-defense that you shot Willie."

"What kind of a chance do you give that scenario, Frank?"

"About the same chance as a snowball rolling through hell and it making it out the other side. But," he added, "it's something to hope for."

"Yes," Jack said. "If we could get them to have a trial in court, it would be a cinch to prove that I shot Willie in self-defense."

"Don't be too sure about that."

"What do you mean by that? You questioned a dozen people who saw the shooting, and they all agreed that I had no choice but to draw against him. And they'd testify to that in court."

"Are you sure about that, Jack? When they were talking about it then, they didn't have the Dalton gang looking them in the eyes."

"You really think that the people would refuse to testify on my behalf?"

"I can't say either way for sure. But I don't think we'll get to find out because unless I miss my guess, the Daltons will ride in here hell-bent for a killin' and shooting up the place, along with anyone else that gets in their way."

"Is it hopeless, Frank?"

"Close, Jack. Close. But I have been thinking about it and have decided on what the first step will be."

"What's that?"

Frank reached in his vest pocket and pulled out a badge. He handed it to Jack. "I don't want anyone to know about this yet, so just hold it in your hand."

Jack took the badge and said, "Okay. Now what?"

"Hold up your right hand."

When Jack held his hand up, Sheriff Morgan proceeded. "Do you solemnly swear to uphold the law with the power invested in you by this office, so help you God?"

"Yes, I do."

"Now," Frank said, "put that badge in your pocket and don't show or tell anybody about what just happened."

"Okay, Frank. But why this?"

"When the time comes, you'll already be deputized. Otherwise, we might not have time to go through the formalities. On the other hand, you won't lawfully be able to go gunning for them. But you will have the law on your side if trouble comes your way. Meantime, keep out of trouble and keep your eyes peeled and your ears open. If you hear or see anything of the Daltons, let me know. If any news comes my way, I'll get in touch with you."

"Right," Jack said. "And … thanks, Frank."

"Don't thank me yet. We still got to come up with a plan because I don't think we're going to be able to talk the Daltons into going to any court." A couple minutes later, Frank said good-bye to Jack and left Murdock's Saloon.

Jack looked around for Rusty but couldn't see him anywhere. That was all right with him. He'd enjoy the ride home, and he could think in peace.

Jack didn't venture from the ranch all the next week. The following Wednesday night, he saddled up and rode out to the crossroads. He entered the woods and stopped at the big oak tree. He reached inside the hole, and there it was, another message from Shannon. Having the feeling that this meant bad news, he hurried home to his room and read the note.

> Dear Jack,
>   The Daltons will be here in four days. Come and see me.
>   Love, Shannon

Despite the seriousness of the matter, Jack slept well that night. The next morning, while dressing, he figured he'd tell Rusty about the Daltons and how they had said that they were coming after him. It would be interesting to see how he would react to the news, if he didn't already know all about it. *If Rusty is truly a friend, he might want to help.* He would need all the gun power he could get.

After breakfast with Dan and Martha, Jack sat and talked with them for a while. Dan hadn't gotten out much since the accident in the line shack because he was mending so slowly.

"I was pleased at how well we came out last winter," Dan said, "what with how long the snow lasted."

"Yes," Jack agreed. "I'm surprised we didn't lose more cattle than we did. Last winter was just about as bad as five years ago when we got caught out in that blizzard and had to hole up in that line shack."

"Did you get out there to repair that line shack yet?"

Jack laughed. "Yeah. Hank and I took a load of lumber out there a long time ago and fixed it up. We practically had to rebuild the whole place. Hank said he couldn't see how you got out of there alive. The place looked like it had been blown apart with dynamite."

Now that the ordeal was over with, they could sit back and laugh about it. And every time it was brought up, Martha would grin and say, "I told you not to go out there, but no. You wouldn't listen to me."

On the way out to the bunkhouse to talk to Rusty, Jack figured he'd also tell Hank and the boys about the Daltons. *That way, if and when lead starts flying, they can be ready to take care of things here while I'm in town.*

It was early, about five thirty in the morning, when Jack stepped inside the bunkhouse. The cook, a Sioux Indian named Ira "Black Horse" Hill, had breakfast on the table. Hank and the crew were just sitting down to eat. Ira started to fix Jack a plate.

"I've already had breakfast, Ira, but I'd love to have a cup of your coffee. Go ahead and eat," he told the men. "I've got something to share with you, and I don't want Dan and Martha to hear about it because I don't want them to be worried. This is my problem, and I don't want them involved. Does everyone understand?"

Everyone nodded to show they understood, so Jack told them what was happening. They all knew about the shootout where Jack outgunned Willie Dalton, and this news didn't take them by surprise.

Hank took a drink of coffee to wash down a mouthful of food. "We were just talking about that yesterday and saying that Willie's brothers would probably be coming after you."

"Well, I just got word that they'll be here in about four days. Course, it could be a day sooner or later. I'm just giving you a warning in case you go into town. Keep your six-shooters loaded and your holsters greased.

"What are you gonna do, Jack?" one of the men asked.

"I don't really know yet. Some people say I should leave town."

Hank slammed his coffee cup down on the table and stood up. He looked around at all the men and then back at Jack. "Hell no! There ain't no bunch of outlaws, including them Daltons, gonna run any of us out of town! Right, men?"

They all agreed to that, and someone said, "We got enough firepower to handle whatever comes along. We're behind you one hundred percent, Jack."

Jack was pleased at the willingness of the men to fight for him, but he said, "I really appreciate that, men. And I didn't doubt for one second that you'd all feel that way, but it just might be that I'll have to leave town."

"And why is that?" they wanted to know.

"Well, I felt the same way when I first heard about them coming after me, but I have to think about the people. This is their town, and if it comes to a war, a lot of people are going to get hurt and some killed. For that matter, some of you could get hurt too. So rather than let that happen, I'll leave town."

"But you're not going to leave right away, are you?" Hank asked.

"No. I'm not going to leave unless I have to. I'll let you know if it comes to that. I've already talked to Sheriff Frank Morgan, and he says *not* to leave now. We're in the process of trying to come up with a plan to take care of this mess. In fact, I'm going into town now to talk to Frank about it. He's going to call a town meeting to see how the people feel about it."

Rusty spoke up then. "I don't think you should go into town alone until this thing is over and done with. I'll ride in with you if it's okay with you."

Jack was hoping that he would say that, but he declined the offer for now. "Why, thanks, Rusty. But right now, there's no need. It will be a few more days before it comes to that. When the time comes, I'll let you know." Then, looking at Hank, Jack said, "Is that all right with you, Hank? Can you spare a man for a few days if I need him?"

"Sure. We'll manage here just fine. But you know where you can get more help if you need it."

"Thanks again, Hank."

On the way to town, Jack thought over what all was said during his chat with Hank and Rusty and the men. He had kept his eyes on Rusty to see his reaction about the news. Rusty had held a poker face, and it was impossible to tell what he knew or felt. Of course, Rusty did say that he would back him up if it did come to gunplay. When he got to Frank's office in the jail, Jack told him about his feelings about Rusty.

"Well," Frank said, "I don't know if you can depend on Rusty or not. He's good with a gun, and he's got plenty of nerve. But I myself don't put much stock in him. I'm sorry, but that's the way I see him."

"I respect your opinion and your judgment on men, Frank. And between you and me, I don't have much confidence in him either."

Frank took his gold pocket watch out, looked at it, and glanced at the big clock on the wall. "Eight fifteen, and right on the dot," he said. "Town meeting's at eight thirty, so we better get going. We don't want to be late."

Jack was a little nervous walking into the meeting. He had no idea what would happen. He thought back how a few times he and Rusty had gotten into trouble in town and sometimes even wound up in jail. He shuddered to think about that. He figured, *These people are going to crucify me.* Then he thought, *I have done some good here too,* although he couldn't think offhand just what it was.

A loud voice brought his thoughts to the present.

"Order! Order! The meeting's about to commence!"

The town hall was packed to the rafters, so now he could see who all was here. Seated at two long tables at the front of the room, facing the crowd, were the town leaders. Presently, the meeting began, and there were hours of discussion—some for supporting Jack, and some for telling him to leave town.

Ed Banner and Toby Jacobs said in agreement, "I vote that we stand with young Jack and shoot the outlaws down the minute they come riding into town."

Some of the men yelled, "Hell no. I vote that he leaves town. You remember what a hellion he was just a few years ago, and now he's brought this down on us."

"Yes," another yelled. "Get out of town, Jack. You're gonna bring death to our town."

On and on it went. When the debate was starting to lean some-what in Jack's favor, Frank stood up.

"Hold on a minute," he said. "I've already telegraphed the cavalry at Fort Benton and—"

Jim Wilcox cut him off, yelling, "Hell, Sheriff, Fort Benton is a three-day ride from Billings. We'd all be dead by the time the cavalry got here."

Frank slammed his fist down on the table. "Shut up, Jim, and let me finish." The room got real quiet, and Frank said, "Now, as I was saying, I've already checked with the cavalry at Fort Benton, and they informed me that they have a whole platoon of troops in Hardin. They're there on a training mission." He paused there and looked at the fellow who was protesting. "Jim, do you know where Hardin, Montana, is?"

"Yes,"

"Well, where is it, Jim?"

"Hardin is north of Billings here, about an hour and a half's ride."

"Thank you, Jim. Now you can sit back down please."

Everyone started to laugh.

Frank let them carry on for a minute, and then yelled, "Okay. That's enough."

By the time the meeting broke up, they had all the plans laid out. From now 'till the ordeal was over with, they would have guards posted at every entry into town. As soon as anyone heard the guards sound the alarm, there would be riflemen on every rooftop. Frank, Jack, and Rusty, along with a few more men, would be in the street to stop the outlaws from coming into the town. If any of the outlaws got through, the riflemen on the rooftops would pick them off.

Walking out of the meeting, Frank told Jack, "You can put that badge on now. The town officials know that I already deputized you. Now the townspeople need to see you wearing it. You and Rusty probably should stay in town until this thing is over."

CHAPTER 7

It didn't take long for everyone in town to notice the badge on Jack's vest. Most everyone approved of it and accepted him as Frank Morgan's deputy. Frank immediately posted the guards in the prearranged places, and they put barrels and bales of hay in strategic places for cover to shoot from in preparation of the Dalton's arrival. Finally, the town was ready.

At eleven thirty the next morning, the guards sounded the warning. "The Daltons are coming!" Immediately, the riflemen were in place on rooftops. Frank and Jack were ready to step out into the street and face the outlaws and try to talk them into turning around and riding away. In the last tense minutes before the outlaws actually rode into town, Jack was thinking about his last conversation with Rusty. He had told Rusty, "Just because we're friends, I don't expect you to face death for me."

Rusty had told him, "Hell, Jack. I don't think the Daltons will try to get past you and Frank. I think they'll leave town when you face them. But," he said, "we been friends for a long time, so I'll be there to back you up. I'll take cover behind the hay bales, and if they want to shoot it out, I'll fill them full of lead."

Well, there it was. He knew now that Rusty wasn't going to be of any help, but he still couldn't believe that Rusty wanted him to be killed. Still, why would Rusty take cover behind the hay bales? He knew it wasn't because Rusty was afraid of gunplay. It could be because he didn't want the Daltons to see him for fear that they would let it out that it was he who informed them about him. Then, thinking about what all Shannon had told him about Rusty left him undecided what to believe.

Willie Dalton's brothers—Nate, Jed, and Bob—were notorious gunfighters, and they had every bit of confidence that they could and would tree this town and make that young punk pay dearly for killing Willie. "Nobody messes with the Daltons," they said.

The three of them rode boldly into town, a frightening sight for the townspeople, for the Daltons were all big, hard-looking men. They came in riding slowly, three abreast, on three huge, black horses. The three brothers had their hats pulled down to shade their eyes, and their long frock coats were pushed back on their right side to expose their holstered guns. As they entered town, Jack and Frank stepped out into the street and started walking toward the three outlaws.

Frank stepped out first, and then Jack stepped past him and to his right so that they were about ten feet apart. That gave them a slight edge. Two people standing close together would make easier targets than being spread out. They lucked out on the position of the sun too. By now, it was after one o'clock, and the Daltons entered town from the east. That put their faces to the west and the sun directly in their eyes while the sun was at the lawmen's back.

When there were about twenty paces between them and the out-laws, Frank held up his left hand, signaling Jack to stop. The outlaws stopped their horses, and Frank spoke first.

"You Daltons ain't welcome in this town, so just turn your horses around and head out the same way you came in and nobody will get hurt."

Bob spoke for the outlaws, ignoring Frank's warning. "Well, well," he sneered. "What a nice little reception we got here. Where is the bastard that back-shot Willie? Just trot him out here so we can take care of business. Then maybe we'll leave town."

"You got your information all wrong," Frank said. "Willie wasn't shot in the back. He got it up front where it counts. He was just too slow to cut the mustard."

"You're a damned liar," Bob yelled. "Where is the yellow sumbitch?"

Jack wasn't cocky, but he had confidence after his shootout with Willie because he knew Willie was a fast gun. After the shooting, they had counted nine notches on the handle grip of his pistol. "What's *your* handle, tough guy?" Jack asked.

Bob scoffed. "Dalton is the only name you need to know, law-man! What difference does it make to you? And what's *your* name?"

"Jack Montana, and I would just like to know what name to put on the tombstone of the man I'm going to kill. I put one badass in boot hill a couple weeks ago, and his tombstone reads 'Willie Dalton.'"

"You're the sumbitch that killed Willie!" Bob yelled, and they all went for their guns.

Jack and Bob cleared leather at about the same time, but Bob's horse got spooked by the sudden movement and reared up, causing the outlaw's shot to miss the intended mark and take off Jack's hat. Being on the ground enabled Jack to adjust his aim as he saw the horse rear up. His bullet slammed into Bob's chest, and the gunman was blasted from the saddle. He was dead before he hit the ground. Confident that his bullet did its job, Jack turned slightly to the left and put a slug into Nate's gut. At the same time Jack fired, a rifle bullet from a marksman on a rooftop caught Nate right between the eyes. He landed on the ground close to Bob's lifeless body. Frank took some lead in the shoulder from Jed's six-shooter, but he put two bullets into him—one in the neck, and the other in the center of the forehead. He died within seconds.

When the smoke cleared, Nate, Jed, and Bob Dalton lay dead in the street. Their horses ran wildly away with empty saddles, the stirrups flapping in the breeze.

Moments later, the men who were there with guns for backup emerged from behind the cover of barrels and bales of hay. Rusty was the first to approach Frank and Jack.

"We sure made short work of the Dalton gang, didn't we?"

Jack was about to say, "What do you mean we?" It was then that he noticed that his hat was gone. "That must have been a close call," he said. "Shot the hat right off my head."

While the townspeople cleared the bodies out of the street, Frank and Rusty helped Jack look for his hat, but they were unable to find it.

"That's strange," Frank commented. "It has to be here some-where. It couldn't have just flown away."

"Aw. Come on," Rusty said. "Let's go to Murdock's and celebrate. Someone probably took it for a souvenir."

Frank gave Rusty a disgusted look without trying to mask it at all. "Rusty, you go join the celebration. My deputy and I have some paperwork to do."

Rusty shrugged his shoulders and laughed. "Okay," he said. Then, mockingly, he said to Jack, "I'll say hi to Shannon for you."

That didn't irritate Jack one bit, because he noticed that Rusty didn't call her a whore anymore. Ignoring Rusty, he said to Frank, "Yeah. Let's go get that paperwork over with."

By the time Frank and Jack finished filling out reports, stating the facts on the shooting and describing the who, what, and why of it all, it was late when Jack got to Murdock's. The place was just about cleared out. Shannon was patiently waiting for him upstairs in her room.

"Oh, Jack," she said as she fell into his arms, "I was so worried about you. I'm so glad you're okay." Then she quickly pulled away from him. "I'm sorry. I know where your heart is and for whom it beats."

The truth of the matter was Jack really liked her company and the feeling he got every time they were together. The reality was that his heart was really with Cindy, and to just let his feelings fade away would be unfair to her. He had already told Shannon that if it weren't for Cindy he would ask her to marry him in a heartbeat.

Considering how complicated the situation was between him, Shannon, and Cindy, he decided not to make a comment on what she had just said. Instead, he opted for, "If this is getting too hard, maybe I'd better stop coming to see you because—."

Before he could finish the sentence, she quickly put her hand over his mouth. "No, Jack. No. I'll try to control myself better from now on."

It nearly broke his heart to see her like this, so as he turned to go, he said over his shoulder, "Okay, Shannon. I'll see you this Saturday night."

As he stepped out of the room and pulled the door shut behind him, he heard her whisper, "Just don't stop coming to see me, darling."

Jack stepped away from her door very perplexed. On the one hand, he was happy about the way things turned out with the shootout earlier, but on the other hand, he was very sad because of this relationship with Shannon. He couldn't see how she could love him so much. It was probably because all her life men had just used her. He couldn't understand that because she was a beautiful woman and it seemed to him that loving her would be easy.

Things went on as usual at the ranch and in town. At the ranch, Jack got back into the swing of things pretty quickly, riding fence lines and rounding up cattle that had wandered too far away from the watering holes. It seemed that the work had piled up during the short time that he was busy in town dealing with the Dalton gang. In town, Frank had to take Jack's badge because the trouble had ended and there was no more need for a deputy. When he turned in his badge, he told Frank, "Thanks. I don't know what I'd have done if it wasn't for you."

Frank had just said, "Hell, Jack, it wasn't anything."

However, Jack knew better. It took a lot of courage for Frank to do what he did. He could have just told Jack to leave town, and he wouldn't have had any choice. The townspeople seemed to have more respect for Jack too, and he was proud of that. But for some reason, he and Rusty seemed to be growing more and more distant all the time. A confrontation was inevitable. One day about two weeks after the shootout, he was out in one of the horse barns cleaning stalls when he heard a horse galloping into the barnyard toward the house. He stepped out of the barn to take a look. It was Shannon.

"Shannon!" he shouted.

Hearing his voice, she rode up to the barn and dismounted. "Jack, something terrible has happened!" She was upset and very excited.

He ran to her side. "Calm down, Shannon. What's wrong? What has happened?"

"Last night," she gasped, "someone broke into the bank and tried to rob the safe. Sheriff Morgan was making his rounds and spotted the robber, but he got away."

"Did Frank recognize the guy? Was anyone hurt?"

"No one was hurt, and Frank couldn't tell who it was. The man had a mask on, and it was dark. He got away."

Jack felt relieved. "Well, the would-be robber didn't get any money, and no one was hurt. That's not so terrible."

"But that's not all," she said. "The intruder dropped his hat while climbing through the window. Frank picked it up for evidence. And, Jack, Frank says the hat is yours."

"Well, that's easy to disprove," Jack said. "My hat had my name stamped on the inside of the sweatband."

"But it is your hat, Jack. It does have your name in it. I saw the hat myself, and I recognized it. It is your hat!"

"That's just crazy," Jack said. "I haven't left the ranch all week!"

Still very upset, Shannon asked, "What are we going to do? Frank might have to arrest you."

"It will be okay, Shannon. I know what's going on now. The day of the shootout with the Daltons, remember? My hat was shot off my head, and I couldn't find it. Someone picked it up, and now that someone is trying to frame me for the bank job by planting my hat there."

Again, Shannon asked, "What are we going to do?"

"Just stay calm, Shannon. I'm not going to be arrested. Go back to town and tell Frank that I'll come in tomorrow and talk with him. Meanwhile, I'll have to inform Dan and Martha about this."

After Shannon calmed down some, she left the ranch and headed back for town. Jack finished cleaning the barn and went in the house. After dinner, he told Dan and Martha about what was happening. They both became upset over this turn of events.

"I'll bet," Martha mused, "Rusty had something to do with this. I told you that someday he'd get you into trouble, Jack!"

"Now, Martha," Dan said, "don't go jumping to conclusions. Frank's a good lawman and a good friend. He'll know what to do." Then, looking at Jack, he said, "I'll ride into town and talk to Frank with you."

Jack knew Dan wasn't healthy enough to make a trip into town, so he told him that it would probably be better if he went alone and he probably wouldn't be in town long enough to make it worthwhile anyway.

Jack had started sleeping in the bunkhouse again so that he wouldn't bother Dan and Martha with his coming and going. After talking with them for some time, he went out to the bunkhouse for a game of cards before going to bed. Hank and the boys had just started a game, so he sat down at the table while Hank started shuffling the cards.

Bob Marshall, a happy-go-lucky guy with a joke always ready, sat down at the table beside Jack. "Have you heard the one about the Injun and the cowpoke, guys?"

"I would say yes, but I'm sure we're going to hear it anyway," Jack said as Hank dealt the cards.

"Well," Bob says, "this cowpoke was riding across the prairie, and his horse fell and broke his leg. So the cowpoke shoots him, right?"

Hank Shaw mumbled, "Yep."

"So," Bob continued, "the cowpoke starts walking, and pretty soon he's burning up and about to die. Then he sees this big cactus and lies down in its shade and goes to sleep. Right?"

"Yep."

Then Bob started to laugh.

Impatiently, Hank says, "Finish the damn joke, Bob!"

"Okay, okay!" Bob says between bursts of laughter. "Well, sir, suddenly, the cowpoke wakes up and there's this Injun, see, and he's sitting on his horse with an arrow pointed right at him. The Injun says to the cowboy, 'You tellum how to keep cool, or you die.' The cowpoke thinks real quicklike and tells the Injun, 'You make your horse run real fast, and the wind blowing in your face will cool you off.'" Bob again burst out laughing.

Jack was trying to keep a straight face, but Hank and the other guys just wanted to play cards.

"Damn it, Bob!" Rusty roared. "Either tell the joke or get the hell out of here so we can play cards."

Bob managed to control himself long enough to finish the joke. "Well, sir, the Injun whacks his horse on the rump, and they takes off in a dead run. After a while, the Injun comes walking back and sits down under the cactus beside the cowpoke. Pretty soon, the cowpoke asks, 'What happened? Where's your horse?'

"The Injun says, 'Ugh. Him run so fast him freeze to death!'"

Jack and Bob began to laugh, and then Hank joined in. Finally, Rusty and the others began to laugh too, and they all heehawed and slapped each other on the back for a half an hour.

Finally, wiping his eyes, Jack said, "Thanks, Bob! That's just what I needed: a good laugh."

The card game got serious then and lasted for a couple of hours. Finally, Jack stood up and stretched. "I've had enough for one night. I'm going to bed. Besides, you guys just about broke me." He lay down in his bunk, stretched again, and began to doze off. He was barely aware of the sounds of the other men as they were getting ready to go to bed. The last thing he was aware of was someone saying, "It's going to be another long day tomorrow."

CHAPTER 8

Frank was exasperated. "Hell, Jack. I know it wasn't you that I saw in the bank the other night, and I don't need any proof to convince me of that. But I saw someone drop that hat. And when I picked it up and examined it, I saw your name in the sweatband. I saw the bullet hole in it from when it was shot off your head in that gunfight. I would have recognized it anyway without all of those markings. So I know that it *is your hat.*" Frank then went and got the hat. "Here it is. You can examine it yourself, but I have to keep it locked up. It's evidence."

Jack took the hat and examined it. "I know you have to keep it locked up, Frank. And I appreciate anything you can do to help me in this. But I don't think it will amount to much. Do you?"

Frank didn't respond to the question, so Jack asked the question again and added, "Am I under arrest, Frank?"

Frank hesitated and then began to curse. "Damn it, Jack. My hands are tied right now. I sent a wire out to the presiding judge of this district, Judge Hoffman, and he ordered me to lock you up."

Jack was shocked. "Well, Frank, if that's what you got to do then I won't try to resist." He stood up, unbuckled his gun belt, and handed it to Frank. "Let's get it over with."

Reluctantly, Frank took the gun belt and put it in his desk drawer. Jack walked over to the back of the jail where the cells were and opened one up. He took a deep breath, stepped inside, and pulled the barred door shut. He could see that Frank didn't like this any more than he did, so to relieve some of the tension for both of them, he grinned at the sheriff. "You'd better lock this door before I decide to break out."

"I'm glad someone can see humor in this," Frank remarked. "But I don't think locking the door is necessary. When the judge returned my wire, he said he needed to come out this way anyway so he'd try and hear your case as soon as possible."

That gave Jack a little relief. "So how long do you think that might be?"

Frank shrugged his shoulders and stepped inside the cell with Jack and sat down on the small cot. "I don't rightly know offhand, but I'd guess two days. Meanwhile, I will investigate this matter thoroughly. If you can think of anything that will help, just give me a holler."

They talked for some time going over the whole incident. "Frank, I don't think Rusty would do such a thing as that to get me into trouble with the law, but still, I am beginning to have doubts about him. You might talk to him, you know, check him out."

Frank got up from his seat on the cot and walked toward the cell door. Before closing the barred door behind him, he commented, "I won't bother to lock this door. I know you won't try to leave." Frank stood on the other side of the cell door as if he hated to leave Jack in the cell. "I was already thinking of checking up on your pal Rusty. I never did trust him any further than I could throw a horse. If you need anything, let me know and I'll see what I can do."

"I would appreciate you sending someone out to the ranch to tell Dan and Martha where I am."

"No problem, Jack. I'll take care of it myself."

When Frank was gone, Jack had the sudden urge to leave the cell, get his horse out of the stable, and take off. He shrugged that urge off right away and began to think about what his next move would be. He realized that he was powerless to do anything as long as he was locked up in jail. He lay down on the cot and stretched out. Maybe that would help him think. Someone took his hat and was framing him for the bank job. But why, and who?

As he lay there, he dozed off, and then suddenly, he was startled by someone yelling, "Jack! Jack!" It was Shannon, and she was upset. "I just heard about you being in jail. The sheriff was over at the saloon, asking questions, and told me you were here. What can I do to help?"

Jack was glad to see her, but he knew there wasn't anything she could do. "Shannon, there is nothing you can do at this point. The only person who can help me right now is the sheriff. And he's doing all he can."

Shannon bit her lower lip, showing her determination. "I'm not leaving here 'till you're out of that cell."

He didn't want her to see that the cell door wasn't locked for fear that she would try and drag him out of the cell or that she would come inside and refuse to leave. "Okay. There is something you can do for me."

"What? I'll do anything."

"Well, I guess Frank forgot about me, and I'm hungry."

"I'll get you something to eat, and I'll be back as soon as I can," she declared excitedly and was out the door even before she finished the sentence. Thirty minutes later, she was back, and Frank walked in behind her. "I'm sorry. I forgot about getting you something to eat, Jack."

Jack grinned. "That's okay, Frank. I have someone else who won't forget me."

Since they were all joking about it, Shannon decided she'd join in. Before she handed Jack the plate she'd fixed for him, she held it out to Frank and said, "Well, aren't you going to take the towel off and check to see if I didn't put a gun or something in the food?"

Frank started to say, "Hell, the cell ain't even locked," but he caught Jack's facial expression signaling not to let her know about that, so he just laughed and said, "No. I trust you."

Shannon asked Frank questions about what the judge would say or do.

"I have no idea, Shannon. All I can say is that I've known Judge Hoffman a long time. And so far, I've found him to be a hard but fair man."

Finally, Jack told her that he needed to talk to Frank alone and that she really should go now. "But," he added, "promise me you'll come to see me tomorrow."

That seemed to make her feel better. "Okay. I'll be back in the morning with breakfast for you."

She left then, and Frank told Jack that he sent word out to Dan Walker about him being in jail.

Jack was hesitant to respond but finally asked. "How did Dan and Martha take the news?

"Not good from what I hear," Frank replied. Finally, Frank said, "I'm going to bed. See you in the morning. Do you need anything now?"

"Nope. I'm okay."

Early the next morning, just as Shannon was leaving the jail after bringing Jack his breakfast, Dan and Hank came in to see Jack and to talk to Frank. "How much is Jack's bail, Frank?" Dan asked.

"I can't let Jack out of jail, Dan. That's an order from Judge Hoffman. He'll be here tomorrow morning to hear some other cases. In his wire, he said he'd hear Jack's case first. Personally." Then Frank added, "I think he'll be acquitted."

"Damn it, Frank! We don't need no trial. Jack is innocent. You know that."

"Of course I know he's innocent, Dan, but it's not up to me. Anyway, who said anything about a trial? This is just a hearing to see if there's enough evidence to take him to trial. Let's just be patient until we see what happens at the hearing."

Dan continued to grumble about the situation. "I thought we were longtime friends, Frank."

Hank and Jack both tried to calm him down, but he kept on ranting. "I don't trust these courts or the judges no how."

"Now Dan," Frank said. "You know damn good and well that I'd let Jack go if I could, but you have to understand something. This is not like the old days when Jack and Rusty were just kids and would get into trouble. You would come into town and we'd talk about it, and then I'd let them go. Well, Jack is an adult now, a grown man, and he's been involved in four killings in the last couple months."

Dan interrupted Frank by reminding him, "They weren't killings. They were shootouts ... against outlaws."

"I know that, Dan. And now Jack is in jail, charged with suspicion of attempted bank robbery. So Judge Hoffman is demanding a hearing."

That caused Dan to think the situation over. "Okay, Frank. Hank and I will stay in town tonight and see you in the morning." As he and Hank were walking out of the jail, Dan turned back to face the sheriff. "I'm sorry for yelling at you, Frank."

Frank nodded his head. "It's okay, Dan. I understand. Forget about it."

Again Dan hesitated. "It's just that ... aw, hell, Frank, you know what I mean."

Frank nodded at him again, and Dan and Hank left the jail.

Once outside the jail, Hank said, "I wonder where Rusty's at. He should've been in to see Jack by now. He was supposed to be Jack's friend."

"I'll tell you where Rusty's at," Dan retorted in disgust. "One of two places. Either in a saloon somewhere or back at the ranch in the bunkhouse, with his damn head safely resting on a pillow. I'm thinking mighty hard on cutting him loose. I'll tell you that for sure."

Hank hesitated and then replied, "I don't blame you, Dan. But it be me, I'd wait and keep an eye on him, just to see what he's up to."

Neither of them mentioned Rusty's name again.

As she had promised, the next morning, Shannon brought Jack's breakfast to him. He thanked her, and this time, he opened the cell door. "Come on in, my fair lady," he said with a grin.

"Has this door been open all this time?" she asked as she stepped inside. Then she laughed. "You stinker. Why didn't you tell me?"

He was about to answer her when Frank came into the jail. He walked back to where the cells were and stood there, watching Jack and Shannon sitting on the cot, laughing. "You're not supposed to be in the cell with dangerous criminals, ma'am. You leave me no choice but to lock you up with him."

"It's okay with me," Shannon said, "if you leave us alone, lock this cell door, and toss the key away."

They all got a laugh out of that. In a more somber tone, Frank said, "Judge Hoffman is here. He'll hear your case at eleven o'clock sharp. He always holds court in Murdock's Saloon, but he don't allow any liquor of any kind while court is in session. I'm going to go over to Murdock's now and get things set up. I'll stop at the hotel and tell Dan and Hank that they can come and stay with you until I come back to get you."

"Okay. Thanks, Frank."

"You're welcome," Frank said as he left the cell.

"Well," Shannon said, "I guess I'd better leave before Dan gets here."

She leaned over to kiss him on the cheek, and Jack pulled her close to him and kissed her on the lips. She didn't pull away from him but lingered until he stopped kissing her. She was enjoying one of the few real intimate moments she ever had with him. "Thanks for that!" she said.

"No need to thank me, Shannon. That was pure selfishness on my part because I really needed something that only you could give me."

The kiss and his explanatory speech overwhelmed her. Even so, she had sworn to herself that she would win his love and it wouldn't be because she was doing something for him. It had to be strictly because he had fallen for her. To hide her emotions from him, she held back the tears and turned to leave. "I'd better go. I don't want Dan to see me here."

However, Jack was insistent and held onto her hand. "Why don't you want Dan to see you here?"

"Because of the way I am. Everyone knows that I'm referred to as 'your whore,' and I don't want to be an embarrassment to you or to Dan."

This rare outburst of emotion caught Jack off guard, and for a moment, he loosened his grip on her hand. She then pulled away from him and ran out of the jail.

Judge Tobias W. Hoffman was very tall, old, gray, and bent. He looked just as Jack had pictured him: well over six feet tall, gray, bushy eyebrows, and a muttonchops beard.

He was stoop-shouldered from old age. Jack figured the judge must be at least eighty.

Remembering that Frank had told him that the judge was hard but fair in his handing out sentences caused Jack to be a little bit nervous. When he stepped inside of Murdock's saloon on the heels of Sheriff Frank Morgan, he noticed that all eyes were turned toward him, making him even more nervous.

During the trial, a bank representative who also was a lawyer presented the evidence against Jack. He didn't have a lawyer, so Frank called several people to the stand as character witnesses, and had them tell what they knew about Jack and the shootings.

Finally, the judge said, "We'll take a twenty-minute recess, after which I'll announce my decision on this case." Then he told Frank to bring Jack back to the judge's quarters. "Talking to the accused might shed some light on Jack's case."

After the twenty-minute recess, the judge came out of his quarters and took his seat at the bench. When everyone in the room was seated, the judge made his announcement. "I am declaring this man innocent of any crime if"—the judge paused there, and everyone held their breath—"he agrees to carry out certain conditions, which I have placed in Sheriff Frank Morgan's authority." The judge then pounded his gavel on the table and announced, "People of the court, I now call this case closed. Next case please."

Immediately, Dan and Hank, along with some of the other people who were friends of Jack, came up to him, shook his hand, and congratulated him on the outcome of his hearing. He looked over their shoulder and saw Shannon sitting in the back row of the area designated as the courtroom, where she had been all during the trial. He held out his hand to her, and hesitantly, she came to him. He hugged her in front of everyone in the room, including Dan.

"Thanks to you people, and to Shannon here. I really thank you for your support."

To her surprise, there were no angry looks or words shown toward her. It was just one big, happy moment for all of them.

Outside the courtroom, Jack thanked Frank again and asked, "What are the certain conditions that the judge placed on me?"

Frank paused before answering. He cleared his throat and said, "I don't know. The judge left that up to me. I told him that you once acted as my deputy and that you were a good one. I asked if I could use you again to satisfy his requirements, but he said no because it would be inappropriate after this court hearing. It would have to be something else. So consider yourself a free man until I figure out what I can have you do to fulfill your obligation."

"Well," Jack said, "that's fine, Frank. I know you'll be fair. I trust your judgment, and I'll agree to whatever condition that you decide on."

"Wait a minute, Jack. It's not going to be that easy."

"How so?"

"Judge Hoffman left the certain condition up to me, but he ordered that the length of the condition be for the period of one year."

"One whole year?"

"Yes, one year. That's what makes it so difficult. That's why I need time to think about it. I'll let you know as soon as I figure out what I'm to have you do."

Dan's arthritis, caused by the accident, grew worse. It was winter again, which aggravated his condition all the more. His trips to the doctor became more frequent. Jack put on his heavy mackinaw and was going outside to hook up the buggy to take Dan into town to see Doc Green again.

"It's damn cold out there, Dan," he said. "You sure you want to go? I think the doctor will give me your medicine, considering the weather and all."

Despite his pain, Dan grinned. "Hell, Jack. It ain't even snowing. I remember the time when you and me went out in a snow blizzard to save a couple cows."

Martha knew that nothing would keep him from going with Jack, so she agreed with Dan. "You have your longhandles on, don't you?" she asked as she started helping him button up his mackinaw.

Dan pretended to get upset. "Damn it, Martha! Can't I even get dressed by myself without you fussing over me?"

Jack laughed. "I'll have the surrey ready by the time you get outside, Dan." As he stepped out into the cold and shut the door behind him, he heard Dan say in a softer voice, "Thanks, Martha. Sometimes these old fingers just don't want to work."

Jack finished hooking up the surrey and drove it around to the door. He got out and helped Dan onto the seat. He clucked to the team, and they were off. All the way to town, Dan talked about the things they used to do together, never forgetting the time they got caught in the blizzard and had to hole up in that line shack. He spoke of Jack gutting that cow and crawling inside its carcass to keep from freezing to death. He shook his head in admiration of Jack's perseverance.

When they got to Doc Green's, he talked to Dan and gave him some laudanum. "Only take this in small doses, and only when absolutely necessary."

Dan agreed, and they left the doctor's office. As always, they stopped in to chat with Frank.

As they were about to leave, Frank told Jack. "Come in to see me tomorrow morning. Something's come up."

Jack said he would, and they left the sheriff's office and went over to the general store. Jerry greeted them and said he had two letters for them. They were both from Cindy. One was addressed to Mr. and Mrs. Daniel Walker, the other to Mr. Jack Montana. They were both anxious to read the letters, so they left for home right away. Later, when Jack was alone, he remembered his letter from Cindy. He opened it and read it over two or three times. It was more of a note than a letter, but that was all right with him. He was pleased with its contents. Cindy was coming home for a long-overdue visit, and she wrote that she was very anxious to see him.

As Jack rode into town the next morning, he had no clue as to what Sheriff Morgan was going to throw at him. He could pretty well bet that it was something about that condition that the judge had spoke about. As to what the condition was, he had no idea.

Jack stepped inside Frank's office at the jail just after the sheriff had sat down behind his desk with a cup of coffee. "Hello, Jack. Come on in and grab a cup of coffee and we'll get down to business."

Jack took a cup off the hook by the coffeepot and poured himself some coffee. "Well, Frank, I hafta tell you I been kind of dreading this, but, yeah, let's get it over with." He sat down in the chair beside Frank's desk and waited for him to speak.

"Well," Frank said, "it occurred to me that you're pretty handy with horses and guns."

"So," Jack said, his interest rising.

"It's pretty risky business. You don't have to accept it if you don't want to."

"Come on, Frank. Quit stalling. Spit it out! What's the job?"

"Okay, Jack. Here it is. There are these five men; not just outlaws. They're real tough guys, and the law doesn't have the kind of men we need to go out after them. Oh, there are a few lawmen capable of going after them, but these guys are never in one place for very long. What makes it worse is that sometimes these guys work as a team and other times they work alone. So it makes it very hard to even find them, let alone bring them in." Frank paused there and, for the first time, looked directly at Jack. "Are you interested?"

"That depends, Frank. Under whose authority will I be working? Didn't you say that the judge said you couldn't use me as a deputy?"

"That's right. Judge Hoffman said nix to that. The only way that you can ever be used in law enforcement in the future is if you execute the conditions laid out to you. The only consolation you will have is if you have to kill any of these men, no one can prosecute you."

After a moment, Jack said. "Then I'd be a bounty hunter, under the protection of a clause in the law that says I can't be arrested for the murder of these particular five men?"

"Yep. That's about it," Frank agreed.

"Do I have a choice?"

"I told you that you don't have to accept the job if you don't want to. No one will blame you if you turn it down. You proved that you weren't a coward when you took the Daltons on."

"But the judge said he was placing the certain condition under your authority."

"Yes, he did, but he didn't say I had to make you risk your life carrying out the condition. He just said, 'When something substantial comes up, you have the authority to command that Jack does what you ask.' So, if you don't want to take on this assignment, then I won't ask you to do it. We'll wait 'till something else comes up."

"Damn it, Frank. I wish you had said that I *didn't* have a choice. I would've just agreed to the assignment and that would be that."

"I wouldn't demand that anyone do this job, especially not a friend."

"I appreciate that, Frank, but what makes you think that *I* can bring these outlaws in?"

The sheriff paused to study on that for a minute. "Jack, I've watched you grow up from an eight-year-old boy to manhood. You just appeared one day from out on the prairie, and Dan and Martha took you in and raised you as their own child. Since then, I've seen you in trouble, and I've seen how you handle yourself. You're a good and honest man, and you're damn good with a gun. I've been a lawman for twenty years, so I've seen many a gunman in action. And, Jack, you are one of the best, maybe *the* best, I've seen. Even so, sometimes even the best isn't good enough, and I'd blame myself 'till the day I died if you got killed while doing this assignment." Frank paused again and then sighed. "And by the way, the warrants that I received on these outlaws say dead or alive, so that lessens some of the risk if you know what I mean."

Frank was sure that Jack was quite able to bring these men in, but he didn't want to try to force him into accepting the assignment. He would give him one more chance to turn it down. "Don't give me your answer tonight. Sleep on it and see me tomorrow."

"Okay, Frank. That's just what I'll do. I'll see you tomorrow." Jack left the sheriff's office and headed straight for Murdock's Saloon. He stepped inside and crossed the large room to the bar, where he ordered a whiskey. He downed it and ordered another. "Keep it coming, Mac."

McDaniels poured another, and he downed that one. About that time, Shannon had come and was standing beside him.

"What's the matter, Jack?"

"I just talked to Frank and found out what my assignment is. You know, the condition that I have to fulfill in order to be a free man."

She pulled gently on his arm. "Come with me. You need a little Shannon time."

He set the glass down on the bar and followed her up the stairway. "I guess you're right." In her room, he told her about his talk with Frank Morgan. "What do you think, Shannon?"

She was moved that he would consult her on such an important matter. "I don't want to say anything that might lead you to get hurt or killed. I couldn't go on living after that. You know I love you."

"I know how you feel about me. That's why I'm asking you. I know you won't just say what you think I want to hear."

"Well, I do have a solution to this problem."

"What is it?"

After hesitating, she said, "Jack, why don't we just run away from all this, just you and me together. I'll go anywhere with you, under any condition."

"You know, Shannon, I'm very tempted to take you up on that. In fact, that was my first thought. We could just disappear. But running away never solves anything. We'd probably be feeling guilty and quarreling over everything. In a matter of months, we'd be enemies."

She knew he was right, but she couldn't help but think, *At least I'd have you all to myself during those few months.* Finally she said, "You're right. We can't run away. I know your heart, and you won't rest 'till you get this all behind you. So I guess I'd say take the sheriff's offer and go after those outlaws. Just be careful and come back to me."

Chapter 9

The door to Sheriff Morgan's office squeaked as Jack opened it the next morning. The clock on the wall read eleven o'clock when Jack stepped inside the jail.

"Morning, Frank. I've decided to take that assignment you offered."

Frank looked up from the pile of papers on his desk. "Morning, Jack. I never thought that you wouldn't take it. Fill a coffee cup and sit down."

Jack grabbed a cup of coffee and straddled a chair. Looking over the back of the chair, he asked, "What kind of leads can you give me, and what's your advice?"

"Leads or advice? I have none. You'll have to go on your own hunches. But I do have a poster of the five outlaws, containing pictures and descriptions. I also have a cover for you. You will be known as a representative and salesman for the famed Samuel Colt's Patent Firearms Manufacturing Company."

Jack took the wanted poster of the five outlaws, looked it over carefully, and read their names aloud. "Hal Colby, Ralph Simmons, Bill Taggard, Art Cummings, and Jess Barker." After a moment, he looked at Frank and asked, "Why do I need a cover?"

"Because this assignment will probably take quite a while to complete. As you said yourself, basically, you're going to be a bounty hunter, and if these men find out that you're after them, they'll be gunning for you. Needless to say, that will make your job more dangerous so that it will take longer to complete. As a gun salesman, you can move about as you please and ask questions as you go."

"And how do I become a gun salesman?"

Frank reached under his desk, picked up a small briefcase, and set it on the desk in front of Jack. "I've got it all under control. Take a look."

Jack opened the briefcase. Inside were two matched, beautifully handcrafted Walker Colt .44-caliber six-shooters. The briefcase itself was tailor-made for the two six-shooters to lie in separate compartments that were lined with thick, red velvet. There was a pocket of the same material in the upper part of the case that contained several order blanks just in case someone actually wanted to purchase some of the handguns. After looking at the six-shooters and the blank order forms, Jack looked questioningly at Frank.

"It's all legal, Jack. I've spent a couple weeks getting this all worked out. I got in touch with Samuel Colt personally, and he authorized the whole thing. You are listed in his company record books as a salesman for his company, just in case someone should decide to check up on you. There are authorization papers inside the briefcase if you need to show them."

Jack carefully looked over everything again. "Well, I guess you came up with a pretty good cover, Frank. Thanks."

"Don't mention it. I just wish I could do more."

Jack picked up the briefcase and the wanted poster of the outlaws. "You've done plenty, Frank, and I'm not forgetting all the times you looked out for me while I was growing up either." As he was going out the door, he said, "Thanks again, Frank. I'll be leaving first thing in the morning. See you later."

When Jack got back to the Walker Ranch, he was greatly surprised to see Cindy there. After they embraced, she said, "I took off work and got here as soon as I could when I heard that you were in trouble."

"But how did you get here from town?"

"Since I came home unannounced, I knew that no one would be in town to meet me, so I rented a horse from the livery stable." After answering questions about her job and how she liked staying in Boston, she wanted to know all about the trouble he was in.

He started at the beginning and told her everything—how he had had the shootout with Willie Dalton, and then later with Willie's brothers, and how someone had gotten hold of his hat and planted it in the bank while attempting to rob it.

She was very concerned. "What will you do?"

Jack told her about the hearing they had had and its outcome. "But that's not fair," she said. "What kind of an assignment did the sheriff get for you?"

Jack explained to her that he had to comply with the obligation that the court put on him in order to clear his name and what all the obligation entailed.

"That's outrageous," Cindy scoffed. "Why should you have to risk your life by facing five outlaws when everyone knows that you're innocent? It isn't fair."

"Sure. Everyone who knows me believes that I'm innocent, but other folks don't know me, so they feel that I'm probably guilty—folks like Judge Tobias W. Hoffman. So, if I want to clear my name and be counted as a good citizen, I have to earn that right."

Later in the evening, Jack told them that he had to leave the next morning. Dan and Martha were disappointed that he had to leave on this dangerous assignment so soon. In telling them about the assignment, he had watered it down as much as he could, hoping that it would lift some of the worry from them.

Cindy let it be known that she wasn't happy in the least. "You mean that we'll only get to see you one night before you have to leave, and you won't be coming back 'till the job is finished or maybe not at all?"

"Well," Jack said, "when you were in Boston, you wrote and said you had a job and that you wouldn't be home for two or three years."

Martha forced a laugh. "Oh, stop it, you two! Neither of you has changed one bit. You argue over everything, just like you did when you were kids!"

Finally, Jack said, "Okay. I can't leave in the morning, not with Cindy being here. My assignment will just have to wait a couple more days."

After that, the conversation became normal as they enjoyed the rest of the evening, talking about old times.

Dan and Martha were early risers, so they always went to bed early. "Since you're not going to be leaving for a couple more days, we'll be going to bed now," Martha said. "It will give you two some time to spend alone."

Dan wouldn't admit it, but pain usually put him to bed much earlier that this, yet he grumbled about going to bed anyway, adding, "You know these women, Jack. They can't take these late-night hours. They have to get their beauty sleep."

Jack and Cindy sat by the fireplace in silence until Cindy moved closer to him and put her hand on his and said, "Jack, do you remember when we were kids, how we used to sit here and play by this fireplace?"

"Yeah," he said. What he wanted to say was, "*I think I fell in love with you then,*" but the words just wouldn't come. He silently cursed himself for not being able to tell her because this was the perfect time and place.

There was another period of silence in which he was trying to muster up the courage to tell her how he really felt, but she ruined it by giggling and saying, "I remember the first time I ever saw you. You were a little skinny, freckle-faced boy. You were so funny-looking back then." She was about to say, *"But now I think you are the most handsome man that I've ever seen, and I love you."*

When she laughed and said she thought he was funny-looking, it embarrassed him. Before she could finish what she wanted to say, he got up suddenly and turned away from her. "I been thinking. I promised the sheriff that I would leave the first thing in the morning, so I had better get to bed. I'll be leaving right after breakfast. Good night." He then quickly left the room and went to the bunkhouse.

He had no way of knowing it, but she sat there and cried 'till daylight. Over and over, she told herself, *You stupid woman. Now you've driven him away, maybe forever.* She figured her only recourse was to get him alone in the morning right after breakfast and just come out and tell him that she has always loved him and she wanted to marry him. Then she said to herself, *Damn you, Jack, for being so shy and bashful.* Suddenly, a thought occurred to her. *Maybe he doesn't love me. After all, we were raised together like brother and sister.*

Jack lay in his bunk, unable to sleep, thinking. *I should have known that she wouldn't be interested in me. I can't face her in the morning knowing what a fool I've been.* After sleeping for about an hour, he got up and got his gear together. Quietly, he went out to the barn, saddled up, and left. He figured it was just better this way.

The next morning at the breakfast table, Cindy sat by Jack's empty chair. Her eyes were red from crying, but she was determined to at least tell him that she was in love with him, even if she had to do it in front of her mother and father. She would make any sacrifice to let him know how she felt.

After the three of them were seated and waiting for Jack to come in from the bunkhouse and join them, Cindy kept saying, "I wonder what's keeping him."

Martha said, "Maybe he decided not to eat breakfast this morning."

Dan laughed. "Martha, my dear, have you ever seen one time when that boy didn't show up for breakfast?"

However, when he didn't show up, Dan went out to the bunk-house to check on him.

"I don't know, boss," Hank said. "When he came in last night, he did seem a little distant, but I figured he was thinking about this assignment that he has to take care of. He didn't say much except, 'See you in the morning.' But then this morning, I noticed he wasn't in his bunk, so I went out to the barn and his horse and gear was gone. So I figure he musta headed out last night sometime."

Dan went back inside the house and told the women the news. Martha and Cindy both cried. Dan left the room with tears in his eyes.

Cindy knew why Jack had departed last night without saying good-bye after he'd promised he would stick around for a couple more days. However, she didn't want to upset her parents more, knowing that it was on account of her that he had left like he did. "Maybe," she suggested, "he just couldn't stand saying good-bye." Wanting to be alone so she could figure out how she could open this door that she had closed between Jack and herself, she said she was going out for a ride.

Hank and Rusty and some of the other men were out by the barn, working at the forge, forming horseshoes. They wanted to have their mounts ready for the big roundup that was coming up in the spring after the winter thaw.

When Cindy came out of the house to get her horse out of the barn, she talked to them for awhile, and then said she wanted to go for a good ride before she left to go back to Boston. They offered to get her horse ready for her, but she said, "No thanks. I can manage."

The stable horse she had rented in town wasn't as high-spirited as she liked, so she picked one of Jack's favorites, a big piebald stallion that he had named Charger. She loved that horse because of its beautiful, shiny coat blotched with black and white. Its wild spirit reminded her of Jack. Although a gentleman, Jack sometimes seemed to have a wild side to him. She chose Charger, but she chose her own bridle and saddle. She slipped the bridle bit in the horse's mouth, took her heavy saddle from its rack, and heaved it up onto the horses back. As she was tightening the cinch strap, she noticed a piece of paper stuck in one of the folds of leather in the saddle. She took the paper and smoothed it out. It was a letter from Jack.

> Dear Cindy,
>
> I have loved you since the very day we met. All these years, I wanted to hold you in my arms and tell you that I love you, but since we were raised like a brother and sister, I was afraid you couldn't return my love. I didn't have the nerve to tell you how I felt about you. Last night, when we were sitting by the fireplace, my love for you was overwhelming. I was going to tell you then that I loved you and ask you to marry me, but when you laughed at me and said that you though I was funny-looking, I knew that we could never be together. Please don't show this letter to anyone else. Just destroy it and forget that I ever wrote it. This is the last time I will ever say to you I love you. However, if you ever need anything, I'll be there for you.
>
> Jack

By the time she finished reading the letter, it was tearstained and she was sobbing. With trembling hands, she folded the letter and slipped it down in the top of her boot. *Cindy,* she said to herself, *you have pushed him away and closed the door between us for good. Now you'll never have him.*

CHAPTER 10

Three days from the Walker Ranch in Billings, Montana, Jack's horse came up lame. Somehow, the horse had bruised the right front pastern bone. Jack could tell this by feeling up and down the horse's right front leg. The horse would show tenderness whenever Jack put a little pressure just a little above its right front hoof.

"Well, hoss," he said, "we'll both have to hoof it now." He loosened the cinch strap on the saddle and began walking, leading the horse. After walking a couple of miles, he saw a road and followed it for a half mile more, after which he saw several buildings, a corral, and a stagecoach parked in front of a larger building. He noted the weather-beaten sign over the door. "Butterfield Stagecoach Lines."

The stagecoach had just pulled up and stopped, the dust still swirling up behind it. About that time, the hostler came running out and started unhooking the six-horse team. As Jack got closer to the coach, he saw four men step out and go inside the stationhouse. He could see two female passengers still sitting inside the coach. He tied his horse to the hitch rail and went inside the building. He was tired and hungry and needed to find out if he could buy passage on the coach to the next town—wherever that was—and also if he could leave his horse there at the stationhouse until he could come back after it. When he went inside the stationhouse, he saw that it was a pretty good setup. There was a man scurrying around, doing what he could to help the passengers get their food so they could get going again.

"Privies outback, folks, if you need it," he said. "Stage leaves in twenty minutes. If you want to eat, you better get to it in a hurry!"

The food consisted of cold beef sandwiches, a pot of beans, and cold cornbread displayed on a homemade lunch counter.

Jack noticed that of the four male passengers, three of them seemed to be together. The fourth one seemed to be a loner. Jack was concerned about the other passengers and asked the station manager, "What about the two women still sitting out there in the coach? What about food for them?"

The man hesitated for a moment and then said, "Listen, mister. The food's here if they want to come and get it. I ain't gonna fetch it out to them. They're no better'n anybody else!"

Jack walked out to the coach and opened the door. Peering inside, he said, "Ladies, if you want to get out and stretch or get something to eat, you better hurry. There's not much food left, and the coach will be leaving soon."

The younger of the two answered, "Thank you, mister, but mother doesn't walk well. An accident, you see. And three of those men are very vulgar and were making advances toward us."

"But aren't you hungry? Don't you want to get out and stretch while you have the chance?"

The younger woman looked at her mother and motioned for her to get out, but she shook her head no.

Jack gently took hold of the young woman's arm, "Come on, ma'am. You need to eat. I'll take care of those men."

She looked at him and somehow figured that he was trustworthy. She let him help her out of the coach. "I can't leave mother out here by herself," she said and started to get back inside the coach.

Again, Jack gently took hold of the young lady's arm to stop her from getting back inside the coach. "Let me try to persuade your mother to come with us," he said as he climbed inside the coach and sat down by the older lady. "Come on, ma'am. I promise I'll protect you." Reluctantly, she rose up and let him help her to the ground.

Once inside the stationhouse, Jack escorted the women up to the crude counter where the food was. There were only two plates left, and as the women reached for the plates, one of the three men that were passengers on the coach stepped in front of them and made a grab for one of the plates.

"Excuse me!" Jack said. "You've had your fill. These plates are for these ladies!"

"Go to hell," the man said. "I'm still hungry."

Suddenly, Jack's easygoing tone disappeared. "I'll only say this once, fellow. Get back to your table or go outside—whatever you want. Just leave us alone."

The man looked over at his two friends, but they offered no help. Then he looked over at the fourth man, the loner. There were no takers there either, so the man just turned his head and looked the other way. "The damn food's no good anyway," the man muttered and turned away.

Jack picked the two plates up and escorted the ladies to another table and set the plates down. "There you go, ladies. Please sit and eat." After he held their chairs for them, he sat down too. The younger woman said, "Mother and I thank you very much, sir, but . . ."

Jack was puzzled. "But what, ma'am?"

She lowered her voice to a whisper and looked over at the three men in question. "I'm afraid you might have made more trouble for us."

"When you get back on the stagecoach, you mean?"

"Yes."

Jack hadn't had time yet to inquire about passage on the coach for himself, and he didn't know how he was going to work it, but he knew right then that he was going to be on that coach. "Oh, didn't I tell you? I'll be on that coach when it leaves here." That was stretching the truth some, which he didn't normally do, but he wanted to make the ladies feel better. He could probably catch a ride on that coach even if he had to ride shotgun or on top of the coach with the luggage.

After hearing that he was riding with them, the women did feel better. They opened up to him, and they began to talk like old friends.

"We don't even know whom to thank for all the kindness," the younger woman said.

"Oh. Excuse me," he said. "I'm Jack Montana."

The older woman spoke to him for the first time. "I'm Margaret Holts," she said as she held her hand out to him, "and this is my daughter, Amanda."

Jack gently shook her hand, and then Amanda held out her hand to him. As he took her hand, he said, "I'm honored to meet you ladies."

Margaret Holts was a very refined woman of great dignity. She had white hair and spoke eloquently. One could tell by her appearance and manner of speech that she had excellent breeding and had been highly educated.

Jack guessed that she had given birth to Amanda late in life.

Amanda was a different story. She had long, flowing, brown hair, which when seen in the sunlight looked almost golden. She had a striking figure, which was apparent through the many folds and pleats of her apparel. He couldn't help but wonder how she would look in riding jeans. He doubted though if he would ever see her in riding jeans, since rarely would a lady be seen in such a garb as that.

Amanda, suddenly realizing that Jack wasn't eating, moved her plate between them. "Here. I'll share with you."

"Thanks, but I'm not hungry. I had myself some deer meat just a while ago." *There I go fibbing again,* he thought. *This woman really does something to me. I can't eat their food. They look very hungry the way they are eating.* He went on to explain to them how he was traveling horseback and his horse came up lame. "So that's why I'll be riding on the coach along with you."

The three men had been listening in on their conversation, and the one with whom Jack had earlier argued with spoke up.

"Well, you ain't gonna hitch a ride on this coach, stranger, 'cause there ain't no more room."

Jack smiled pleasantly. "There's always room on top of the coach with the luggage."

The man laughed. "Yeah. I guess you can ride up on top with the luggage and eat dust all day."

Jack laughed too. "Well, I'm going to be on that stage when it leaves here, but it ain't going to be me that's riding on top, eating dust all day."

In the brief silence that followed, Jack spoke to the driver of the stagecoach about booking passage.

"Okay by me," the driver said. "The coach is full though. You'll have to ride shotgun or on top of the coach with the luggage."

Jack paid the driver. "I'll feel right at home with riding shotgun. Thanks."

At that time, the hostler stepped inside and yelled, "The stagecoach is ready to leave, and Sam is driving it out of here in ten minutes, whether or not everyone's on it."

The tension over the dispute between Jack and the other passenger lightened up then, and everyone got up from their seats and filed outside to board the coach.

As Jack helped the women out to the coach, the three men started to climb in. "Hold on there," Jack said. "Where I come from, it's ladies first. Don't you men have any manners?"

Before they could respond, he helped the ladies inside and climbed in and sat down beside them, leaving room for three people to sit on the other side, facing them. The three men started to protest, but when they looked around, the fourth man, the loner, was nowhere to be found. So the men climbed in and sat down, grumbling to each other.

As everyone settled down then for a long ride, the station manager came running out to the coach. "Hey, mister, what about your horse?"

Jack leaned out the window of the door. "Take care of him for me. I'll be back for him as soon as I can."

"Okay," the man answered, "but after thirty days, he's mine."

Jack nodded in agreement, and the man tossed Jack's saddle and bridle up on top of the coach. "Take your gear with you. I don't need it."

They heard the driver crack the thirty-foot bullwhip over the horses' heads and felt the coach launch forward with a jolt. They were off.

As the coach left the station yard, Jack looked around to see if he could see the fourth man who had been on the coach, but he was nowhere to be found. The coach rattled and creaked along for four long hours. The men who were seated facing them never spoke a word. Jack, on the other hand, used the passing time to his advantage. He and the women chatted as if they had known each other all their lives.

He avoided talking much about himself. He only told them that he was a gun salesman. They already knew that his name was Jack Montana. They, in turn, told him that they had a ranch, the Lazy H, that was just on the other side of Laurel, Montana, which was only a short distance up the road. Steve Holts, Margaret's husband, had stayed at home to take care of the ranch while the two of them went back East to visit a sick sister of Margaret's. While there, Margaret fell and broke her ankle. Now, finally, they were almost home. Margaret's husband would be in Laurel with a buggy to drive them home.

"We would like to repay you for your kindness and protection if you'll stop by the ranch for a visit."

Margaret made the offer, and the look in Amanda's eyes made the offer hard to turn down, but he did decline, saying that he had better keep going.

"After all," he said, "that's how salesmen make money: going from town to town."

An hour later, the stagecoach rolled onto the dusty street of Laurel and stopped in front of the livery stable. The hostler came out and took charge of the team and the coach. Jack stepped out of the coach and helped the women out.

As the three men stepped onto the ground, they brushed past Jack and muttered, "We'll be seeing you again, mister."

Jack didn't bother to acknowledge them. He knew that they were all bluff and were just trying to impress each other. Hating to leave good company, especially Amanda, Jack decided to wait 'till they were in their buggy and on their way out to the Lazy H.

After fifteen minutes, when Steve had not shown up, Margaret began to worry. "It's not like Steve to be late," she complained.

Another twenty minutes passed. Jack looked around. He saw the jail just across the street, also noting that Laurel was a very small town. He figured that everyone who lived in this town would know if anything had happened around here. "Wait right here, ladies. I'll go inquire about Steve at the sheriff's office."

Jack stepped into the sheriff's office and introduced himself.

The lawman said, "I'm Sheriff Eli Blake. What can I do for you?"

Jack asked if he knew Steve Holts.

"Hell yes, I know Steve. I've been waiting for the stagecoach to arrive so I could tell his wife that he's laid up over at the doc's office."

"Well, his wife and daughter are here right now. I'll go tell them where he's at. Oh. By the way," Jack said as he showed the sheriff the poster of the five men, "have you ever seen these men around here?"

The sheriff looked at the posters. "No. Haven't seen 'em. Why? Are you a bounty hunter?"

Jack hated the term bounty hunter even more so now that he was one himself. "Actually, Sheriff," he said, "I'm a gun salesman. But until I catch up with these five outlaws, I guess I am one."

Sheriff Blake seemed to respect that answer and then repeated what he had already affirmed. "Nope. Don't recollect that I've ever seen those men around here."

Jack went back over to the livery stable and told Margaret and Amanda that Steve had gotten hurt and was over at the doctor's office. Very much alarmed at hearing this, the women hurried on over to the doctor's office. Jack went with them but waited outside in the anteroom while Margaret and Amanda went in to see Steve.

Presently, the women came out, both of them in tears. Margaret couldn't talk. She sat down in a chair and wept.

Amanda took Jack by the hand. "Come outside with me, and I'll tell you what's going on. Mother can stay here until she gets herself under control."

Outside, she told Jack what happened. "My father has had an accident. He breaks and trains wild horses and sells them. He's got ten wild horses now that he's been working with. One of them bucked him off and trampled him. He managed to crawl under the poles in the corral and escape being killed." She began to weep again. "Jack, I don't know what we're going to do. The doctor says he will be laid up for a long time."

Jack's soft heart spoke up even before he could think of what to do. "Don't worry, Amanda," he heard himself saying. "I'll stay out at the ranch with you and keep things going. A couple of weeks won't hurt none." They went inside, and Amanda told her mother what Jack said.

"But," Margaret said, drying her eyes, "you've done so much for us already."

"Is your husband awake and able to talk?" Jack asked.

"Yes, he is," she said.

"Well, I'll go in and talk to him and see if we can work something out."

Steve Holts was an older man, but age had not prevented him from working his ranch and catching and breaking wild horses. He had started his Lazy H ranch twenty years ago and was shaping it into a well-run outfit. He was also a proud man, but he knew when he was down and needed help. Right now, he needed a lot of help, so he conceded to Jack's offer. He was a little worried about a stranger staying out at his ranch with his wife and daughter, and he told Jack so. "But," he said, "I need a helping hand, and the women told me how you helped them already, and they said they would trust you with their very lives. That makes you okay by me."

By now, Steve was getting weak.

"You need to get some rest, Steve," Jack declared.

Quickly, they made a deal.

"If you will work at the ranch and see what you can do with those horses of mine, I'll give you any three of those horses that you choose."

"It's a deal," Jack said. He then left Steve to join Margaret and Amanda. Next, he rented a horse and buggy from the livery stable to take the women home.

The Lazy H ranch was nicely laid out—twelve hundred acres of good grassland, which was mainly flatland with the exception of a few rolling hills. The house was situated amongst some trees, and water was close by. Steve had built a small bunkhouse but so far had never hired any ranch hands to help with the work. Up 'till now, he had always managed to run things by himself.

The first day at the ranch, Jack moved into the bunkhouse and just went around checking on what all had to be done. The corrals and outbuildings looked to be in good shape, so the only thing that needed to be taken care of right now was the breaking of those wild horses.

Steve Holts had rounded up ten head of fine-looking horseflesh. He had already been working with a couple of them and had them green-broke, halter-broke. You could feed and work around them without spooking them too much, but they had not been broken to ride yet.

At suppertime the first day, Jack had a long talk with Margaret and Amanda. Margaret had been a mail-order bride from back East.

She had been well-educated, which accounted for her eloquent manner and speech. In spite of the difference in their background and the way each had been brought up, Steve and Margaret's marriage had been good. They had Amanda, who was now twenty years old and about to be married herself. Her future husband was away on a business trip at this time.

Jack asked about supplies, so Margaret checked the cupboards and said they were about out of everything.

"Steve must have forgotten to keep things replenished while we were gone."

"We need to return the team and buggy that we rented," Jack said. "Tomorrow morning, we'll go into town, and you two can do that while I take care of the supplies."

Right after breakfast the following morning, they headed for town. The two women drove the rented buggy while Jack followed in their wagon. They would need the wagon to get the much-needed supplies back home. When they arrived in Laurel, they stopped at the doc's office. The women went in to see Steve while Jack returned the buggy to the livery stable. There were a few people at the stable talking to the hostler, so he showed them the posters and inquired of the five outlaws that he was after. No one remembered ever seeing any of them.

From the livery stable, he went to the saloon called the Red Horse and ordered a whiskey. While the bartender was pouring his whiskey, he showed him the poster.

"Nope," he said and moved on down the bar, pouring someone else a drink.

Jack didn't think that was very friendly but decided not to make an issue of it. There were several other men in the saloon, and for all he knew, one or all five of these outlaws could have somehow changed their appearance—a beard or mustache, a patch over one eye, or dyed hair. *They could be in here right this minute.* He sort of hoped that would be the case. It sure would save a lot of work.

Because of this issue, he decided that it wouldn't be a good idea to continue showing the poster around.

He was about to leave the saloon when one of the barmaids came over and struck up a conversation with him. "You're new in town, ain't you, cowboy?"

"Been here a few days," Jack said. "How long you been around here?"

"Are you interested in me or just conversation?"

Jack knew she was a working gal and would only be interested in money. "Right now, all I want is conversation that will give me information."

"I figured as much. I saw you show José a wanted poster." Lowering her voice and leaning closer, she asked, "Are you a bounty hunter?"

"No, I'm not bounty hunter. I'm a gun salesman for Samuel Colt and Company. The reason I'm after these five men is they held up and robbed a stagecoach that was carrying several cases of Sam Colt's newest models of specially engraved six-shooters. In the process, they killed the driver."

She looked around to see if anyone was watching them. "Show me the poster."

Jack handed her the poster.

She took a quick look and handed it back to him. "I've seen one of them around here."

"Well, how about some information? Tell me what you know about these men."

"Cowboy, that kind of conversation comes high."

"I'm willing to pay if it's worth it."

"It's not healthy to give out that kind of information. So we can go upstairs to my room, like we're going to do my kind of business, or we can meet someplace else after I leave here."

"Okay," Jack said. "I'll buy a bottle, and we'll go up to your room." He bought the bottle of whiskey, and on the way up to her room, he thought about Shannon back in Billings. "This is getting to be a habit," he muttered.

"What did you say?" she asked.

"Nothing," he answered.

In her room, the barmaid sat down on the bed. Jack poured them a glass, and after a healthy drink, she brushed her hair back with what she thought was a sexy motion and patted the bed beside her. "We might as well get acquainted. My name is Wanda. What's yours, cowboy?"

"Jack," he said.

After a lengthy conversation, he paid her for their time in the room and then settled with what they both thought was a fair amount for the information that she gave him.

She had pointed to the one outlaw, Hal Colby, and said that she had seen him in the saloon several times. She added that he was a very mean and sadistic beast, so she wouldn't let him get close to her. Therefore, she didn't really know much about him.

After that, he left Wanda's room, saying that if she should find out more information about Hal Colby, he would make it worth her while.

"You're on, cowboy," she assured.

The next few days Jack spent working with the wild horses. Steve had a couple of them halter-broke, so he figured he would halter-train the rest of them. That way he wouldn't have to fight with each horse just to tie them up and saddle them. He thought he'd be done with all that by the end of the week and the following Monday he would start breaking them to ride.

On Saturday morning, Margaret asked Jack if he would go into town with her to bring Steve home from the doc's.

"Sure," he said. "I'd be glad to." He would like that because while she was getting Steve prepared for the journey home, he could go over to the Red Horse Saloon to see if Wanda had any more information about Hal Colby.

As it turned out, Margaret decided to stay home and get things ready for Steve's return. She sent Amanda with Jack to get Steve. This was the first time that he had ever been alone with Amanda for more than a few minutes at a time.

It was about an hour's drive to Laurel, and after some small talk, they grew more comfortable with each other. Jack asked Amanda if she had a lot of friends.

"Yes, I do," she acknowledged. After a moment she asked, "I find it interesting that you would ask me that."

"Well," he said, "I don't think I'm much older that you, if you'll pardon my assumption. It's just that I like to get acquainted with and keep in touch with people of my generation."

For the next few minutes, Amanda told him about herself and her friends, including the man she was going to marry. Finally, when the moment was right, he took the poster of the five outlaws from his pocket and showed it to her.

"Have you ever seen any of these men while you were in town shopping or visiting your friends?"

After looking carefully at the poster, she said, "I think I've seen this one, this Hal Colby, a few times around town." Then, hesitantly, she asked, "Why? Are you a lawman?"

Jack shook his head. "No, I'm not a lawman. I was a deputy awhile back, but not now."

"Are you a bounty hunter?"

"No, I'm not a bounty hunter either. I'm a gun salesman. I told you and your mother that when we first met, remember?"

"Then why all these questions? What's all this about these men on this poster?"

Jack laughed and then told her same story he told Wanda about these five men robbing the stagecoach and getting away with several cases of Sam Colt's specially engraved pistols and killing the stage driver. It was a cock-and-bull story, but it went over well and sure saved a lot of explaining.

"That sounds logical," she admitted. Then she laughed. "You know, Jack, I think you're a very exciting man!"

Jack wasn't totally sure if he read her right or not, but the way she looked at him when she said that sent a chill up and down his spine. He didn't want to get romantically involved with her or any other gal right now. Oh, she was a looker all right and a damn nice girl too, but he only had eyes for one lady, and that was Cindy. If he'd wanted to have another woman, he would have had his way with Shannon. She was one of a kind. Although he didn't want her to get attached to him, he didn't want to get on her bad side either.

"Well, Amanda," he said, "I think you're exciting too, but you're about to be married, ain't you?"

"Yes. I remember that I'm about to be married, and I remember his name too: Carl McBride. But you're much more exciting than he is."

They were only minutes outside of Laurel, so at that point, Jack changed the subject. "Your mother sure will be glad to have your father home again."

"Yes, and so will I."

When Jack and Amanda got to the doctor's office, Steve told them that the doc had just left and said he'd be back in an hour. Jack figured that would give him time to go to the saloon and check in with the barmaid, Wanda.

When Jack stepped inside the saloon, it was dark, so he did as he usually did. He stepped to one side of the batwing doors and paused for a moment to let his eyes get accustomed to the dimly lit room. He saw Wanda seated at a table with a couple of customers, so he went to the bar and ordered a bottle and two glasses. He paid the bartender and took his drinks to a table where he could see Wanda and still have his back to the wall. He hoped that she and her clients were just talking and wouldn't be going up to her room. He didn't have time to wait 'till she was through servicing someone. Presently, the two men got up from their table and left.

When Wanda looked over in his direction, he held the bottle up so she could see it and she came over and sat down. She reached over and picked the bottle up and poured them both a drink. After taking a sip of whiskey, she said teasingly, "I see you haven't forgotten the rules. If you want something from Wanda, you have to pay." Fluttering her eyelashes, she added, "And Wanda has everything you could possibly want, if you know what I mean, cowboy Jack."

Playing her little game, he said, "Yes, I guess you could meet the needs of most any man, but right now all I have time for is information."

"You want to know about Hal Colby, right?"

Jack leaned forward in his chair. "You got it. That's what I'm after."

"Well, I'm sorry to say you just missed him. But Hal loves to brag a lot, so I got an earful." She poured herself another drink and belted down the whole glass in one swallow.

Jack was getting a little impatient. "What about Hal Colby?" he coaxed.

She poured herself another glass of whiskey and started to pour him some. He put his hand over his glass. "No thanks. Tell me about Colby. Do you think he'll be back?"

"Well, Hal spends quite a bit of time here in Laurel because he has connections somewhere around here. I don't know who he's with or what that someone does. Also, he does business in a town called Red Lodge, which is about a two-day ride from here. When he's not here in Laurel or in Red Lodge, he crosses the border and goes into Wyoming. Hal talks a lot about Jackson Hole—you know, that outlaw town in Wyoming? I think he spends some time in the Big Horn Basin. But the answer to your question is yes. I heard him tell someone that he'd be back this way in a couple of months."

Jack thought for a moment about all that Wanda had told him. "I'm not really familiar with those areas," he acknowledged.

Wanda laughed. "I am. In my profession, a woman has to go where the money is. I've been all over Montana and Wyoming. As the cowboys all say, 'If you cross the border by way of the Big Horn Mountains, you'll come down into the Big Horn Basin,' and it's a rancher's paradise."

Jack stood up. "Thanks, Wanda. The bottle's all yours." He reached in his pocket and pulled out a double eagle. He flipped it to her and said, "Keep the information coming."

She caught it in mid-air, and her eyes widened when she saw the coin was a twenty-dollar gold piece. Slipping it between her cleavage, she smiled and said, "Thanks, Jack Montana. The way you pay, I'm yours body and soul. I'll definitely keep my eyes and ears open, and I'll let you know as soon as I hear that Hal Colby's back in town."

"Good. I'll keep in touch."

From there, Jack went back to the doctor's, where he found that the doc had returned. Amanda and her father were ready to leave. After some last-minute advice from the doctor, Jack and Amanda got Steve outside and into the back of the wagon. They made him as comfortable as possible in some hay that Jack had put in there just for that purpose, along with blankets to cushion the bumps and jolts the way home. None of the three hardly said a word, each alone with their own thoughts. After they arrived at home and had Steve in bed, he wanted to have a few moments alone with Margaret. He then wanted to talk to Jack in private. Jack went in and shut the door behind him.

"It's good to be home," Steve said, smiling as he looked around the room with almost the same intensity, as if it was the first time he had ever been in the room.

"Yes. I suppose it would be." Jack could just about know how he felt, seeing as how he would love to be at his home right now. "But that's not what you wanted to say to me, is it?"

"No, it's not. I guess I was just stalling so I could think about how to say it."

Jack didn't know what to expect, so he sat down in a chair and waited.

"Jack, you're a good man. When Margaret told me how you watched over them while on the stagecoach and then said that you were going to stay on and run this ranch for a few weeks while I was laid up, well, let's just say I was a little bit worried. I figured that you must have an ulterior motive. But now that I've met you for the second time and heard my wife and daughter say that they'd trust you with their very lives, well, I just want to say thanks. I told you the first time I saw you that I'd give you the choice of any three horses in the pack. And I will stand behind my word."

They talked for quite a long time. Jack told Steve about his background, how he'd come to be raised on the Walker Ranch, and that he was now working for Samuel Colt, the gun manufacturer. He stopped short though of telling him about the five outlaws that he was after. No need to worry him. Jack changed the subject by telling Steve that he had green-broke the rest of the horses and that he planned to start breaking them to ride the next day.

He could see that Steve was getting very tired now, so he told him he'd check in on him again and let him know how it was going.

At last, Jack had some solid information to go by. Hal Colby would be back in Laurel in a couple of months or so. In addition, hopefully Steve Holts would be well enough to take over running his ranch again so that Jack would be free to go after Hal Colby. He was sure that if he played his cards right Hal would lead him to the other four outlaws: Ralph Simmons, Bill Taggard, Art Cummings, and Jess Barker.

CHAPTER 11

The next few weeks at the Lazy H were enjoyable for Jack. He liked working with horses, especially wild ones, and the ten head that Steve had rounded up were real broncos. Amanda loved horses too and was fascinated with the way Jack handled them. From the first day, she would go outside with him to watch and help in any way that she could. Margaret wasn't fond of her being outside with Jack all the time, and she complained to Amanda that she should be inside helping her with the cooking and cleaning. Amanda made it plain to her mother that she would much rather be outside with Jack.

Jack explained to Amanda that since her dad had already green-broke some of the horses, it didn't take long to halter-train the rest of them. Now he could get right to the work of getting them used to the saddle and then breaking them to ride.

"What do you mean by 'green-broke?'" she wanted to know.

"That means the horse is halter-trained. You don't have to waste time trying to catch him and put a halter on him."

They stood at the corral, looking at the horses. The large corral was divided into two sections so that you could have some of the horses in either of the sections or all of them just in one, as they were now.

"Well," Jack said, as he took a bridle and saddle from the rack and stepped inside the empty section of the corral, "we might as well get started."

"Which one are you going to ride first, Jack?"

He looked at her and said, "You pick. The first one will be your choice."

"Wow. This is exciting," she declared. She looked at the horses.

They were all fine-looking horseflesh. Seven of them were mares, bay in color, and all with good markings. The other three were stallions. One was an appaloosa, One was a black, and the third was a strawberry roan. She pointed to one of the three stallions whose body hair was chestnut in color with white hairs interspersed. "What's that one called?"

"Good choice. A horse with a color combination like that is called a strawberry roan. Now open the gate carefully and see if you can let him out without the rest of them stampeding."

At that time, another horse came forward from the herd. He was black with four white socks and a perfectly shaped diamond in the middle of his forehead.

"Oh, look, Jack! The black one! Ride that one first."

Jack laughed. "I was afraid you'd pick that one to start with."

"You told me to pick, and I choose that one. Why? What's wrong with that one?"

"He's the meanest one in the whole heard. That's all. But you picked him, and they all got to be rode, so open the gate and let him out."

The black stallion was already next to the gate, so when Amanda opened it, he came out and she closed the gate behind him. Jack sat the saddle down and walked over to the horse. While talking and petting him on the neck, Jack slipped the halter off and immediately slipped the bridle on in its place. Next, he eased the saddle blanket onto the horse's back. The black horse started to move away from Jack but calmed down again when he felt Jack's gentle hands petting and rubbing his neck and withers.

"Whoa, boy. Steady now." Jack eased the saddle on and reached underneath the horse's stomach, got hold of the cinch strap, and hooked it up but left it loose. Jack then stood in front of the horse and petted and talked to him, settling him down.

Amanda came over and began petting the black horse too. After a few minutes, Jack slowly began tightening the cinch strap. When he felt it was tight enough, he took his bandana off and slowly and gently put it over the horse's eyes and loosely tied it to the bridle.

"Now the fun starts," Jack said. "You better stand outside the corral, Amanda."

She did as she was told. And as soon as she was on the outside of the corral, Jack put a foot in the stirrup and eased himself up into the saddle. As the horse snorted and began to move around nervously, Jack reached forward and quickly pulled the bandanna from the horse's eyes. The black stallion stood perfectly still for about ten seconds, and then all hell broke loose.

The black stallion reared and went straight up in the air. He came down on the ground with all fours in one little bunch, arching his back so that he looked like a huge black cat with its hair all frizzed up. When they hit the ground like that, it gave Jack a tremendous jolt, but he was in perfect form and stayed in the saddle.

That wasn't all that the black horse had to dish out though. Jack soon found that out because about two minutes later, he found himself lying on the ground. The horse came at him, shaking his head angrily while still bucking and pitching. The bridle reigns were flying every which way in the air, and the saddle stirrups were bouncing up and down with each pitch of the horse.

Jack landed close to the corral railing, so he quickly rolled over a time or two and stood up on the outside of the corral. Dusting himself off, he explained, "I didn't want to give the horse time to stomp on me like he planned to."

When he looked at Amanda, she was laughing. "I'm sorry, Jack, but you were riding so well I thought you had him beat. Then, the next minute, you were on the ground."

Jack grinned. "Well, you and the horse can laugh now, but I'll have the last laugh when I ride him off down the trail."

As he climbed back in the corral, Amanda yelled, "It was a good ride though."

"Yes, it was a good ride. It just wasn't good enough. But I ain't finished yet." Jack hitched up his belt and climbed right back in the saddle.

The black horse again went wild and bucked for all he was worth, but in the end, it was like Jack was glued to the saddle and, ultimately, the horse stopped bucking and began to lope around the corral.

After a few minutes, Jack reined him in by the gate and dismounted. He grinned at Amanda and bowed, making a swooping gesture with his hat. "There you go, ma'am. Your black steed is ready for you."

Amanda gave him a look that showed more than just admiration. "Jack, you're so exciting. I think—."

He had to change her mood, so he interrupted her before she could finish what she was going to say. "I know what you think. You think I'm crazy for getting back on that black tornado. I just hope that he got all the bucking out of his system."

Her mood and her look changed, turning more serious. "What do you mean by that? He stopped bucking, didn't he? Isn't that it?"

"Yes. Normally, when you ride a horse to a standstill, that's it. But sometimes when a horse has as much spirit as this horse has, it might buck every time you get on it."

"But that's not good. What do you do then? What can you do?"

Jack paused and took a long breath. "In that case, you have three choices. One, you can keep him and just be prepared for a wild ride every time you put a saddle on him. Or two, you can turn him loose on the range again so someone else can catch him someday. In that case, if that person isn't a lover of animals, they'd probably shoot him."

"We can't let that happen to him." Cindy said. "What's our third choice?"

Jack laughed. "We can bottle-break him."

Amanda laughed and said, "You're teasing me, Jack Montana. What is the third choice?"

"I'm not teasing you, Amanda. It's a trick I picked up from Dan Walker."

"Then tell me about it," she urged.

"No. You wouldn't like what you hear. Let's wait and see if any of these horses has to be bottle-broke. If not, then I'll tell you about it. If I have to use that trick on one of them, then you'll see firsthand what bottle-breaking a horse means."

Jack led the black horse out of the corral and put him in the barn. He then stripped the bridle and saddle off him, rubbed him down real good, and went back into the corral.

"We'll try to break one more horse. That'll be enough for today. Turn another one loose."

This time, Amanda picked the appaloosa. He stood about seventeen hands, and his body color was golden brown with black main and tail. His white spots were confined to his hindquarters. They were all the same size, as if each one had been perfectly measured and cut and then placed there strategically. It was very unusual to find wild horses with such good conformation and color markings.

When the appaloosa was close to the gate, Amanda opened it. As soon as the horse ran out to the other side, she closed the gate behind him. Since he was halter-broke beforehand, he stood still and let Jack put the bridle and saddle on him.

Jack put the bandanna over the horse's eyes and eased himself into the saddle. He sat for only a second, and then jerked the bandanna from the horse's eyes. Again, the fight was on. The corral was like one big cloud of dust, and this time Jack was ready for every trick the appaloosa tried. The contest between horse and man was long and grueling, but at last, Jack came out the winner. He walked the appaloosa to cool him down and curried and brushed him real good, just as he did the black horse. Jack put him in a stall next to the black horse. After he forked some hay into the manger for the horses, he hung the pitchfork up and began to brush himself off.

"Well," he said to Amanda, "that was one hard day's work. Tomorrow, we'll see if we can break a couple more horses."

In two week's time, Jack had broken all ten horses. Steve was elated and told him so. Jack had to admit it was good.

"But," he said, "I still have to ride each horse one more time to make sure that there's no more buck left in them. Then I have to train all ten horses to neck reign, stop, back up and lope, and everything that makes a good cowhorse."

"But I'm in no hurry for you to finish," Steve suggested. "Take all the time you need. Besides, I'm getting up and around now. In a couple more weeks, I can help do the training."

"And I can help with the training too," Amanda put in.

"That will help," Jack agreed. "I really need to be on the road before long."

Amanda knew full well why Jack wanted to finish up with the horses. He wanted to be ready to go after that outlaw, Hal Colby. Although she didn't want Jack to leave, she knew that that's what he wanted.

"Well," she said, "we can't get those horses finished off sitting here talking, now can we? So after you've finished eating breakfast, you can go out and get things ready. I'll help Mother clean up the kitchen, and then I'll come out and help you."

Jack didn't need any help with the horses, but he declined to say that. He was just glad that Amanda had changed the subject. The first chance he got, he would tell Steve and Margaret that he was after those outlaws, but now was not the time.

As soon as he finished eating, he excused himself from the breakfast table and went outside. A few minutes later, Amanda came out to join him.

"Are we going to finish with the black horse first?" she asked.

Jack grinned at her. "Your choice!"

Laughing, she answered with. "You know which one I'll choose."

"Go get him, and let's see what the big fella will do!"

Amanda ran inside the barn and soon came out leading the black stallion. After petting and talking to the horse, Jack put the bridle and saddle on him. The black horse didn't flinch at all.

"See," Amanda said excitedly. "He's going to be okay! I can't wait 'till I get to ride him."

Jack eased himself into the saddle, and suddenly, the black horse turned into a raging wild beast. Amanda barely made it out of the corral in time. Wildly bucking and trying to rid himself of his rider, he ran into the corral poles. Then, rearing high and slashing the air with his hooves, he threw himself over backward. Jack vaguely heard Amanda screaming in fear of his safety, but Jack was ready. When the horse went down but before he could roll over on him, Jack kicked his feet out of the stirrups and stepped out of the saddle. Then as the horse was scrambling up, Jack swung back into the saddle. The black horse continued to buck for several more minutes, and just as suddenly as he started bucking, he stopped and stood perfectly still.

Jack stepped out of the saddle, and Amanda came running over to him and threw her arms around him. "Oh, Jack, I thought you were going to be killed!"

Gently, Jack pushed her away. "Don't get to close to this horse yet. We have to educate him, and right now too."

Amanda was shaking from the excitement and fear for Jack's safety. "By educate, you mean you have to bottle-break him?"

"I hate to break him that way, but, yes, that's exactly what I mean."

"Okay, but why don't you want to break him that way?"

"Because sometimes it breaks the horse's spirit, and when that happens the horse is no longer good for anything."

"How can it break a horse's spirit? And how does this bottle-breaking a horse work anyway?"

"Just watch," Jack said. He hooked the reigns over the saddle horn, and as he put the bandanna over the black horse's eyes again, Amanda scrambled over the top of the corral to safety.

The horse knew what was coming next. This man was going to get on his back. He began to dance around nervously, but Jack managed to get a foot in the stirrup and ease himself into the saddle.

Amanda hadn't noticed, but Jack was already prepared for this. He had a bottle of warm water in his back pocket, and as he swung into the saddle, he pulled the bottle out of his pocket and wedged it in between his leg and the saddle. As soon as he was seated, he got a good grip on the neck of the water bottle and jerked the bandanna from the horse's eyes. The black horse immediately started to rear, but as soon as his front hooves were off the ground, Jack slammed him over the head with the bottle of warm water. The bottle broke, and the warm water came flowing down all over his head and into his ears and eyes. Immediately, the horse stopped bucking and stood perfectly still and began to tremble. Jack quickly stepped out of the saddle and began to pet the horse and talk to him.

Amanda's concern for the horse overcame her fear for her own safety. She climbed back into the corral and began to pet the black stallion.

"Jack, that was so cruel. I wouldn't have thought you would ever do anything like that. He's hurt and trembling. What was in the bottle? Is he going to be all right?"

"Don't worry, Amanda. You just saw the art of bottle-breaking a wild and stubborn horse at work. No, the horse ain't hurt. Yes, he is going to be okay. Feel the wetness in the horse's hair? That's just warm water. The reason he's trembling is because he thinks the warm water is his blood. Believe me. He'll never buck again."

Weighing all that in her mind against turning him loose or shooting him, she thought it was a good choice. "I guess I overreacted a bit, Jack. I apologize."

"No apologies necessary," he said. "I understand."

"Do you think this will it break his spirit?"

"I don't really know, Amanda. We'll have to wait to find the answer to that. My guess is no, but let's give him a couple days and then we'll see."

They continued to pet and talk to the horse until he had calmed down and then put him in the barn and went back out to the corral.

"Okay," Jack said, "Turn another one loose. We got a lot of work to do."

They worked at riding and training horses the rest of the day. Jack liked the black horse, but he figured that if Steve did give him his choice of any three horses, his first choice would be the appaloosa, then the strawberry roan, and then the black. Finally, the two of them decided to call it a day. They finished up in the barn and were about to go into the house. Amanda suddenly threw her arms around his neck and gave him a long, hard kiss full on the lips. Then she turned and ran out of the barn.

Jack stood there stunned for several moments, and then he put a finger to his lips and grinned. "I sure didn't see that one coming," he muttered aloud. "But I can't say that I didn't enjoy it."

It took another two weeks to finish the training of the horses. Each morning, before starting to work with the other horses, Amanda and Jack spent a few minutes with the black stallion, petting and talking to him.

After the usual petting and talking, Jack said, "Well, let's take him out and see what he'll do."

Amanda led the horse out into the corral, and Jack put the bridle and saddle on him. All the while, the black stallion danced around a bit, but seemed okay.

"Well," Jack said, "that should do it. Now let's see what he'll do."

Jack then put his foot in a stirrup and eased himself into the saddle. There was no bucking, so he reached down and patted the horse on the neck.

"Good boy," he said and loosened the reigns and touched the horse gently with his heel.

The black stallion moved out smoothly and reacted perfectly to every command.

"Amanda! Open the gate!" he called.

She opened the gate, and Jack again touched the horse with a heel. The black stallion leaped forward, leaving a shower of dirt flying high into the air.

He rode the black horse out of the ranch yard and down the road. He left the road then and headed out on the open plain. He let the stallion run full out for a few minutes and, with a slight pull on the reigns, slowed him down into a lope and then to a canter.

"Good boy," he said aloud as he headed back to the ranch.

He rode into the corral and stepped out on the saddle. He handed the reins to Amanda.

"You want to try him out?"

Amanda took the reins. "You just know I do. That's all I've been thinking about ever since we started working with these horses."

He watched Amanda ride out on the black stallion. "She'll do to ride the river with," he said under his breath. Then he thought, *How lucky this Carl McBride is to be marrying up with her.* He wondered if he would get to meet her intended before he had to leave.

Steve was pretty well recuperated now, and for the last few days, he had been coming out of the house to watch Jack and Amanda work the horses. Today, as they were finishing up and getting ready to quit for the day, he came out to tell them that Margaret had supper ready and waiting for them.

"Okay, Dad," Amanda said. "Tell Mom we'll be there in about ten minutes."

A little later, during the evening meal, Steve talked about how he was pleased with the way the horses turned out.

"You sure have a way with horses, Jack. I had never heard about your technique on how to break a horse from bucking again once he was broke and trained for riding. I had a horse turn out like that once. If that ever happens again, I'll know what to do."

Jack enjoyed the flattery for a moment and then became embarrassed by it. "Thanks," Jack said, "but the credit goes to Dan Walker. He showed me everything I know about horses."

"Well, you've done a great job breaking and training the horses for me. I really appreciate all you've done here. I don't know what I would have done if not for you."

Again, he became embarrassed. "Well, Steve, most of the credit goes to Margaret and Amanda. I was just helping out."

Margaret laughed. "You're kidding of course. We were down and out until you came along and—."

Amanda could see that all this talk about him, although true, was embarrassing him. So she intervened on his behalf. "Yes, Jack. you did pretty well after a few tips from me!"

Margaret and Steve looked at her and started laughing, but they got the message.

"Well then," Steve said. "Let's just say thanks. We'll talk about the payment that I promised you. Have you picked out the three horses you want yet?"

Jack remembered that Steve had promised him any three horses. He recalled that earlier he'd decided that he would pick the appaloosa, the strawberry roan, and the black. However, he knew that Amanda really loved the black stallion, so he would leave him for her. He also knew that Steve might sell the black horse because he was a fine-looking animal and would bring a good price. He decided to wait and make a choice about the black horse later.

"Well, Steve, I'm a little undecided as yet. I'd like to work with the horses for a couple more days before I make a decision. Okay?"

"Fine with me," Steve agreed. "Meanwhile, I'll ride into town and see about a buyer for the other horses."

CHAPTER 12

While Steve was searching for a buyer for the horses, Jack and Amanda took the horses for long rides daily. It was the best way for him to determine which of the horses he would choose. The first day out, they stopped by a stream to water the horses. Jack stepped out of the saddle, knelt by the water's edge, and dipped a hand in the cool water for a drink. His thirst quenched, he sat down under a tree to watch the horses while they grazed on the thick grass. For a moment, he was lost in his thoughts of home and Cindy.

Amanda sat down beside him. After a moment she said, "Jack."

"Yes," he answered.

"Do you remember the other day in the barn, when I kissed you?"

"Yes."

"What did you think? Did you like it?"

He had to be honest, so he spoke accordingly. "Yes, I liked it, but you are spoken for, and you don't even really know me. So how could you possibly care for me in that way?"

Ignoring his question, she continued. "Do you like me? I mean, enough that you could learn to love me?"

Jack knew that he had to settle this right now or just leave, but he wasn't ready to depart just yet. He wanted to stay and help Steve run this ranch 'till he was able do it on his own again. In the meantime, he would have a place to stay while waiting for Wanda to find out about Hal Colby.

"Amanda," he said, "I'm sure I could learn to love you. You're a fine woman and, I must say, beautiful too. Any man would be lucky to have you love him, but you shouldn't settle for a man who had to *learn* to love you. Besides, how about Carl McBride? Don't you love him?"

"I thought I loved him. But ever since I met you, I can't imagine being with anyone but you. Carl now is just another person to me."

"Okay. You've got second thoughts about Carl now. But what is there about me that makes you think you want to be with me?"

"Oh, Jack, you're so exciting. I just swoon every time I think about being with you."

Jack didn't know what to say or do now, so they were silent for some time. Finally, he decided he'd have to tell her about Cindy. If she took it too hard, he'd just leave. "Look, Amanda. I'd be mighty proud to be your husband. But I already have someone that I love in that way, and I hope to marry her as soon as I get back home."

Another silence. Then she said, "I understand, Jack. I had no idea you were in love with someone else. I won't bother you about us anymore."

"You're okay with it then?"

Wiping her eyes, she said, "Yes. I'm okay. And thank you."

"For what?"

"For being honest and not taking advantage of my loving you and for showing me what true love is about. I ... I would have done anything you wanted." After a moment, she said, "We can still be friends, can't we?"

"Amanda, I'd really be heartbroken if we couldn't remain good friends."

The weeks went by, and Steve was completely recovered. Jack got word from Wanda that she had news about Hal Colby for him, so it was time for him to move on. He had grown close to the Holts family, so he decided to tell them what had brought him out this way. They all wished him good luck, and Steve wanted to know which three horses he had chosen. He knew from talking to Steve that Steve had planned to sell the black horse, so Jack said, "My first choice is the black, then the appaloosa, then the strawberry roan."

Steve was hoping that he wouldn't choose the black, and he said so. "But," he said, "I said you could have any three horses that you wanted, so you can have the black stallion too."

"Fine. Then I'll be leaving first thing in the morning."

Amanda was shocked at this sudden decision. "Couldn't you stay just a few more days?"

"Yes," Margaret said. "Give us a little more time to say good-bye."

Steve was in agreement with the women but said, "We would like you to stay a little longer, but if you have to leave now, we understand."

"I've already got everything packed," Jack explained, "but I'll wait and leave tomorrow morning."

"Tomorrow morning is still too soon," Amanda objected, "but we'll accept that."

The next morning, after breakfast, Jack finished his coffee. "Well, I'd best be going," he said. He picked up his war-bag, and they all walked out to the barn together. Jack bridled and saddled the appaloosa, which he called appy, and tied his belongings behind the saddle. Next, he put a lead line on the strawberry roan and tied it to the saddle horn of the appy.

When he mounted the appy, Amanda asked, "Can I ride the black horse one more time before you leave?"

"Why, of course," Jack said. "You can ride him anytime you want to. He's your horse!"

"My horse?" she exclaimed.

Jack laughed. "Yep. He belongs to you now."

Amanda threw her arms around him and began to kiss him. "Oh, thank you," she said. "This is the best gift I've ever had."

Between Amanda's kisses, Jack looked over her shoulder and saw her father watching, and it occurred to him that he'd forgotten to talk to Steve about giving the horse to her. Since Steve had planned on selling the black stallion, he might be a little peeved.

"Oh, but," he said, "I clean forgot to—" At that point, he made eye contact with Steve.

Steve mouthed the words, "It's okay."

After a couple more kisses, Jack laughed and gently pushed her back at arm's length. "You really need to thank your father because he had planned on selling the horse. He's worth a lot of money."

Amanda then turned to her father and gave him a big hug and kiss. "Thank you, Dad. You won't be sorry."

"Will you want to choose another horse?" Steve asked.

"No," Jack said. "You gave me the three I asked for, and I gave one away. Besides, it will be easier with only one horse to lead."

Margaret had been watching from her kitchen window, and now, seeing that Jack was about to leave, she came outside to say good-bye. She hugged him and kissed him on the cheek. "I really hate to see you go, Jack. You've been such a great help to us." Jack returned Margaret's hug, shook hands with Steve, and mounted up. He reigned the appy around, and left the Holt's ranch for what might be the last time.

Jack hated to leave the Holts family because he had grown very fond of them. Now on the trail to Laurel, he thought that maybe he would stop in to see them again on his way back home to Billings. He'd really like to meet Carl McBride, Amanda's intended, and see if she went ahead with the marriage. He thought of Cindy and how much he loved her, but he drove those thoughts from his mind, thinking that she would never marry him. He knew he'd have to stay focused while on the trail of the five outlaws. The realization that he might wind up dead before this manhunt was over made his problem with Cindy Walker seem just a little easier to put on the shelf for now.

He had trained Steve's wild horses well, so the trip to Laurel wouldn't be bad at all. It was a day's ride by buggy or wagon, but only a half day on horseback. He enjoyed being out in the open country, so he decided to take his time and make it in two days.

The first day out, he rode the appy, leading the strawberry roan, making camp at the end of the day in a little wooded area by a small stream of cold, swiftly running water. He built a fire and made coffee and ate some of the prepared food that Amanda had packed for him. He was surprised to find a note inside the package. He opened it and read,

> Dear Jack,
> When Carl gets back from his trip, I'm going to send him packing. I'm still in love with you, and I won't settle for less. The only way that I'll ever marry is for you to come back to me or if I find someone else who could fill your boots.
> Lots of love and good hunting,
>
> Amanda

Jack sat by his campfire and read the note several times. "Boy," he said aloud. "Amanda, you sure ain't making it easy for me to walk away from you, are you?"

Late in the evening of the second day out, which he spent atop the roan, Jack rode down the street of Laurel. It was starting to snow, so he headed first for the livery stable. After tending to his horses, he headed for the Red Horse Saloon to see Wanda. He was anxious to hear the news she was supposed to have for him about Hal Colby. He went inside, and as he made his way to the bar, he looked around for her. Not seeing her anywhere, he ordered a beer. It went down smoothly, and he felt a little refreshed after his two-day ride.

As he set the glass down, he looked in the mirror that was hanging on the wall behind the bar. Wanda was coming down the stairway and walking toward him. She didn't want anyone to overhear their conversation, so she acted surprised to see him. "Hi, cowboy," she said. "Long time no see."

"Yep. It's been a while, Wanda. Let me buy you a drink."

"Anytime, cowboy." She motioned to the bartender. "Give us a bottle and two glasses." He set the bottle and the glasses on the bar, and she picked them up. "Thanks, José." To Jack, she said, "Come on, cowboy Jack. Let's find a table."

Jack followed her to a table in a corner, and they sat down. She filled their glasses and turned hers up and, drinking it down in one swallow, poured another one. As he watched Wanda drink the whiskey like it was water, he noticed that she looked more haggard than the last time he saw her. She actually was a pretty woman, but he knew what the results of too much drinking would do to a person. He knew it was really none of his business, but he felt the urge to say something about it. "Wanda, don't you think you drink a tad too much?"

She slammed her glass down, filled it again, and drank it down in one gulp. Then she looked at him and forced a smile. "Honey," she said, "I have to drink like this to cope with life."

Jack knew it would do no good to say any more about her drinking problem, and he had his own worries. "Sorry," he said. "Pour yourself another drink, and tell me about Hal Colby."

She wiped her mouth with her handkerchief. "I'm sorry too, cowboy Jack. You just missed Hal by about two hours."

He didn't know if she was sorry about his missing Hal by two hours, or if she was sorry about her drinking problem, or if she was sorry about his mentioning it. He decided it wouldn't be worth asking.

"Well, it's really better this way," he said, "because it's snowing now, and I can track him. And hopefully, he'll lead me to the other four outlaws. Can you tell me where he was headed when he left here?"

"I heard him say that he was headed for the border, into Wyoming."

"Did he mention the name of any towns he was going to?"

"He didn't say exactly where he was going, but he mentioned Red Lodge, Powell, Big Piney, and Greybull. Sometimes he goes to Fort Washakie. He never did say why he goes there."

Jack picked up the bottle and took a big drink. "Thanks. That's a big help." He then set the bottle back on the table. "You can keep the bottle, Wanda. I'll need to stay sober." He reached in his pocket and, pulling out a double eagle, flipped it to her. "Here. Keep this warm 'till I get back. It will more than cover the price of a bottle."

Wanda grinned as she dropped the twenty-dollar gold piece into her cleavage. "It will be right here waiting for you 'till you get back, cowboy Jack. You can retrieve it yourself."

Jack didn't figure on coming back here, but she had been a great help to him, so he didn't want to hurt her feelings. "Maybe I'll take you up on that, Wanda. Yeah. I might just do that."

He was hungry and tired and still a little cold from the two-day ride. The weather had turned colder, and it had started to snow, so he dreaded setting out on Hal Colby's trail. However, he knew he had to get started now or the snow would cover the outlaw's trail and he would have to wait 'till Hal came back to Laurel again. God only knew when that would be.

He could not postpone the inevitable. He had to get this job started, so he left the saloon reluctantly and went to the livery stable for his horses.

The hostler brought the horses out and said, "Here you go, mister. That'll be two bits."

He paid the hostler the two bits and gave him a nickel for a tip. He figured that that might encourage the hostler to answer some questions. He decided not to show him the wanted poster because that might intimidate him so that he wouldn't want to answer any questions or he might give the wrong answer to throw Jack off track.

"I was supposed to meet a man today in the Red Horse Saloon here in town, but I was told that I missed him by about two hours. He was here for a couple of days, so he must have put his horse up here. I wonder if you could tell me what kind of horse he was riding and where he went, or at least in what direction he was headed."

"Yep. I probably could. What'd he look like?"

"He's a big man, heavy moustache, bushy eyebrows, and has a large scar on his left hand."

The hostler seemed proud of himself as he said, "Yep. I know him. He's a businessman. Comes into town every couple of months or so. His name is Hal Colby."

Jack was amazed that the outlaw used his real name or alias, whichever Hal Colby was. Anyway, he used the name that was under his picture on the wanted poster. "Yes. That's the man I was supposed to meet. Now can you tell me what kind of horse he was riding?"

"Sure can," the hostler said. Then he laughed. "If you get within eyesight of that horse, you'll know him right off. Hal rides a jackass. He kinda looks like the standard bay-colored horse, but his tail and ears give him away. Skinny tail and great, long ears, you know, just like a jackass. Is there anything else you need to know?"

"Nope," Jack said. "I was going to ask you to show me a set of his horse's hoof prints so I could track them in this fresh snow, but now that I know he's riding a mule I'll know them as soon as I see them."

The hostler laughed. "Yep. If you ever saw the hoofprints of a mule, you could easily tell the difference betwixt them and a horse's hoof prints. Hell, a blind man could tell the difference just by feeling the prints with his fingers."

By this time, Jack had his horses ready to go. He mounted the strawberry roan, and leading the appy, which was carrying his gear, he headed out of town. He forgot about his being cold and hungry from the two-day ride to Laurel because of his good fortune in being able to find and follow the mule's tracks so easily. Anyone who knew anything about horse's hooves could follow the trail of a mule. Making it even easier yet, the ground was covered with snow. Of course, if it started to snow much harder, he would have to shorten the distance between himself and Hal. That would make the job more intense, for he would have to be careful not to alert the outlaw that he was being followed.

Jack located the mule's hoof prints as soon as he left the livery stable. He had already switched his light jacket for his heavy mackinaw, so he just sat back in the saddle and watched the trail. He wouldn't even have to get down every now and then to make sure he was following the right trail. He could read the sign easily from the saddle. He could tell that the mule was moving slowly by observing the distance between the hoof prints, so it was going to be an easy trail to stay on. As he had told Wanda, he wasn't familiar with the Wyoming territory, so he kept in mind what she had told him: "If you cross the border by way of the Big Horn Mountains, you'll come down into the Big Horn Basin."

For three days, he followed the mule's trail through the Big Horn Mountains, making dry camps at night. He didn't want to do anything that might cause Hal Colby to suspect he was being followed. Then, on the fourth day, just like Wanda had said, they crossed the border into Wyoming. On the fifth day, they dropped down out of the mountains into the Big Horn Basin, and Jack noticed that it was getting colder and starting to snow much harder. The mule's tracks were getting fainter all the time. Jack knew he only had a couple hours of daylight left, but he felt that he was only about an hour behind the outlaw, so he was getting anxious to close in on him.

While descending from the mountains, Jack estimated the Big Horn Basin to be about ten miles wide, but it stretched out as far as the eye could see. The Big Horn River flowed across the southeast corner of the basin, and at this point, Hal changed his path for some reason. Maybe he became confused or had a hunch that he was being followed. Maybe it was just a precaution that he rode around in a big, wide circle, making a few crisscross patterns, and doubled back for a mile or two, entering the Big Horn River at a shallow ford. Although it took a little while to follow the pattern and find where Hal entered the river, it was easy because Jack knew all the tricks of tracking. He knew that following a horse's track was opposite of a person's track. A person walking in the grass, for example, would kick the grass down in the direction of travel, Whereas a horse, or in this case a mule, because of its swinging gait, would knock the grass down in the direction from which he had come.

Jack entered the Big Horn River at the same point as Hal did. He rode slowly, watching closely to see where Hal exited the river. After a quarter of a mile, Jack saw the mule's hoof prints leading up onto the riverbank. Following slowly, he saw a wooded area, and he sat there on his horse, looking around at the trees. The branches were heavily covered with ice. The snow was coming down harder and thicker, but he could still make out the mule's tracks. After a moment, he again followed the tracks, and suddenly, partially hidden by the trees, he noticed a trapper's cabin. It was dark now, and Jack could see a light shining through the cloth that was covering a window at the side of the cabin. It was for that reason that Jack noticed the cabin.

He tied his horses to a tree and, taking off his boots and spurs, hung them on the saddle horn. He then put on his high-topped moccasins, which he kept in his saddlebags. He wanted Hal to be completely surprised when he made his grand entrance. If possible, he wanted to take Hal as a prisoner. Otherwise, he could just sneak up and shoot him. Jack made his way to a side of the cabin where there wasn't a window and quietly moved down the wall of the cabin to the corner. He looked around the corner. There was a window, and next to it was the door.

He paused there for a moment to prepare for his next move. Suddenly, the door opened and Hal stepped outside. He took a couple steps away from the doorway and then began to relieve himself.

He had no idea that he wasn't alone, and he was so engrossed in watching the white snow turn yellow and melt as he urinated that he failed to hear Jack step up behind him.

Jack eased his .44 from its holster, and cocking the hammer back said, "When you're finished, raise your hands and turn around. Don't make any moves that might shorten your life. On the other hand, that's okay with me if you do."

Hal was a big man, but he wasn't slow. When he finished relieving himself, he stood still for a moment. Turning swiftly, he tossed an Arkansas toothpick at Jack with deadly accuracy. At the same time, he dodged low and to the right. It was a good move, but when he turned, the light from the doorway, which was at Jack's back, was shining right in his eyes and caused him to miss. The thin-bladed knife stuck in the doorjamb right where Jack had been standing. Fortunately, the light and the fact that Jack had anticipated the outlaw's move saved Jack from injury or death. When Hal turned and tossed the razor-sharp blade at him, Jack brought his Colt .44 down and across Hal's, head knocking him out cold and face down in the snow.

Jack grabbed Hal by the belt and dragged him inside the cabin, got him in a chair, and tied him up. It was almost morning when Hal woke up. Jack had been awake for a while and had coffee made.

"Damn, man. You didn't have to bust my skull open, did you?"

"Don't matter to me," Jack said. He figured the more ruthless he sounded the more fear Hal would have, and that might take a little of the sassiness out of him. "Five hundred dollars dead or alive is what it says on your reward poster."

"So you're a damned bounty hunter?"

"Call me what you like, but at least I ain't no robber or killer of innocent people."

Hal was silent for a while, then he asked, "How 'bout some coffee and some grub?"

Jack was hungry anyway, so he cooked for both of them and poured two cups of coffee. He untied Hal and let him sit at the table with him. "Try anything, and you're a dead man."

Hal drank some coffee and took a few bites of food. "Are you aiming to take me in alive or dead?"

"Would've killed you last night if I'd a mind to. However, it's up to you." Jack showed the reward poster to Hal. "Tell me where these other four guys are, and maybe it will help me decide on how I take you in: sitting in a saddle or lying belly down across it."

Hal looked at the poster and said, "Don't even know those guys."

Jack eased a .44 from its holster and pointed it at the outlaw's head. He cocked the hammer back. "This forty-four has a hair trigger. Any movement at all could cause it to go off."

The outlaw began to sweat. "Okay, okay. I know them. Just put that hogleg back in the leather."

Holstering the pistol, Jack grinned. "Now we're on the same page. Start talking."

"First," Hal said, "just who the hell are you?"

"I'm Jack Montana if it means anything to you. I'm a gun salesman for Samuel Colt and Company."

"So why the hell are you after me?"

"Let's just say I don't like you. Now, back to the question. Where are your sidekicks?"

Hal had no idea who his captor was. He knew who Samuel Colt was, but he had never heard of this Jack Montana.

"Say on!" Jack demanded.

"Okay! All I know is they're somewhere in Montana. We meet here every year at this time to plan our next move. We wait here about a week. If we're not all here after one week, whoever is here heads on over to Fort Washakie and stays there 'till the rest join us. Then we stay there while we plan our next job."

"Why not just meet at the fort in the first place?

"Because it's more private here. But after a week, this place gets freezing cold, so we go to the fort and stay there for as long as it takes. It's a hell of a lot warmer there."

"So your four buddies should show here up at any time?" A grin played across Hal's thin lips. "Yep. That's what I'm counting on."

For two days, Hal and Jack stayed in the cabin. Jack couldn't trust the outlaw even one second out of his eyesight. During the day, he had to watch him just about every minute. At night, Jack would tie Hal to a chair while he slept. During the day, if Hal wanted to sleep, Jack would allow him to lie on the bed. They took turns preparing meals and keeping the fireplace going. It had turned bitter cold, and the snow was still coming down. If Hal's cohorts didn't show up soon, Jack would have to think about getting more firewood.

On the third day, just after daybreak, Jack was contemplating taking Hal on to Fort Washakie and waiting for the other four outlaws there. Suddenly, his thoughts were interrupted by the whinnying of horses outside.

"Unless there's a wolf or a bear out there prowling around, we've got company," Hal said.

"Yep," Jack acknowledged as he listened to the noise.

Grinning, Hal said, "What're you gonna do now, bounty hunter?"

Quickly, Jack gagged and bound Hal to a chair behind the table. Anyone opening the door wouldn't notice at first glance that he was tied up. With a couple of hurried steps, Jack was standing behind the door. He eased the Colt out of its holster and leveled it at Hal. "If you make a sound, you'll be the first one who gets it."

A few minutes later, they heard footsteps at the door. The doorknob turned, and in stepped a tall, thin man with a pockmarked face. He was shivering in his heavy mackinaw from the cold. Seeing Hal, he glanced around the room. "Where're the rest of the boys? I saw three horses in the barn."

It was dark in the room, but he sensed something was wrong. Before he could react, Jack slammed the door shut behind him. "Don't turn around. Just unbuckle the gun belt and let it drop.

Slowly, the man did what he was commanded. When the gun belt hit the floor, Jack said, "Now turn around and kick it over to me."

When the man had complied with the order, he looked at Jack questioningly.

"So you're Jess Barker?" Jack said.

"You know me, but I don't recall ever seeing you before. Who are you?"

"Jack Montana. And you're right. We've never met before. But we can get acquainted later." Jack stepped close to Jess and, with one hand, patted the outlaw down for more weapons. Finding none, he stepped back. "You can relax now and take a seat at the table with your friend Hal there."

CHAPTER 13

Jack kept his two prisoners, Jess Barker and Hal Colby, in the cabin for the rest of the week. He remembered Hal telling him that they only waited one week for everyone to show up. If they weren't all there by then, those who had arrived went on to Fort Washakie for the previously arranged rendezvous. He figured that it just might be a good thing that Ralph Simmons, Bill Taggard, and Art Cummings were, for some reason, delayed. Just getting these two outlaws to the fort alive would be trouble enough. He'd get these two crooks to the fort and watch for the other three there. Hopefully, they would show up at the fort before too long, and with luck, he might even get the post commander's help in capturing them.

The next morning after breakfast, he shrugged into his heavy mackinaw and commanded Hal and Jess. "Get bundled up. We're heading for Fort Washakie."

"The hell you say!" Jess yelled. "You ain't taking me anywhere!"

Jack knew that it was the hope of Jess and Hal that the other three outlaws would show up before they left the cabin. Chances were they thought that Jack would never be able to handle all five of them.

In a flash, Jack's Colt was in his hand. "It'll be a hell of a lot easier for me to get you there tied to your saddle belly down or dragged behind your horse. But," he said, cocking his gun, "if that's the way you want to be remembered, it's fine with me."

The two outlaws grumbled, but they hurriedly got into their mackinaws. It had stopped snowing, but the wind was blowing, and it was freezing that morning when the three men left the warm cabin and made their way to the barn for their horses. Jack herded Hal and Jess into the barn and told them to get saddled up. He watched as they finished getting their horses ready, and then he made his own preparations. He bridled and saddled the appy and began to saddle the roan so he could fasten his gear onto its saddle, all the while keeping the horses between himself and his two captives. He reached down under the roan's stomach to get the cinch strap so he could tighten the saddle. When he reached for the strap, he looked down just for a second. When he looked up again, Jess was sitting on his horse and had a .44 pointed right at him, already squeezing the trigger.

Jack dropped, rolled, and went for his revolver all in the same motion. Jess, shooting down from his horse, got off three shots, all three slugs going into the floor. The first one hit where Jack had been standing, and the other two hit the empty spaces he had just rolled through. Jack, rolling and shooting in the same motion, got off four shots. Jess hit the floor dead, four slugs in his hide.

Quickly, Jack focused on Hal, covering him with his .44. However, Hal hadn't moved a muscle. He just sat there on his horse, grinning like possum eating peach seeds.

"Damn," he said. "I was sure hoping Jess would fill you full of lead. I knowed he had a hideout gun. Kept it in his saddlebags." Then as Jack reloaded his Colt, Hal said, "I must say that was damn good shooting."

With a little prodding from Jack, Hal helped get Jess's body loaded onto his horse. Then Jack motioned toward the big door of the barn. "You know the way to Fort Washakie, so lead the way." As he followed Hal out of the barn and onto the trail to the fort, Jack thought to himself, *Two down and three to go. Sure hope my luck holds out.*

They rode 'till late in the evening. When they came across a running stream, they followed it for about a quarter mile until they saw a grove of trees.

"We'll camp here," Jack said. "The trees will give us some protection if it starts snowing again."

Entering the grove of trees, Jack spotted a good place to make camp. After tying their horses and rubbing them down good, he got the feedbags out of the gear he'd packed on the roan horses and put some grain in them for each horse. He gathered up branches and crisscrossed them in a pile so the air could get underneath. Next, he threw some chunks of pitch pine on top and touched a match to it. In no time, he had a good fire going. He made some coffee, dug some jerky out of his saddlebags, and hunkered down to a decent feeding. He untied Hal so he could fix his own meal, but he shared his coffee with him. After eating, they finished off the pot of coffee and Jack tied Hal up and covered him with a blanket. Then he made himself as comfortable as possible and went to sleep.

Jack woke early in the morning and prepared a quick breakfast. After they had their coffee and some jerky, they got underway again. At two o'clock in the afternoon of their second day out, they were less than a quarter mile from the fort. The lookouts spotted them through their spyglass. The commanding officer was alerted, and, looking through the long glass, he saw four horses. The fourth horse seemed to be carrying a dead man, judging by the way that the man was tied across the saddle. The rider of the lead horse seemed to have his hands tied to the saddle horn, which indicated to them that he was a prisoner. The middle rider seemed to be in charge. He was leading a horse with a packsaddle on it.

The commanding officer, a man named John Goodman, motioned to one of the cavalry sergeants. "Take six men, Sergeant Calhoun, and check those riders out. We don't want trouble coming in from outside civilians."

"Yes, sir," Sergeant Calhoun responded. He then quickly named six enlisted men and commanded them to get mounted. Sergeant Calhoun gave the order to move out, and they rode out from the fort two abreast, with Sergeant Calhoun in the lead.

Jack saw the soldiers leave the fort from afar and was hoping he wouldn't be turned away. In that case, he'd have a big problem. When Sergeant Calhoun was within twenty feet or so of Jack, he commanded his men to halt. Jack rode out in front of Hal Colby and halted his prisoners. Looking at the soldier's insignia on the uniform, he said, "Good afternoon, Sergeant."

"Good afternoon," Calhoun returned. "State your name and what business you have at Fort Washakie."

Jack rode in closer to the sergeant and carefully reached back in his saddlebags for the wanted poster of the five outlaws. Handing him the poster, Jack said, "I'm Jack Montana, and these guys are two of the five wanted men. And I have reason to believe that the other three will be coming to the fort expecting to meet up with these two."

"You have papers to identify yourself?"

"Yes, sir," Jack said, handing the sergeant the papers showing his name and that he was a gun salesman for the Samuel Colt Firearms Corporation of Hartford, Connecticut. The sergeant returned all the papers to Jack and held out his hand. "Sorry about the delay, Mr. Montana. I'm Sergeant Calhoun. We'll escort you and your prisoners to the fort."

Jack readily shook hands with the sergeant. "Thanks. I appreciate that."

Sergeant Calhoun then positioned two of his men at the rear of the party and escorted them to the fort.

Once inside, the sergeant had Hal Colby locked up in the fort's stockade and ordered a detail to take care of Jess Barker's body. He then escorted Jack to see the commander of the post.

The post commander shook hands with Jack. "I'm Captain John Goodman, Mr. Montana. Jack, if I may be so informal."

"Certainly, Captain Goodman."

Smiling, the captain said, "Please call me John. If you're not comfortable with that, just call me captain. While the men and I are on duty here at the fort, we salute and address one another in military manner, but we like to be informal when we can."

With the formalities out of the way, the captain looked over Jack's papers, including the wanted poster with the pictures of the five outlaws. "Sergeant Calhoun informed me about the outlaws, but I'd be interested to know why you're after them. You have papers to show you are a representative of the Samuel Colt Firearms Corporation. Are you also a bounty hunter?"

"No. I'm after these men because they held up and robbed a stagecoach that was carrying several cases of Sam Colt's newest models of specially engraved six-shooters. In the process, they killed the driver."

"I see. I'm glad you cleared that up." The captain looked at the poster and said, "As for the other three outlaws, Ralph Simmons, Bill Taggard, and Art Cummings, I'll have my men on the lookout for them. When or if they do show up here, they'll be placed under arrest."

"I'd appreciate that, Captain. It would sure take a load of off my mind."

"Then consider it done. What do you intend doing in the meantime?"

"The first thing I'd like is a bath and a shave and then something to eat and then about twenty-four hours of sleep."

The captain laughed. "I can believe that. I've been in that shape a time or two myself. Just make yourself at home during your stay here at Fort Washakie. If you need anything, just ask Sergeant Calhoun or myself."

Jack thanked the captain again and left the captain's quarters. He went to the sutler's store, where he bought some needed supplies, and then found the barbershop. His next stop was the bathhouse and finally the civilian quarters, where he found a place to bed down and slept clean through 'till eleven o'clock the next day. He woke refreshed and, after dressing, had breakfast at the mess hall. After eating, he looked up Sergeant Calhoun and asked if he'd heard or seen anything of the three outlaws who were supposed to meet up with Hal Colby.

"No, sir," the sergeant said. "Haven't seen hide nor hair of any of them."

That became the routine for the next few days. Finally, Jack went to the captain's quarters and spoke with him. "I can't just sit here and wait for them to decide to show up."

"Whatever you say, Jack. What are your plans?"

"Well, Captain, I figure I'll backtrack all the way to that trapper's cabin in the Big Horn Basin if I have to and visit some of the towns between here and there. Maybe for some reason they stopped over for a few days somewhere."

Captain Goodman handed him documents that stated that two outlaws, Hal Colby and Jess Barker, had been delivered to Captain John Goodman at Fort Washakie by the hand of Jack Montana and the outlaw Jess Barker had been killed while resisting arrest.

"Here. Take these documents with you," the captain explained, "just in case you, for some reason, decide not to come back to Fort Washakie. It will save you some traveling time. Along with the documents, I included a map of the towns between here and the Big Horn Basin. Jack, I wish you luck and good hunting."

"Thanks, Captain, I appreciate that. But if I can't locate them, I'll come back anyway to see if they did show up here."

They shook hands, and Jack went to the stables and loaded his gear on the appaloosa, bridled and saddled the strawberry roan, and, after shaking hands with Sergeant Calhoun, mounted up and left the fort.

The temperature was only five degrees above zero, but the early morning sun was shining brightly and the wind had stopped blowing. Jack felt comfortable bundled up in his heavy mackinaw. Wanting to keep as warm as possible, he had put his heavy fur chaps on over his trousers. They were for heavy brush, but they also kept the cold off his legs.

The horses were feeling frisky in the crisp, cold air. He could see their breath as it was exhaled from their nostrils. The scene reminded him of the dragons in the fairytale books when they expelled fire. Around noontime, he entered some canyons, which offered a pretty good windbreak, so he made a quick camp to make some hot coffee. While the coffee was coming to a boil, he led the horses to a small stream that was nearby. Then he ate some jerky and washed it down with the hot coffee.

After being on the trail a couple more hours, the temperature began to drop again, so he started looking for a good place to camp for the night. He was tempted to head back to the canyons, but he pushed that thought out of his head and kept moving forward. At long last, he came to a wooded area and found what he was looking for. A huge tree had fallen to the ground. Its trunk and roots, matted with dirt and sod, reached to about seven feet high, making a perfect windbreaker.

"There," he said aloud as he brought the horses in closer so they would be sheltered too. "I'll gather enough tree branches to keep us warm all night." He put on another pot of coffee and hunkered down between the fire and the tree real cozylike, holding a steaming hot cup of coffee. Late in the night, he put some more logs on the fire and dozed off to sleep.

His luck was still holding out. By morning, the wind had died down again, and the rising sun brought warmth. He had studied the map that Captain Goodman had given him, so he knew in his head which direction to go and what trails to ride. According to the map, he was now entering an area called Shoshoni. Actually, the whole Wyoming region was a favorite hunting ground for many Native American tribes—mainly the Crow, Arapaho, Shoshone, and Cheyenne. The famous Wind River wound in and around this whole area. Captain Goodman had told him that there were still some bands of hostile Indians in the area but if he was careful he shouldn't have any trouble.

At about mid-morning, he came to a small cluster of old buildings. As he rode in, he noticed that the buildings were very old and weather-beaten. The writing on the signs was so dimmed that he had to look twice to read what they said. The best-looking building in the small settlement turned out to be the livery stable. Compared to the other buildings, it seemed quite impressive. It was a very large structure and had two huge sliding doors in the front like most other livery stables and appeared not to have been painted for some forty years or so. Oddly, the paint on other buildings looked to be at least twice that old. He needed to care for his horses anyway, so he headed for the livery stable. He dismounted at a hitching rail in front of the establishment.

A young Indian boy, who Jack judged to be about sixteen, came out of the stable. He looked at the two horses and then at Jack. "That'll be two dollars a day, in advance."

That is kind of high, Jack thought, but he decided not to quibble over the price for the care of his horses. "Okay," he said, "but make sure both horses get rubbed down good and grained." He paid the young man the two dollars and then paid him a tip. He wanted to make sure that his horses were well taken care of.

The Indian took the money and squeezed out a half smile. In a barely audible voice, he said, "Thanks."

Jack couldn't tell if that was a sneer, or if politeness around here was taboo, or if people around here just weren't used to good manners. At any rate, he decided to see how much information the tip would get him.

He showed the Indian the poster of the five outlaws. "Have you seen any of these men around here?"

The hostler looked at the poster but quickly shook his head and abruptly said no.

"Well then. Where can a man get a drink and something to eat?"

The Indian pointed across the street at an old, adobe building and said one word: "Saloon."

Jack took the risk of saying thanks, and taking his rifle and war-bag from his saddle, he walked across the street. It was dark inside the saloon, but it only took a couple of seconds for his eyes to focus and record every detail in the room—how many men there were, where each man was, and the slight hand movement of each one of the men as their hands eased toward their guns. There were seven men besides the bartender, who appeared to be either Indian or Mexican. Of the seven customers, four were Indian and one was Mexican. The other two looked like white men, but he couldn't tell for sure because of the dirt. They stank and looked like they hadn't had a bath in a couple of months. The only real difference in the appearances between any of the men was their clothes. A couple of the Indians had on discarded army shirts or jackets, leggings, and high-top moccasins. Most of the men were wearing sidearms and knives around their waists. The two white men, as well as the Mexican, plainly were gunmen. Each was wearing a gun belt with their six-shooters low on the hip and tied down. They only made a slight movement when he came in, but Jack's keen eye saw it. All three gunmen had slipped a hand down and thumbed the leather thong from the hammer of their six-shooters.

The bartender was sitting on a stool behind the bar. The four Indians were sitting at a table. The two white men and the Mexican were standing at the bar. Just before he had stepped inside, he had heard talking and someone laughed. Now, as he stood there, no one turned to look at him, but the room got deathly quiet.

His intentions had been to go inside, have a drink, and maybe show the wanted poster and ask if anyone had seen any of these men. However, judging from the looks of these men, more than likely, they were wanted by the law themselves. He changed his mind about the poster, dusted some of the trail dust off his clothes, and walked up to the bar. "Mescal," he said.

The bartender brought out a bottle, held it up for him to see, and said two words: "Dinero primero."

Jack put some money on the bar and said in Spanish, "There you go."

The bartender shrugged his shoulders and, setting a glass on the bar in front of Jack, filled it from the bottle of mescal.

Jack emptied the glass, and set it back on the bar top. As he set the empty glass down, he looked at the man and said, "As I stepped in here, I heard you speaking English. The next time I come in here, you damn well better speak to me in English!" Jack half-turned from the bar so that he could observe the bartender and the three gun-slingers beside him. The Indians at the table were sleeping it off in their chairs. Jack looked eye to eye with the three gunmen to see if they would make a fight of it. The one closest to him just grinned, nodded his approval, and turned back to the bar and continued drinking. With that, Jack turned and left the saloon.

Standing on the sidewalk in front of the saloon, he looked around for a hotel or someplace he could stay for a day or two. He didn't really want to stay here in this place, but he had to stay long enough to decide whether or not Ralph Simmons, Bill Taggard, or Art Cummings had ever been around here.

Three doors down the street, there was a building with a sign hanging by one nail. He could barely read the faded word *Hotel*. He figured that he might as well give it a try, so he headed in that direction. The outside of the hotel didn't look any better than the rest of the buildings; however, it wasn't too bad on the inside. He crossed the small lobby to the desk to register for a room. There was a cowbell setting on the desktop, so he picked it up and gave it a shake. The noise that came out of that little cowbell would just about have wakened the dead. He figured that if there was a cow within a hundred miles of there it would have come running.

No cows showed up, but a minute later, a woman stepped out of a room behind the desk. In Spanish, she asked if he wanted a room. He said yes.

She had him sign the register and handed him the key to room number eight. She then asked, "With or without?"

He figured he knew what she meant, but just to make sure he asked, "With or without what?"

"With or without a *puta*, whore," she answered calmly.

He had to admit that sounded kind of tempting, but he declined the offer. He took the key and his rifle and war-bag and went down a hallway she had indicated. He found the room and went inside. He set his gear on the bed and made a complete search of the room. On one inside wall, he noticed a door. He turned the doorknob and found that it was locked. *Probably leads to another room*, he figured. *Maybe it makes it easier to clean the rooms that way.* By now, he was really getting hungry, so he went back to the saloon. When he entered the saloon, he again took notice of his surroundings and saw that the same men who were there earlier were still there and in the same place.

He again ordered mescal and then made his way to a table where there was a big plate of cornpone and a pot of beans. After dishing up all the beans that he wanted, he took his food and mescal and sat at a table where his back was to a wall so that he could see the door. Anyone coming inside would be completely visible to him. He had studied the wanted poster 'till he knew he would recognize any of the three outlaws, even if they were in disguise. He sat in the saloon 'till past midnight, and there was no sign of the men he was looking for. He finally decided that he would go get some sleep and come back the next day.

Jack had always been a light sleeper, but since he'd been on the trail of these five outlaws, he realized that he had become almost an insomniac. He lay awake most of the night, thinking and trying to get a glimpse of his future. He still thought a lot about Cindy and wondered if he would ever be able to get over her and find a woman whom he could love and settle down with. Sometimes he found himself thinking about Shannon, the pretty fallen angel at Murdock's Saloon back in Billings. He knew that she really loved him, so he figured she could give up the saloon life and cease being a whore. He knew he could trust her to be a good wife and mother to his children. Then, sometimes, he thought about Amanda Holts. She said she loved him and was going to tell her intended, Carl McBride, to get lost. Amanda was a beautiful young lady and would make a good wife too. Minutes later, he was asleep, dreaming of being married to a beautiful woman and having his own ranch and a whole passel of kids.

Jack woke up at the crack of dawn, got dressed, and headed for the saloon. There was no sign or anything that he could see that indicated the place had a name, so he was content to call it "the saloon." When he stepped inside, two of the Indians were still there. They were lying across a table, still sleeping it off. The same fat bartender was behind the counter, sitting on the stool.

Jack stepped up to the bar and said, "I'll have mescal and some breakfast."

The bartender set a bottle and a glass on the bar and said in English, "Sure. Help yourself."

Jack said thanks and took the bottle and a plate, filled it with cornpone and beans, and went to the same table he had sat at the night before.

As he sat there looking out the swinging doors at people going to and fro, he noted that there were more people around than yesterday. *That's right*, he thought. *Today's Saturday. If there are any ranches around here, they'll be cowhands coming in for a drink.* Within another half hour, there were several men coming into the saloon.

He nursed his food and drink as long as he could, hoping he would see at least one of the outlaws step through the door. At last, with his patience growing thin, he thought it was time to leave this Shoshoni area and look someplace else. Deciding to have a cup of coffee before he left, he went to the bar. The bartender thought he was going to ask for another drink and held up a bottle of mescal. "This is what you drink, ain't it?"

Jack thought, *What the hell. I might as well have another drink before I hit the trail.* "Yep," he answered.

As the bartender poured him a glass of mescal, he asked, "You're new around these parts, ain't you?"

"Yeah. Rode in yesterday. The livery stable was my first stop and then here."

"You looking for work, are you?"

Jack considered saying yes to see what the bartender's response would be but then opted for keeping to the original plan. "No," he said. "I have a job."

"Oh," the bartender said, getting a little braver. "What is your line of work?"

Jack picked up the briefcase containing Sam Colt's newest model of specially engraved six-shooters, and placed it on the bar. Opening it up to expose the matched pistols, he said, "I'm a salesman for the famous Samuel Colt Firearms Company." Handing the bartender a card, he said, "Here's my calling card. I'm Jack Montana."

"Damn," the bartender said, as he looked at the twin colt .44's glistening in the specially crafted briefcase and velvet lining. "What a fine-looking set of pistols."

"They're not just fine-looking, mister. They're fine-working forty-fours too."

Eager to get his hands on a matched set of Colts like that, the bartender began to get friendlier. "Call me Carlos, Jack."

By now, there were four or five men crowded around to see the new Colt .44's.

One man said, "How do we know that these guns are as good as they look? How 'bout I try one out 'n see how it shoots?"

"Can't let you do that," Jack said, "because then it would be a used gun, and I'm not in the used gun business." He then drew one of his own Colt .44's and did some fancy twirling. "Except for the fancy engraving, this Colt is exactly the same as the ones in the briefcase. Its balance is perfect." Pointing to a picture of a naked woman that was hanging behind the bar, he said, "Watch." As they were watching, he fanned the hammer six times in six seconds, maybe less, and both eyes in the picture disappeared—three slugs in the left eye, and three slugs in the right eye.

"Damn," Carlos said again as he stared at the holes in the picture where the eyes had been.

Jack twirled the colt one time so that the gun's butt was toward the man who wanted to check out the pair of new colts. "Here. Try it out for balance," he said.

The man backed away. "I'll take your word for it, mister."

Reloading the Colt, Jack looked at Carlos. "I'll pay for the damage to the picture."

After the shooting exhibition, more men came over to look at the Colts that were in the briefcase. Jack placed three orders for the Colt .44's. After that surprising and exciting event, Jack decided to spend one more day there before moving on.

The next morning, Sunday, Jack was in the saloon, sitting at the same table. More men were talking to him about the fancy colts when a stranger came in that Jack hadn't seen in the saloon before. Instantly, Jack recognized him as one of the outlaws on his poster, Art Cummings. Jack would know him anywhere. He had studied the pictures on that poster for hours on end, just in case he lost it or would have to get rid of it. He could pick any one of the outlaws out of a crowd by day or night. Art was a smaller-built man, thin, and had the look of a professional gunman to him.

As he talked to the men around his table about the guns, Jack watched the outlaw go to the bar. Jack heard Carlos saying, "How's it going, Art? Where's Hal and Jess and the rest of the boys?" Jack couldn't hear Art's response to Carlos's question, but the look on his face told Jack that Art wasn't in a good mood. He wondered if it was because the rest of the men weren't showing up at the meeting place at the time they were supposed to. Art ordered a bottle. Carlos gave one to him. He paid for it and turned and walked out of the saloon.

Jack's first impulse was to get up and go after Art. He sure didn't want to lose track of him now. His better judgment, however, told him to wait. He didn't want any of these men to suspect that he was after Art and his sidekicks. Jack talked to the men a while longer and then made an excuse to leave the saloon. He headed straight for the hotel, wondering if a town no bigger than this one would have more than one hotel. He didn't think so. When he reached the hotel, he went to the desk. The same woman was there. "Hello," he said. "Do you remember me?"

"Yes," she said, "I remember you. Would you like to have company sent up to your room?"

Again he declined the offer of a *puta* sent to his room. He reminded her that he was a gun salesman and said, "I was wondering if I had any business contacts call for me while I was gone today?"

"No. No one called for you."

"Well," he said, "I'm not really familiar with all my clients, but I think one of their names is Art something or other."

"Oh," she said, "a man by the name of Art Cummings did register about ten minutes ago."

Jack faked a long sigh of relief, and said, "Finally one of them showed up. What's his room number?"

"Nine," she said.

"Oh. Right next to mine. Thank you," he said, and he left the lobby and went to his room. He figured his luck was still holding true, what with Art showing up at this hotel and even renting the room right next to his. He unlocked the door to his room, entered, and went to the door that was in the partition that separated the rooms. He bent down and peered through the keyhole into the adjoining room. Number nine; Art Cummings's room. Art was sitting on the edge of his bed, taking long drinks from the bottle he brought from the saloon. There was someone with him, a man that Jack couldn't see. Jack could hear the other man's voice, but he desperately needed to see him to identify him. Jack kept peering through the keyhole, trying to get a glimpse of the other man. At last, the man moved to a position in line with Jack's vision, and Jack recognized him immediately. It was Bill Taggard.

Jack watched the outlaws for a few minutes. Art would get up and pace back and forth across the room a few times, all the while talking to Bill. Then he would sit back down on the bed, take a couple more pulls from the bottle, and do the same thing all over again. Jack grew tired of watching them. Fortunately, the outlaws were not quiet people. Every move they made seemed to be magnified ten times, so Jack went to the chair that was by his bed and sat down. If he waited 'till they left Art's room for something, maybe he could figure a way to get into the outlaws' room. Perhaps he could go to the lobby, get the spare key to Art's room, let himself inside, and wait for them to return.

After an hour and a half, Jack was starting to doze off when he heard the door to Art's room slam shut. He peered through the keyhole again and saw that Art and Bill were both gone. It was time for action, but he really didn't like the idea of creating a ruse to get the spare key. Suddenly, he thought of a better plan. He went over to the door in the partition and, taking his knife, removed the pins from the door's hinges. He pulled the door out of its frame and leaned it against the wall. He entered Art's room and searched every corner, under the bed, and all of Art's gear. He couldn't find anything that would give him a clue to the outlaw's plans.

The only thing to do now was to wait until Art returned and then take him in. It would be harder if his friend Bill came back with him, but either way, Jack would be ready. He didn't want the cleaning lady or anyone else coming in before Art returned, so he opened the door, hung the "do not disturb" sign on the outside doorknob, and closed the door again.

CHAPTER 14

It felt strange to Jack to be sitting in another man's room alone and uninvited, but this business had to be taken care of, and this was the best way to do it. He pulled a chair up close to the door and made himself comfortable. For a while, he sat there looking out the window at the setting sun. It began to grow darker outside, and as it grew later, he knew that Art would eventually be back because all his gear was here in this room.

Figuring he might as well get some rest, he allowed himself to fall asleep. He awoke sometime after midnight and saw that the room was flooded with moonlight. He wanted the element of surprise when Art returned, so he shut the window and closed the blinds. He stretched and sat back down again. About an hour later, he heard someone at the door. Quietly, he got up from the chair and moved it between the door and himself. He lifted his gun from its holster and waited for Art to open the door and step inside.

When Art pushed the door open, it was dark, and it took a moment for him to notice the outline of someone in his room. "Who the hell—" he blurted and simultaneously went for his gun. Jack didn't want to shoot him, so he was ready and shoved the chair hard into Art's legs. Art fell over the chair, losing his grip on his six-shooter, which fell on the floor.

"Don't move, Art, or you're a dead man." Completely caught off guard, Art obeyed the command of the voice and lay where he had fallen. Jack picked up the pistol that Art had dropped and stuck it in his waistband. "Now get up slowly," Jack ordered, "and close the door behind you."

Again, Art did as he was told. As the door closed, Jack gave Art a quick pat down, relieved him of all weapons, and opened the blinds. Still covering the outlaw with his .44, he lit the lamp.

Art glared at Jack for a moment. Looking around, he saw the opening in the wall and the door off its hinges. "Who the hell are you, and what are you doing here?"

"In view of the present circumstances, Art, I don't think you are in the position to ask any questions. Do you?"

On the other hand, Jack figured it wouldn't hurt to at least converse with the outlaw. "I'm Jack Montana, and I'm taking you to Fort Washakie."

Art looked puzzled. "I don't know you. Do you know me from someplace?"

"You don't know me," Jack acknowledged, "but I know you from the wanted posters; you and Hal Colby, Ralph Simmons, Bill Taggard, and Jess Barker, your whole ring of wanted-dead-or-alive outlaws. Jess Barker is dead, and Hal Colby is at Fort Washakie in custody and waiting for you, Ralph Simmons, and Bill Taggard to join him.

Art Cummings suddenly sagged at the shoulders. The news certainly took something out of him. "I don't even know them guys," he lied. He looked at Jack again. "Why are you doing this?"

Jack had given Art all the information that he was going to. "Because you and your cohorts are crooks and killers. That's all you need to know."

Art suddenly was himself again, full of hate and defiance. "You're a damned bounty hunter, ain't you?"

"If that's what you want to believe," Jack answered. He began to question Art about his dealings with the other outlaws.

Art again claimed he didn't know any of them.

Jack called him a liar. "That's not what I heard. You guys were all supposed to meet up out at that trapper's cabin at the Big Horn Basin. If you weren't all at the cabin within a couple days of the planned date, then you were to go to Fort Washakie and wait there 'till all of the gang was there. Right?"

"Go to hell!" Art sneered.

Jack would liked to have waited around for a while to see if Bill Taggard would come back to join up with Art, but he knew he couldn't keep Art a prisoner for very long without someone finding out about it. With Art protesting, Jack ordered the outlaw to step through the doorway into his room. Then he put the door back on its hinges. "Now," he said, "no one will ever know. Come on. Let's get out of here."

Art was still protesting. "Go to hell! I ain't going to Fort Washakie or anywhere with you."

"Shut up and get moving. The poster says dead or alive," Jack warned, "and it doesn't make much difference to me. In fact, dead would be easier. It's up to you."

Jack's luck was still with him. His room was at the very end of the hall. The next door was facing the hallway and led outside. He prodded Art out of his door and into the hallway. The coast was clear, so he pushed Art out the second door and they stepped into the alleyway. With Art leading the way down the alley and Jack following close behind, they entered the street. It was three o'clock in the morning, and there was no one to be seen anywhere.

Jack nudged Art with the barrel of his pistol. "Move! Head for the livery stable." They reached the livery with no trouble, and Jack was delighted to see a note pinned to the office door: "Take care of your own horse. You can pay in the morning."

Art *wasn't* delighted to find that no one was around at the stable. He felt his hope for help growing slim.

He started cursing, and Jack nudged him again. "Shut up, Art. Let's get these horses ready to go."

Thirty minutes later and with more prodding from Jack, they were mounted up and headed for the fort. Jack was riding the appaloosa and leading the strawberry roan. He knew that they could make better time if he left one of his horses here until he returned, but he figured someone would steal him, so he chose to take both horses.

He had Art leading the way so he could keep an eye on him. They were more than halfway to the fort by nightfall, and Jack would prefer to have kept going, but he knew it would be easier to keep an eye on Art in the light of a campfire than on horseback in the dark.

They found a good place to make camp away from the trail and under some trees. Jack built a fire and made coffee. They ate jerky to fill the void in their stomachs. As the two men sat across the fire from one another, drinking their coffee and staring into the night, each had just one thought on their mind. One was thinking, *How can I escape tonight?* The other was thinking, *How can I keep him from escaping?* At last, Jack got up and tossed the coffee grounds from his cup onto the fire. He got a piece of rope, which was his pigging string from the gear in his saddlebags. He walked over to a nearby tree and looked at Art. "Come on over here. We're fixing to turn in for the night."

Art looked surprised. "You're not going to tie me to that tree, are you?"

Jack motioned for him to get over here, "You bet your sweet ass I am! One of us ain't going to get any sleep tonight, and it ain't going to be me." He was glad that he had given the outlaws the impression that he was a ruthless bounty hunter and a killer, but he knew that he couldn't shoot a man just because the man wouldn't allow himself to be tied to a tree. If Art thought he *would* shoot him, so be it. Jack put his hand on the butt of his pistol and said, "I'd rather take you in alive, but…"

"Okay, okay," Art grumbled. Cutting loose with a barrage of foul language, he slowly walked over to the tree and allowed Jack to tie him up with his back to the tree and in a sitting position. Jack left enough slack in the rope for Art to move his arms some.

For protection against the cold night, Jack tossed a blanket over Art's legs. He figured, with the campfire being that close and with the blanket, Art would be warm enough.

Jack got his own bedroll and placed it on the ground so that the fire was between him and Art. He threw some more wood on the fire, crawled under his blankets, and went to sleep. He woke up a couple of times during the night. Art appeared to be sleeping, so after checking the fire, he went back to sleep. It hadn't snowed for a couple of days, so at night, the ground was cold but not wet, which made for a more comfortable night. In the morning, Jack threw some pitch pine on the dying coals of the fire and soon had the coffee on.

They reached Fort Washakie around eleven o'clock in the morning that second day, and again, Sergeant Calhoun and some scouts from the fort rode out to meet them and escort them inside. The sergeant took charge of Art, and Jack went to see Captain Goodman.

When he knocked on the door of the captain's quarters, the captain called, "Come in." As Jack stepped inside, he looked up from the paperwork on his desk and grinned. "Hello, Jack. If you keep bringing in these outlaws, you'll fill our stockade."

"I'm doing my best, Captain. Three down and two to go."

The captain put his paperwork aside and leaned back in his chair. "Sit down, Jack. Let's talk for a while."

Jack sat down, "Sure, Captain. I have plenty of time."

"I went to the stockade to see Hal Colby the other day," the captain offered. "He claims that you're a ruthless bounty hunter and a dangerous killer, that you shot and killed Jess Barker just for the fun of it, and that you roughed him up for no reason at all. Is that true?"

Jack grinned. "No, sir. Jess asked me to shoot him, and Hal hit himself on the back of the head and came with me of his own accord."

They both laughed.

"Jack, I'm sure you had a reason for everything you did, but I have to put in my report what Hal Colby said and that I spoke to you about the complaint made against you. You understand?"

"Yes, sir. I understand."

"Okay then. I'll report that I talked to you and you denied all the charges."

"That's correct, sir, and thank you."

Jack and the captain talked for quite a while. There seemed to be a sort of rapport between them. The captain asked him about the outlaws that he was chasing and about how he liked working for the famous Samuel Colt as a gun salesman. He almost told the captain that he wasn't working for Sam Colt and the real reason he was after the outlaws, but he wasn't sure the captain would understand, so he just changed the subject by asking the captain some questions. While they were talking, the captain's wife tapped on the door and came into the room. The captain stood up and introduced them.

"Jack, this is my wife, Kathleen. Kathleen, this is Jack Montana."

Jack was surprised. She looked very much like Cindy Walker, just a little older. He stood, took off his hat, bowed his head, and gently shook her hand. "I'm pleased to meet you, Mrs. Goodman. I hope you will forgive my poor manners, but you look very much like a lady back home that I intend to marry."

After some small talk, Jack excused himself. "I'd best be going. I got a lot of ground to cover."

"Will you be leaving soon, Jack?" the captain asked.

"Yes, sir. I had pretty good luck back there in the Shoshoni territory, so I think I'll head back that way." He shook Kathleen's hand again and said, "Good-bye, Mrs. Goodman." Then he turned to the captain and shook his hand. "I'll see you later, Captain."

Outside the captain's quarters, he paused for a moment, thinking about how much Kathleen reminded him of Cindy. It had been a while since he'd thought about her. Now he probably wouldn't be able to get her out of his head, at least not for a while. He made his way to the chow hall. They were still serving chow, so he ate and had a hot cup of coffee and then headed for the corrals to get his horses.

As Jack left the fort, the weather was good. There was a chill in the air, but the snow melted except where it had drifted into high snow banks. The horses were fresh and feeling good. Jack was riding the strawberry roan and leading the appaloosa. All this in consideration, he could have made it back to that rundown village and that sleazy hotel where he took Art Cummings prisoner if he had wanted to. On the other hand, he felt that he needed time to allow himself to think about Cindy again. When he made camp that night, he unrolled his bedroll by the fire and allowed himself the pleasure to dream about his beautiful Cindy. Although he felt that she could never love him, he still loved her.

When he reached that little settlement in the Shoshoni territory the next day, it was late, so he put his horses up at the livery stable and went directly to the hotel. He had only been away four days, but this little settlement didn't have all that many inhabitants, so his hope was that both his and Art's rooms had been kept open for them.

Jack went into the hotel lobby and stopped at the desk. He greeted the lady clerk behind the desk and asked if she remembered him. "Why, yes, Mister Montana," she said, as she turned around and took his key off the keyboard. Handing it to him, she said, "Number eight, wasn't it?"

Taking the key, he acknowledged, "That would be it. Thank you for holding the room for me."

He remembered that he had left the door to Art's room locked, with the "do not disturb" sign hanging on the door. As he walked past Art's room, he saw the sign still hanging there, and that brought him some relief. Then he realized that someone else could've rented the room and put the sign there themselves. He took a gamble and removed the sign and slid it under the door. He then let himself in his own room and went to sleep.

He woke before daylight, and after dressing, he went to the wall that separated the rooms and bent down at the door and looked through the keyhole into what had been Art's room. There was enough daylight shining through the window of the room that he could see that no one had slept there. There was some personal stuff over in one corner that looked like Art's, so he was sure that they were keeping his room open for him. He knew that Art wouldn't be coming back to this room, but he wanted somehow to keep it open in case Bill Taggard showed up again, looking for Art.

His stomach reminded him that he was hungry, so he decided he'd go have something to eat while determining what needed to be done. As he crossed the hotel lobby, he noticed that there was a different woman at the desk. He had seen her a few times before, so he waved and spoke to her as he passed the desk to leave the hotel.

"Oh. Mister Montana," she called.

He stopped and walked back over to the desk. "Yes?"

"There was someone here asking for you."

"Oh? Who was that?" He couldn't imagine who could be asking about him here.

"Well, actually," she said, "they were asking about your friend Art."

"Do you remember who they were?"

"Yes," she said, "Bill Taggard and Ralph Simmons." She turned the register around for him to see.

He looked at the register, and there were their names, Bill Taggard and Ralph Simmons. They were registered in the room next to his, number seven. "Thank you," he said. "Are they in their room now?"

"No. They just registered and said they'd be back later."

"Okay. I guess I'll see them later. Oh. As I passed Art's room last night, I noticed he had a 'do not disturb' sign on his door. And just now, as I left my room, I noticed the sign was gone, and I thought I heard him moving around inside. I think I'll go up to his room and tell him that Bill and Ralph are here."

The desk clerk nodded her approval. "Okay. When they come back, I'll tell them that you and Art are in his room, waiting for them."

"That'll be great," Jack said and turned to leave. As if by an after-thought, he turned around again and said, "I'd like to surprise them, so just tell them that Art's waiting in his room."

Again, the clerk smiled and nodded her head. "Okay. I won't mention that you're with Art."

"Thanks," Jack said and went back to his room. Once inside, he immediately locked his door and repeated the process he had initiated in this same room just days before when he had captured Art. Once the door was off its hinges again, he stepped inside the room that had been Art's and positioned the door to appear as if it had never been removed. When all was ready, he sat down in a chair and waited.

Jack had learned to be patient, so when two hours had passed and the outlaws hadn't shown up yet, he didn't become anxious. He just relaxed and continued waiting. At length, he heard footsteps in the hallway, ultimately stopping at Art's door. The wooden floor creaked as the person shifted his weight while knocking on the door. Jack rose to his feet and, standing close to the door, drew his gun. He suddenly realized that he'd heard only one set of footsteps.

"Art! Are you in there?" the voice asked.

Not ever hearing either of these last two outlaws' voices, he had no way of knowing which one of the outlaws it was. Of course, it didn't really matter. Muffling his voice, he called out, "Keep your shirt on. I'm coming!"

He waited for a few seconds, jerked the door open, and, motioning with his gun, waved the man inside. Seeing the outlaw's face, Jack recognized him. "Don't try anything foolish, Bill. Just step inside."

The outlaw stiffened with surprise and then did as he was commanded, but not without question. "Who the hell are you? And where is Art?"

Bill had stepped partway in the room. Now Jack pulled him all the way inside. Lifting the outlaw's gun from its holster, he said, "I'll supply the questions. You supply the answers."

Suddenly, Bill's partner, Ralph, appeared in the doorway and opened fire on Jack. It was point blank, but the outlaw had drawn and fired quickly, so only one bullet found its mark. Luckily for Jack, the bullet had merely grazed him in the side, just above the beltline. It burned like fire, but it didn't stop Jack from acting quickly. He dove onto the floor, rolling and firing at the same time. One of his bullets hit Ralph in the gut, and the other bullet entered the outlaw's chin and came out the top of his head. He was dead before he hit the floor. He never uttered a sound.

Quickly, Jack jumped up from the floor, covering Bill with his six-shooter before he could grab his gun and get into the action. He knew that someone would be coming soon to see what the shooting was about. He didn't want to be caught this way. It would be difficult to explain all that his assignment entailed. Meanwhile, if Bill would manage to escape, he might disappear, maybe forever. If that was the case, he feared that his assignment would be a failure.

He motioned with his gun for Bill to pick Ralph up. "Grab your partner, and let's do-si-do out of here," he demanded.

Bill said, "That's just too damn cute! You can grab him yourself and go to hell!"

The gunfire had already alerted the whole town, so one more shot wouldn't hurt. Jack's .44 bucked in his hand, and a bullet plowed through the floor an inch from Bill's foot. "The next one will put you alongside your partner. Now grab him and let's get out of here," Jack ordered.

Bill sensed that Jack wasn't just talking to hear his own jaws flapping, so he grabbed Ralph's corpse, heaved it up on his shoulder, and asked, "Now what?"

Jack heard footsteps running toward them. "Hurry. Get out the door and down the hallway. We'll go out the back door and through the alley."

Outside in the alleyway, Jack ran into another obstacle. It was broad daylight, and there were people walking past the entrance of the alley. Some of them were running, and he heard someone yelling, "There's been a lot of shooting in the hotel. Whoever did it can't be far away."

He ordered Bill to lower Ralph to the ground and covered him up with some tumbleweed and other debris in the alley. "Now," he told Bill, "we'll just sashay over to the livery stable and get our horses."

"Where we going?" Bill wanted to know.

"After we get our horses, we're going to stop back by here, pick up your pal, and head for Fort Washakie," Jack said. "Now let's get moving. And remember, one wrong move and you'll arrive there laying across your saddle instead of sitting in it."

Bill figured he had no choice now but to go along with this bounty hunter. He knew it was a two-day ride to the fort and he could surely find a way to escape when they camped for the night or at some other place along the trail before they reached the fort.

Jack walked about one step behind and to the side of Bill. He had been fortunate so far, and he didn't intend to push his luck.

At the livery stable, the hostler brought out the horses. It was the same young Indian buck who had tended his horses the other time. Just as before, he didn't say more than two words. That suited Jack just fine. He paid what was owed for the horses and motioned for Bill to saddle and bridle his horse. While Bill worked at that, Jack saddled and bridled the appaloosa and tied all his gear behind the saddle on the strawberry roan.

When the horses were ready, they mounted up, and twenty minutes later, they were back in the alley and had Ralph loaded onto the strawberry roan. With Jack hoping no one would notice the body draped over the horse's saddle face down, they rode boldly out of the settlement. When they were out of sight of the settlement, Jack told Bill to stop. He dismounted and lashed the outlaw's hands to the horn of the saddle, mounted again, and put Bill in the lead. "Don't look back," Jack stated. "Just keep heading straight for the fort." Bill cursed and called Jack all kinds of names, but Jack just let him rave.

At noontime, they rode off the trail a ways and built a small fire to make some coffee and eat some jerky. The weather was still clear but chilly, and the fire felt good to them. Sitting there, resting for the first time in a long while, Jack realized how tired he was, and he dozed off just for a second. When he opened his eyes, Bill was just starting to get up.

When the outlaw saw Jack's eyes open, he sat back down and grinned. "I was just gonna stretch my legs," he lied.

Jack got up and washed out the cups with some clean snow from a snowdrift and packed them away. "Come on. Let's get moving," he said.

The thought of falling asleep with Bill and his unshackled hands that close to him startled Jack into a new sense of vigilance. Consequently, he made a slight change. Instead of just tying Bill's hands to the saddle horn and having him in the lead, Jack also tied Bill's feet in the stirrups. Then he tethered the outlaw's horse to the roan, which was in turn lashed to the horn of his saddle.

So went the rest of the day. However, an hour after leaving the noontime stop, Jack began to doze off again. Every now and then, he would snap out of it and look back at the outlaw, and each time, Bill was just sitting there in the saddle, grinning and waiting for Jack to fall asleep. At length, he fell asleep, completely unconscious. The next thing he knew, he was slipping out of the saddle. The movement jerked him awake, and he faintly heard the sound of a horse galloping. Reality hit him, and the adrenaline pumped him into action. He palmed his .44 quick as a flash and turned in the saddle. Bill had worked his hands and feet loose and taken control of his horse. He had his shell-belt with its empty holster in his hand, swinging it around over his head, and was gaining on Jack. Jack knew that heavy shell-belt would knock him out of the saddle and maybe unconscious. He fired two quick shots into Bill, and the outlaw went flying out of the saddle.

Jack jumped out of his saddle, ready to fire again, but the outlaw had fallen face down and wasn't moving at all. With the toe of his boot, he rolled Bill over. He was still alive, but he was seriously wounded. One bullet caught the outlaw in the left shoulder. The other bullet had put a huge, bloody groove in his head, just over his right ear.

Jack holstered his gun and bent down. "Bill, can you hear me?"

The outlaw opened his eyes and looked at his blood-soaked shirt and the red snow around him. He was wounded and weak but still able to cut loose with the profanity. "You ... you sumbitch! You killed me. I'm dying, ain't I?"

"Yep. You just might," Jack agreed. "But I'll do my best to get you to the fort alive and kicking." Quickly, Jack took off Bill's heavy coat and his shirt.

Instantly, Bill started to shake. "Hey," he said weakly. "I'll freeze to death."

"No, you won't. I just want to get your coat and shirt off before they become completely soaked with blood. I'll stop the bleeding, and then I'll get you back into your duds."

Jack went through Bill's gear that he had tied to the back of the roan's saddle and got one of his shirts and managed to accomplish the task of binding the wounds and putting Bill's shirt and coat back on him. Then Jack, riding close beside Bill and steadying him in the saddle, headed for the fort again with one dead outlaw and another one that was wounded.

CHAPTER 15

"So you got all five of them?" Captain Goodman asked. "Hal Colby, Ralph Simmons, Art Cummings, Jess Barker, and now Bill Taggard?"

"Yes, sir," Jack said. "But I'd hoped to bring them all in alive!"

"I can appreciate that, but still, it was a job well done. Two have been buried, one is in the hospital, and two are in the stockade. If that had been a bounty hunter, he would probably have just brought them all in dead. Less trouble that way. And by the way," the captain said, "I have some papers for you to sign. The papers just acknowledge that you, Jack Montana, are the one who arrested and brought in these five prisoners, that you turned them over to me, Captain John Goodman, and in addition, that I have issued to you a government note for the full amount of five hundred dollars reward for each of these five outlaws, as was noted on the wanted poster. The note is redeemable at any bank."

Jack had forgotten all about the reward money. He was risking his life bringing in these outlaws to pay for a crime that he didn't even do. Now with that over and done with, he could go back to Billings with his name cleared. "I had forgotten all about the money, Captain. But I'll take the note for the twenty-five hundred anyway."

Jack stayed at the fort for two days, resting up and replenishing his supplies, which were running low. The two days also gave his horses a much-needed rest.

He started out early on a bright and sunny morning when the snow was all but gone. He was riding the strawberry roan while the appaloosa followed with the supplies. After two days, he entered the Shoshoni area and the familiar settlement. .

He would have liked a bath and a hot meal, but he didn't think it would be worth it to stop. Another two days put him in the Big Horn Basin. He camped along the Big Horn River for a whole day. It was a beautiful place. The winter was gone, and the trees were turning green again. The basin floor was once again thick with lush, green wild grass, beautiful for grazing cattle and horses. The hunting was good. He saw plenty of deer and elk. He bathed in the cold river and washed his clothes.

He left the Big Horn River before the sun was up. A day and a half later, he was descending the Big Horn Mountains into Montana. Another day of continual riding found him entering the town of Laurel, Montana. He was anxious to ride out to the Lazy H ranch and see Steve and Margaret Holts and, of course, Amanda as well—in any case, he decided to stop in at the Red Horse Saloon and have one drink. He would like to thank Wanda the barmaid one more time for tipping him off about the outlaw Hal Colby.

In the Red Horse Saloon, José was tending bar and recognized him. "Mescal is your drink, ain't it, Jack?"

"Sure is, José. And make it your good stuff."

José laughed. "All my stuff is good. You know that."

Jack was about to ask about Wanda when she appeared at his side. "Did I hear someone mention my name, cowboy Jack?"

Jack nodded and put some money on the bar. "José, give us a bottle and two glasses."

"Here you go," José said as he set the bottle and glasses on the bar and scooped up the money.

Wanda grabbed the bottle and headed for the table in the back of the room where they usually sat. "Is our usual table okay, cowboy, or do you want a little more action with Wanda today?"

"I'm not staying for any length of time, Wanda. My assignment is accomplished, and I'm on my way back home. I just wanted to stop by and say good-bye and thanks for your help."

"Oh," she said as she set her drink down. She hesitated a moment and then said, "Well, I'm really glad that you have finished your job successfully. It's just that, well, I don't meet many real good, decent men in my work and I kind of liked talking to you."

"Well, I really appreciate what you did for me, Wanda. You keep your eyes open. I'm sure that one day the right cowboy will ride in here and you'll both ride out of here together." Then he reached over, kissed her on the lips, and put two double eagles in her cleavage. He stood up, said good-bye to her, nodded to José, and went out the batwing doors of the Red Horse Saloon for the last time.

As he mounted up and reined the big appaloosa around and headed out of town, he looked back and saw Wanda standing on the veranda, waving good-bye to him. He waved back and smiled, knowing that beneath that rough language and all that makeup there was a lady just trying to make a living in a hard land.

The appaloosa was a high stepper, and within another hour, Jack was recognizing land markings that told him that he was on the Lazy H range. Another quarter mile and he came to the creek that was only about fifteen minutes from the ranch house. The weather had turned warm, winter was gone, and spring had arrived in full beautiful color. He stopped at the creek to let his horses drink and peel off his jacket. He rolled it up neatly and tied it on behind his saddle. He nudged the appaloosa with the heel of his boot, and they were off again. A short time later, he entered the ranch yard.

Steve Holts was in the corral, working with a new string of horses. Amanda was working with the black horse that he had given her. He could smell a wonderful aroma coming from Margaret's kitchen that made his stomach growl. Amanda was the first one to notice him. Quickly, she tied her horse to a hitch rail and ran to meet him. He stepped down from the saddle, and before he could turn around, she was in his arms hugging and kissing him. Steve came over and shook hands with him.

About that time, Margaret stepped out onto the porch to call Amanda and Steve to dinner. She saw Jack and said, "I'll set another plate on the table," and disappeared inside again.

When the three of them went inside the house, Margaret hugged him. Then all three of them were asking him questions, all talking at the same time.

Jack held up his hands. "Hey, I can only answer one question at a time."

They all started laughing. "Well," Steve said, "I guess you can tell that we're happy to see you again."

"I surely can. And I'm real happy to see you all again too."

They talked during dinner, and afterward, they sat in the parlor and had coffee.

"How long can you stay with us?" Steve asked.

"I figured I'd head for Billings right after breakfast in the morning. I need to get back home."

"Oh," exclaimed Amanda. "You have to stay at least three more weeks because we're having a big party that weekend and you'll get to meet all our friends and neighbors."

"I'm afraid I can't stay that long. I really need to get back home."

"But you have to stay," Amanda insisted. "The big party is to celebrate my bridal engagement."

"That's right. You told me you were engaged to be married. But the way you talked, I figured you'd already had a party to celebrate your impending wedding."

Amanda laughed. "No, silly. That is … well, I'll tell you about it later. Just *please* say you will stay!"

The way Amanda had spoken to him earlier about her intended marriage to Carl McBride didn't sound to him to be a good thing, and he thought that she would call the marriage off.

"Just say yes," she pleaded.

Jack was a little annoyed, but he couldn't refuse her at this time, so he opted for, "We'll talk about it over breakfast in the morning, okay?"

"It's a deal," she agreed.

Steve laughed. "You know women, Jack. They always get their way, and they can change their mind on a minute's notice."

"It's a woman's choice," Margaret said.

"I thought the saying was, 'It's a woman's *privilege*?'" Steve corrected.

Margaret laughed again. "That too."

Jack and Steve both threw up their hands in surrender. "We give up," they said.

After visiting for another hour, Jack excused himself. "I'm about done in. I need to go to bed."

Jack was bone-tired, so he fell asleep immediately. An hour later, he heard a tapping on his door. He got up, opened the door a crack, and peeped out. "Amanda!" he said. "Is something wrong?"

She pushed the door open and stepped inside. "No, silly. Nothing's wrong."

Jack tried to push her back out of the room. "Then you shouldn't be here. Go back to your room."

"It's okay. I just want to talk to you."

Jack grabbed a blanket and wrapped it around himself. "Okay, but make it quick. I wouldn't want your folks to see you in here."

She sat down on the edge of the bed, and Jack sat beside her.

"What did you want to talk to me about?"

"I had been hoping you would stop by on your way back home. For one thing, I needed to know that you were all right."

Jack was impatient. "Amanda."

"Shush," she said. "This is something I have to say. Before you came along, I was about to marry someone I hardly knew. After I met you, I learned what it felt like to really love someone. Then you told me that you loved someone else, and you went away. I was heartbroken, but I understood that you had plans to marry Cindy Walker. Jack, I just want to thank you again for not taking advantage of me. I would have followed you anywhere and done anything you wanted but because you were a good and honorable man. I have found someone else. Jack, he really loves me and I really love him. He has asked me to marry him, and I said yes. But we're going to wait for one year to get to know each other better."

"Oh. Good," Jack said. "That's what the celebration is about. You called off the wedding with Carl McBride, and you're going to announce your official engagement to your new intended?"

"Correct."

"Who's the lucky man? Where did you meet him? What is his name?"

"His name is Victor Boyd. Actually, I met him a long time ago. We went to school together. After he heard that I had broken up with Carl, he started courting me. He told me that he had fallen in love with me a long time ago but he was too bashful to ask my father if he could court me. When he learned that I was no longer engaged, he figured he'd better speak up. We started going together and decided to become engaged."

Jack really couldn't deny her now, and he admitted to himself that he would enjoy spending some time with the Holts before going home. "Okay. I'll stay until after your engagement party. Am I invited to your wedding next year?"

She threw her arms around him and kissed him. "Oh. Thank you for staying for the party. I so much want you to meet Victor and get your opinion of him. And of course you're invited to the wedding. I'd love it if you brought Cindy along with you."

Jack figured that would never happen because whatever had been between him and Cindy was lost forever. Even so, he didn't want to spoil Amanda's moment of happiness, so he took a deep breath and said, "That would be great, Amanda. We'll be there with bells on."

Jack woke up at five o'clock in the morning with the aroma of coffee, eggs, potatoes, steak, and sweet potato muffins filling his nostrils. He got dressed and headed for the kitchen. Margaret and Amanda were busy at the stove when he stepped in and said, "Good morning, ladies. Breakfast sure smells good."

Neither of the two turned from their work to look at him. "Go out on the porch and wash up. Breakfast will be ready by the time you get back in and seated at the table. Steve will be in from the barn in a minute."

That sounded official to Jack, so he stepped outside on the porch. Steve was just finishing washing. "Morning, Jack."

Jack cheerfully returned his greeting. "Good morning, Steve."

He hurriedly washed and dried his hands and went inside and seated himself at the only empty chair at the table. They bowed their heads while Steve said grace over the food, and then they began to pass the food around and eat. Normally, dinner at the Holts' table was pretty quiet, but now that Jack was here, there was a lot of conversation. Jack related the story of his tracking down the outlaws, leaving out the parts that might upset the women. Jack then wanted to know what all happened while he was away.

After the meal, the women started clearing up the table, and afterward, they brought the coffeepot over and refilled Steve and Jack's coffee cups.

"I'm sure glad you're staying with us for a few more weeks." Steve said, grinning. "This way you not only get to be here for Amanda's party but in the meantime you can help me with that new string of horses I brought in. I got a big herd this time; fifteen head."

"So that's what this was all about," Jack teased. "You all just wanted me to stay so I would help break those horses for you."

Amanda turned from her work to face the men. "No!" she protested. "I told you, Jack Montana, exactly why I wanted you to stay."

Margaret turned around to get into the conversation. "You two leave him alone." Looking at Jack, she said, "You can stay with me in the kitchen here and help with all the cooking and dishwashing. How about that, Jack?"

They all laughed, and Jack said, "You know, Amanda, I just remembered, I *really* have to get back home. I'll be leaving just as soon as I finish this cup of coffee ... and another sweet potato muffin."

The conversation turned more serious as Steve said, "You know, Jack, I was only joking when I mentioned about you helping me break that new string of horses."

"Of course I know that, Steve; but on the other hand, I couldn't sit here for three weeks and do nothing. Let's go out and take a look at those horses right now."

CHAPTER 16

Jack laughed as Steve hit the ground and rolled over three or four times to get away from the horse that was trying to stomp him into the dirt. As Steve jumped up and ran for the corral, where Jack was setting on the top rail, Jack reached down and grabbed Steve's arm and helped him over the top and onto the ground on the other side. Just at that time, the horse came bucking and kicking and ran into the fence right where they had been sitting.

Steve took his hat and brushed himself off. "I'm getting too damned old for this, Jack. Going to have to stick to herding cattle. Say, what the hell you laughing at?"

"Sorry about that, Steve, but you got the funniest way of riding a horse I ever seen. Where I come from, the bronc riders stay in the saddle."

Steve grinned. "Well, partner, it's your turn to ride that tornado. Let's see how long *you* can stay in the saddle."

Jack took his rawhide lariat from the corral post and checked the hondo to make sure the rawhide wouldn't hang up while passing through it and cause him to miss a throw. He waited until the horse calmed down a bit and climbed into the corral. As he walked closer to the horse, he spoke softly. The animal seemed to stay calm until he got within ten or twelve feet from it. Suddenly, the horse turned and bolted away, but Jack was ready for that and made a quick twirl over his head with the lariat. With a flick of his wrist, the lariat shot high into the air like a striking snake and settled around the horse's neck.

As soon as Jack saw that he had made a good throw, he ran to the snubbing post and took a couple turns around it with the lariat. When the running horse came to the end of the lariat, he was jerked almost to the ground. He recovered quickly though and started running at Jack with murder blazing in his eyes.

Jack was an old hand at this and knew all the tricks. He simply let the horse chase him around the post, and each time around, he'd take the slack out of the lariat. It didn't take long until the horse had pulled himself in close to the post and couldn't move around much. Jack stood and talked to the horse 'till he calmed down some then began to stroke the horse on the neck and talk soothingly to him. Simultaneously, he was easing the lariat from around the animal's neck. Abruptly, he grabbed the saddle horn with his left hand and swung up into the saddle. The horse, realizing he was loose from the pole, began to rear and buck.

It seemed like an eternity to Jack, but after a few minutes, the horse began to tire out. And just as suddenly as it began to buck, it came to a standstill. Jack dismounted and took hold of the horse's lead rope and led him around the corral a few times and then turned him loose.

After Jack retrieved his lariat from the snubbing post, he and Steve walked over to the well and got a drink of water. Jack took a long drink of the cold water, wiped his mouth, and grinned at Steve. "Well, we're getting the job done."

"We sure are," Steve agreed. "We've broken six horses in one week. It sure goes a lot quicker and easier with two guys working at it. I sure do thank you for your help."

"That's quite all right. This kind of work keeps a body out of trouble … most of the time."

"Yep. It sure does," Steve said.

They were interrupted when Amanda came out and announced, "Dinner is ready, guys. And mother says *now*, before it gets cold."

"Well, I guess we better get in there and wash up. We sure don't want to keep the boss waiting."

"Yeah," Jack agreed. "We better get moving."

The work with the new string of horses was finished. They were all broke to ride and ready to be delivered.

Amanda was very excited and chatted all through breakfast that morning. "I can hardly wait. It's just two more days until my engagement party. I need to get into town and see Abigale Bentley for a dress fitting. Father, are you or Jack going to town today? Oh. I guess I can go to town by myself—."

Margaret interrupted her chatter. "My goodness! Look at yourself, girl. You need to stop talking long enough to breathe and give these guys a chance to answer you."

Steve laughed. "As a matter of fact, Jack and I both are going into town right after breakfast. We need to pick up some supplies, so we'll be taking the wagon if you want to go with us."

"I'll be ready to go as soon as I've finished helping Mother wash the dishes and clean up a bit."

The men had no more than got the team hooked to the wagon when Amanda came running out of the house.

"I'm ready to go whenever you guys are."

Two hours later, they were tying up in front of Roderick's Mercantile Store. Jack got out of the wagon and, as Steve was tying the team to the hitch rail, helped Amanda down. While he was still holding her hand, a man approached them. He was a stranger to Jack. He could tell the man was very angry.

"Amanda, what's this about you getting engaged to someone else? We've only been broken up for a few months. I thought we'd get back together again after you had a chance to realize how foolish you were to break off with me."

Jack immediately determined that this guy was the jilted boyfriend, Carl McBride, and his first impulse was to knock the guy senseless. But he held his emotions back. *It would be better to wait and see how this plays out. If this guy even attempts to lay a hand on Amanda, that's when I will intercede.*

As the man drew near, still talking, Jack sized him up. Jack himself had grown to be a big man, six feet two inches tall and weighing two hundred and fifteen pounds. This man looked to be about six feet five inches and well over two hundred pounds. And he wore a six-gun like he knew how to use it.

Amanda snapped back at him. "Carl, I told you when we broke up that we were through. We could be friends, but our engagement was off. You won't let it go at that. You keep pestering me. I'm telling you again. Never speak to me again. Now, for the last time, it's over. Don't ever approach me again."

Carl was within arm's reach of them now. Looking at Jack, he said, "Who's this, your new boyfriend?"

Jack didn't know what Carl intended to do, but when he reached his hand out toward Amanda, Jack quickly stepped in front of her. "The lady said not to ever approach her again. My advice to you is to turn around and walk away and stay away from her."

In a fit of rage, Carl lunged at Jack, thinking this was the man that Amanda was going to marry. He would beat the man to death right here on the street in front of her. Jack had other ideas. As Carl charged at Jack, he sidestepped, and as his momentum carried Carl past his intended target, Jack grabbed him by the shirt collar and the seat of the pants and propelled him into the side of the wagon. Carl hit the wagon with such force that it knocked him down. He landed in the dust on his back, and he lay there, stunned, for a minute. As his head cleared, he glared up at Jack. The bigger man knew he wasn't a match for Jack in a fistfight, so he got to his feet and went into a slight crouch, his hand hovering over his gun.

"You don't want to do that, fella. It'll get you killed."

That was good advice, but Carl was so full of hatred that it didn't leave any room for reason. He went for his six-shooter, but it was only half out of the leather when Jack's .44 came out of the holster and sent a bullet smashing into Carl's gun, sending it flying into the air. The big .44 bucked in Jack's hand three more times, and Carl's gun jumped through the air like a pebble skipping across the water. While all this was happening, a crowd had gathered, watching every move and thoroughly entertained by the performance.

Carl stood there, holding his hand, fear and astonishment spreading across his face. "Who—who are you, mister?"

As Jack calmly reloaded his .44, he said, "Jack, Jack Montana."

A voice called from the crowd, "Jack Montana? You're the gunman that shot it out with the Dalton gang and killed every one of them."

Another voice rang out, "And you just captured and took in five more outlaws to Fort Washakie."

Another voice yelled, "Hey, Jack. I'll buy you a drink."

Still another voice yelled, "Killer! Gunslinger!"

This was not something Jack was enjoying. He certainly didn't want the title killer or gunslinger tacked onto his name. He didn't want to bring shame to the Walker family in any way.

Steve and Amanda realized just as well as Jack what could happen. This incident could turn out to be disastrous. Obviously, some people admired Jack for what all he did, but some people would accuse him of being a bad guy and would blow this thing up until there would be a mob calling for his arrest and, ultimately, his death.

Before anything else could happen, Amanda hooked her arm in Jack's arm and said, "Come on, Jack. We'd better get away from this crowd. Let's go on into the store."

Steve moved to the other side of Jack to shield him. "She's right, Jack. We'd better get away from this crowd."

Once inside the store, Jack asked Amanda, "Where is this dressmaker's shop that you wanted to see?"

"Just down the street a ways. Why?"

"There's no reason for you not to go, is there? I don't want to cause you to miss out on your appointment."

"No. It's okay. I'll come back tomorrow."

"You only have two more days until your party." He looked at Steve. "Is there a back way out of here that she could use? She could go and take care of her business at the dressmaker's while we take care of the supplies."

"That's right," Steve said. "Amanda, you go take care of that. We'll load up the supplies and then meet you in front of Abigale's dress shop."

After some protest, she agreed and left the store by the back door.

"That was good thinking, Jack, to get Amanda out of the way in case there's more trouble."

"That was the plan, Steve. Sheriff Eli Blake, what do you make of him?"

"Sheriff Blake? He's a good man. Why?"

"Well, I been through things like this before. I know the sheriff will want to know what happened, and he'll want to talk to me. I just want to get to him before the crowd convinces him that it was all my fault. So if you don't mind, while you finish with the supplies, I'll go out the back way and head on over to see Sheriff Blake."

"Sounds good ... and, Jack, whatever happens, we're behind you."

Jack nodded his thanks and left Roderick's Mercantile by the back door. As he walked down the alleyway toward the sheriff's office, he peered out to the street where the incident took place. Carl was still there in front of the crowd, talking and trying to get them riled up. He heard Carl saying, "Yeah. That was the Jack Montana.

We've all heard about him. He's nothing but a cold-blooded killer, a real gunslinger. Why, it's a wonder that he didn't kill me."

Jack didn't linger long enough to hear any more. He hightailed it on over to the sheriff's office. When he got there, Sheriff Blake wasn't in his office. Jack figured Blake was talking to the crowd and that he'd missed him on the way.

"Well, looks like I'll just have to wait," he told himself.

An hour later, Sheriff Eli Blake came in. He looked at Jack. "I remember you, Jack. You came in my office a while back looking for Steve Holts when he was laid up over to the Doc's."

"Uh huh," Jack said. "I suppose you talked to Carl McBride and the crowd?" As he was talking, he unbuckled his gun belt.

Blake laughed. "Son," he said, "I did talk to Carl and the crowd. And, yes, most of us around here have heard of you. I don't want to take your gun."

"But," Jack said, "I figured Carl would have the people all riled up and demanding that you arrest me."

Blake laughed again. "What the hell for? The name *Jack Montana* is practically immortalized around here. If I had realized who you were the first time I saw you, I probably would have taken you around and introduced you to everyone in town. Them five outlaws were no-good desperadoes. Hell, they even tried to rob our bank. But someone tipped me off to their plans, and we were waiting for them when they came riding into town. Them outlaws took off and never did come back. And thanks to you, they never will."

Jack was relieved and said as much. "I figured I'd at least wind up in jail over this."

"Naw. It's over with for now. You see, I've known Carl since he was a kid, and I've seen his bad side as well as the good. He has most folks around here fooled, but not me. He hasn't fooled me one bit. When Amanda broke their engagement off, he went crazy. Every time he seen her in town, he'd pester her and do everything but threaten her. Now he's showing his bad side. Jack, you watch out for him. He'll cause as much trouble as he can.

When Jack left the sheriff's office, Steve and Amanda were pulling up in front of the jail. Sheriff Blake came out, and the four of them talked for a long time. Jack repeated to Amanda and Steve what was said between Sheriff Blake and himself. Presently, Steve turned the team around and they headed back to the ranch.

"When we get back home," Amanda said, "you got a lot of explaining to do, Mr. Montana."

"I'm sorry I didn't explain everything to you when I first got here instead of telling you that I was a gun salesman, but I wasn't sure you'd understand. I thought that maybe you'd think that I did rob that bank back in Billings and that I was just another gun-slinging outlaw."

"Naw," Steve declared. "I would have never thought that I'd have the pleasure of entertaining Jack Montana in my home, let alone him helping me break all those wild horses."

"Yes," Margaret added, "and I thank you for all you did for us before and for putting that Carl McBride in his place when he was attacking Amanda."

"And," Amanda said while hugging him around the neck, "I thank you too. I'm not sure that we will let you leave, even after the party."

Jack's face was beginning to turn red. "I surely appreciate all this, but can we talk about something else, like the party?

"Oh my! Yes!" Amanda shrieked. "I almost forgot about the party! It's the day after tomorrow."

The next day, Friday, was one of hectic party preparations. The women were busy cleaning the house and making sure everything was in order. Jack and Steve stayed out of their way by just staying outside, working in the barn. There were always saddles and bridles or other harnesses to repair and clean.

CHAPTER 17

The big day of Amanda's party came, and the guests were arriving. Jack had borrowed one of Steve's suits. It was a tad tight in the shoulders, but it would do. Laurel was a small town, and the Holts were well liked, so just about everyone was there. Also, the news had gotten out and swept through the town like wildfire that Jack Montana would be there, noted to be a close friend of the family. Sheriff Eli Blake was there, as were Mayor Owen Myers, Judge Isaiah Catkins, Doctor Allen Collins, and Abigale Bentley. Well over fifty people were present. That's not to mention all of the close friends of Amanda. And soon, the intended groom, Victor Boyd, arrived. The evening wore on, people were shaking hands, and Steve had the great pleasure of introducing Jack Montana to everyone.

Late in the evening, an uninvited guest showed up: Carl McBride, along with two friends who were obviously gunslingers. Since this was a party at a respectable home, everyone had checked their guns at the door. It wasn't a demand. It was just common courtesy applied by the guests themselves.

Carl and his two friends walked in unexpectedly, and before anyone knew it, they had covered everyone with their guns. Some of the women were frightened and started to scream. Carl backhanded one of them and yelled, "Shut up,!"

Amanda stepped out from the rest of the people. "Stop this and leave my house now, you coward."

Carl backhanded her too. She was knocked to the floor.

"That did my heart good, you damn floozy."

Jack had been outside in the privy when Carl busted in on the party. As he stepped inside the room where everyone was being held at gunpoint, he saw and realized what was going on.

"Well, well," Carl mocked, "if it ain't our big-time hero."

There wasn't much Jack could say or do since the only ones having guns were Carl and his two friends.

"Come on out here, where everyone can see how you protect your sweetheart, Jack Montana."

Jack knew that this was going to get mighty hairy, but at this point, there wasn't a thing he could do about it.

Carl began to laugh. "Jack, my friend, you ever meet these two guys before? Let me introduce you. Jack, meet Les and Asa Walton. Guys, meet the famous Jack Montana. You don't have to shake hands ... yet." Carl began to laugh again.

Jack stepped forward. "Why don't you let these people go if your fight is with me. Then let's get it on." He had never met the Walton brothers before, but he had heard of them. They were noted gunmen, fast and dangerous. He didn't know how or where Carl had met them, but he knew he was in trouble. He glanced around. Amanda's intended, Victor Boyd, was keeping a low profile. *Well,* Jack told himself, *it's just as well.*

"Okay. Enough talk," Carl said. "Let the fun begin."

He stepped forward and swung a right fist into Jack's stomach. He doubled over, gasping for breath. Carl stepped in again and clubbed him over the back of the neck with both hands cupped together. Jack fell to the floor. He struggled to his feet, and when Carl came at him again, Jack tensed up, ready to defend himself. Carl saw the movement and stopped. He wagged his finger at Jack and laughed.

"No, no, no. This is my party now. You lift one finger to hit me and Les and Asa will fill you full of lead."

He punched Jack full in the face. Jack was knocked back four or five feet from the impact. He stood there bleeding profusely from the face.

Amanda jerked away from Steve, who was holding her back, and ran to Jack's side. She put her arms around him to hold him up and screamed at Carl, "You bastard! Leave him alone!"

Carl stepped forward and grabbed her by the arm and flung her across the room and onto the floor. Steve and some of the other men moved forward to attack Carl, but the other two gunmen, Les and Asa, pulled their guns again. One of them put a couple of slugs in the floor at the men's feet. That stopped them in their tracks. Otherwise, they would have been killed on the spot.

Carl continued to beat Jack until he was a bloody mess. Finally, Jack fell to the floor, unable to get up.

Carl yelled at Les and Asa, "Pick him up!"

After they stood Jack up on his feet, Carl laughed like a crazy man.

"Now, big man, let's see how fast you are. Les, go find Jack a gun."

Les walked over to where the guns were hanging from hooks on the wall. He picked up the first gun belt that he saw, but unknown to him, it happened to be Jack's own pistols. The gunman brought the gun belt over to Jack and held it out for him to take. Jack just stood there, swaying to and fro. "Put it on him!" Carl yelled.

Les did as he was told.

"Now get back over here," Carl yelled excitedly.

Les walked back and stood beside Carl and Asa.

"Now," Carl shouted, looking over at Amanda and the rest of the people. "You're going to see who's the fastest. You're going to watch me outdraw and shoot the great Jack Montana."

Amanda tried to go to Jack again, but her father held on to her tightly.

"No. Please don't," she cried.

Carl was ready for his triumphal moment. "When Les here counts to three, Mister Jack Montana, you're going to die."

"One," Les counted."

At the count of one, Jack knew that, although he was so beaten up that he couldn't hardly stand, he better make it good or he was going to die. He also knew that if he did manage to beat Carl to the draw, Les and Asa would open fire on him. Either way, he knew there was a good chance that he was going to cash in his chips.

When he heard Les say two, something triggered in his mind, and suddenly, it was as though pictures from the past were floating before his eyes. In the first picture, he was a small boy and three men from the past were beating him. After that another picture came before him, one of a cruel man who took him into a saloon and told him, "Get out of my sight … I don't want to see you anymore." Next thing he knew, he was holding onto a horse going nowhere, with the pain of starvation deep and real in the pit of his stomach, but another man, a kind man, and a woman were caring for him.

At the sound of Amanda's voice screaming, "Jack!" the pictures disappeared. At that same time, he heard Les's voice count three. In that moment of time, Jack was still in a state of partial unconsciousness, but his natural instincts awoke into a blur of action. Up and out of their holsters jumped two deadly Colt .44's, spewing smoke and hot lead.

One slug caught Carl between the eyes before his hand even touched the grips of his pistol. Les and Asa managed to clear leather, but their slugs went wild because even as they were pulling the trigger of their guns, they were already dead. Their bullet-riddled bodies hit the floor almost at the same time.

As everyone stared in disbelief, Jack fell to the floor, unconscious. Thinking that he had been shot to death, Amanda ran and knelt at his side. She cradled his head in her arms, crying out his name. Then she realized he hadn't been shot. He was alive. He opened his eyes and was trying to speak.

"What did you say, Jack?" she asked.

She heard his voice weakly calling, "Cindy. Cindy."

Doctor Allen Collins treated Jack's bruises, and a few days with Margaret's care and mothering and he was pretty well healed up. While he was recuperating, several people, including Sheriff Blake, stopped by to see how he was doing and to talk to him about the shooting.

"I don't know how you did it in the condition you were in, Jack," Eli said. "I've been sheriff for almost twenty years, and I'll tell you I've seen plenty of gunfights. And I've seen what I thought was the fastest and the best. But after witnessing you take out those three guys, two of which were noted to be top gunmen, while being almost unconscious, well..." He shook his head uncertainly. "Well...I think that maybe you've topped them all."

"Well, I don't know about me being top of the heap. All I know is that I've had a lot of practice lately at shooting it out with outlaws. I figure that with that and a helping hand from the Almighty, I been blessed. Yes, sir. I been mightily blessed."

Amanda was constantly at Jack's side all during the time he was healing and preparing to start back home. They did a lot of talking, especially about her intended. Victor Boyd had been out to see Amanda and Jack several times. He was ashamed because he had not tried to help when Jack was confronted by Carl and the two gunmen. Amanda had mixed emotions about it too and said as much.

Through their many visits, Jack had learned to like Victor. He thought that Victor would react differently if anything like that was to happen again. He told Amanda, "It's really a good thing that Victor didn't try to interfere because he would probably have been killed."

Amanda agreed and said she wouldn't call off the wedding as yet. She would continue seeing Victor until she had a chance to really make up her mind.

CHAPTER 18

Jack left the Holts' Lazy H Ranch right after breakfast the next morning and headed for the Walker Ranch in Billings. It was his home, and he was anxious to see Dan and Martha. His heart ached to see Cindy again, but he doubted she would be there. Even if she was, he reckoned they'd just wind up in another argument, so he was hoping that she would not be there.

Jack made excellent time riding from Laurel to Billings, much better than his outward journey. On that first trip, his horse had come up lame, and he had to walk a long way to the Butterfield Stagecoach Station. Then there was the trouble with the four men that were on the coach with Margaret and Amanda. Of course, that had turned out good because he met the Holts family. And because of the Holts family, he met Wanda at the Red Horse Saloon, and she got him on the trail of the five outlaws.

Two days after leaving Laurel, he rode into Billings. As much as he wanted to get home, he thought it best if he stopped in town to report to Sheriff Frank Morgan. It felt mighty good to Jack to be back in his hometown again. When he dismounted and tied up in front of the jailhouse, he turned around and looked at all the familiar buildings and things that he missed while away. He grinned as this thought crossed his mind: *I'd probably have gotten homesick if I'd had the time to think about it.*

He chuckled at that thought as he stepped up on the sidewalk and went inside the jailhouse. Frank had only stepped inside and sat down minutes ago, so when Jack walked in, he stood up and, grinning, stuck out his hand. "Damn. It's good to see you again, Jack."

Jack pumped Frank's hand. "It's good to see you too, Frank. And it's good to be home again."

Frank sat back down and motioned for Jack to take the chair beside his desk. "I hope you're here to tell me that you have a good report to make."

"Yep. I'm happy to say I have returned successful." Jack handed Frank the documents that Captain John Goodman had given him that specified all the details of Jack's capture of the five renegades.

After reading the documents carefully, Frank said, "Everything's in order, Jack. You've done your job well. And you're a free man."

"Thanks, Frank. How's everything around here? Has anything changed?"

Jack noticed a wrinkle in Frank's brow as the sheriff cleared his throat. "As a matter of fact, there have been some changes since you've been gone."

Jack steeled himself for the news. "Okay. I'm listening."

"I don't hardly know where to start, so I'll start with your friend, Rusty. Rusty has turned real bad, Jack. I did the best I could to help him out, but he's bent on riding the outlaw trail. Fights, shootings—

you name it, he's in it. He got drunk one night at Murdock's Saloon and claimed that he was twice the man that you were and insisted that Shannon take him to her bed. Said he'd show her what it was like to sleep with a real man. She turned him down, and he went crazy. He beat her up bad and then shot two men that tried to stop him and proceeded to bust up the place. By the time I got there, Rusty had ridden out of town."

Jack was real upset. "How is Shannon, Frank?"

"Oh, she's much better now. She's recovering from the beating pretty good. She has taken time off at Murdock's 'till the bruises go away."

Jack responded with a question. "Do you have any idea where Rusty is?"

"No. I've questioned everyone in town, and nobody seems to know where he is."

"Well," Jack said, "I'll find him!"

"I wouldn't go running off looking for the likes of him just yet, Jack. That's not all the bad news around here."

Jack's shoulders slumped. "What else, Frank?"

"Since Rusty has disappeared, just about all the ranches around this whole area have been missing cows. And not just a few. Dan came in to see me about it. He says he's lost way over half of his herd. Said he don't have enough cows left to make the drive this year. He said he had put a mortgage on the ranch to pay for Cindy's schooling, and now he can't make the final payments. Says the bank's going to foreclose on his loan if he hasn't paid it off by the end of the year."

"Do you happen to know how much the mortgage is?"

"Yes," Frank said. "Eighteen hundred dollars."

"Wow, Frank. That's a lot of money." Moving on, Jack asked about Cindy.

Frank said that Dan hadn't told her anything about the mortgage as yet. He didn't want to worry her. "He's hoping that something will happen that will enable him to make the ranch payment before it forecloses. That way she wouldn't have to know about it." Then he added, "Cindy was very upset with you for leaving like you did. She left to go back to Boston the day after you left town."

Jack sat silently for a while, and then, wearily, he stood up. "I'll spend the night in town and then ride out to the ranch in the morning."

He left Frank at the jail and walked over to Murdock's Saloon. There wasn't anyone in there that he knew except for McDaniels, the barkeeper. When Jack stepped up to the bar, Mac came over with a bottle of mescal and, pouring him a glass, said, "Howdy, Jack. Been a long time. You still a mescal drinker?"

"Howdy, Mac. Yep. I'm still partial to mescal when I drink."

Business was slow in the saloon that night, so Mac, being a good friend, leaned his elbows on the bar and talked with Jack for some time.

"You heard about Rusty, I guess."

"Yeah. I heard."

"You and Rusty came in here for years, ever since you was just kids."

"Yeah. We sure did."

"Funny thing though. You were both young and wild, but Rusty was downright mean where you seemed to be just full of piss and vinegar. You know what I mean?"

"I guess so, Mac."

"Still, I never figured old Rusty would do a thing like beatin' up on a girl like Shannon."

Jack winced at the thought. He didn't want to hear any more about it tonight. "One more quick one, Mac."

Mac poured him another glass of mescal. Jack tilted the glass straight up and drank it down in one gulp. He then set the glass down, wiped his mouth, and walked out of the saloon.

"Night, Mac."

Mac yelled after him, "See you around, Jack!"

Jack walked along the boardwalk feeling pretty low. Things were going real well. Now nothing seemed right. As he passed the sheriff's office, Frank called out to him, and he stepped inside the jail.

"Where you beddin' down tonight?"

"I haven't thought that far ahead yet, Frank."

"You're welcome to bunk here if you've a mind to."

"Thanks, Frank. That's just what I'll do."

On his way out to the Walker ranch the next morning, Jack was anxious to get home to see Dan and Martha, but at the same time, he dreaded facing them. He figured they would want to know why he left that night when he'd said he was going to stay for a couple more days—and why he left without saying good-bye. At least he wouldn't have to explain to Cindy why he had left the way he did because she knew why he left that night. He made sure of that in the letter he left her.

Thinking back to that night when he had left because of that awful moment between Cindy and him, he recalled every word that he had written in that letter to her. Even though he tried to blot out the image of the letter, he still saw it clearly in his mind as if it was right before his eyes.

When Jack rode into the ranch yard, Dan's foreman, Hank, had just ridden in from the range. Two of the other ranch hands, Lucas Duran and Leon Hatfield, were with him. They had been out getting a tally on what was left of the Walker cattle.

Leon was saying, "It don't look good, Hank!"

The foreman was about to agree with Leon when he heard Jack's horses entering the yard. When he saw Jack, he said, "Well, look who's here, boys!"

All the somber looks turned to grins when they saw Jack. They all dismounted and began shaking hands.

Martha heard the racket and looked out her kitchen window. When she saw Jack, she yelled, "Hank! Don't you guys keep him out there all day. Get yourselves in here!" Then, turning around, she lowered her voice somewhat. "Dan, Jack's here! He's coming inside!"

"Go on inside," Hank told Jack. "We'll take care of the horses."

"Thanks," Jack said and went on in the house.

As soon as he stepped inside the door, Martha began to hug him. "I'm so glad you're home, Jack. You are home to stay, aren't you?" she asked as she stepped back and began wiping her eyes with the hem of her apron.

"Yes. As far as I know, I'm home to stay."

Hearing that Jack had returned, Dan had come into the kitchen. He put his hand on Jack's shoulder and began pumping his hand. Then, unashamedly, the two men hugged each other as father and son. Martha wasn't sure, but she thought she saw a little wetness in the eyes of both men. She didn't know if the wetness was because they were so glad to see each other or because, after all these years, they had finally allowed themselves to show their affection for each other.

When the emotional moment was over, Martha called them to the table. She had set cups around the big table in the dining room. As Jack and Dan sat down, Hank and Leon, Lucas, and Bob Marshall were knocking on the kitchen door.

"Goodness gracious," Martha called. "Come on in. I've made enough coffee for an army."

When they were all seated, Martha began to pour the coffee. Then she set a freshly baked apple pie on the table and began to serve generous portions to all the men.

Bob Marshall, the jokester, said, "Gee, Mrs. Walker. You didn't have to go to all this trouble just for me."

Martha laughed. "You're right, Bob ... and I didn't!"

Everyone laughed at that. Then the talk got serious. Dan asked Jack about the outcome with the outlaws, and everyone listened to his account of that ordeal and everything else that had happened while he was away.

Jack wanted to ask Dan just how serious the situation was concerning the mortgage on the ranch, but he decided to wait until they were alone. Instead, he asked about Cindy. Immediately, he regretted asking about her because that brought up the question about the abrupt way he left that night.

He was hoping that Cindy hadn't shown them the letter that he'd written to her that night. "I'm sorry about that," he said. "I just don't like saying good-bye."

Martha shook her head in acknowledgment. "Yes. That's what Cindy said. But we'll be seeing her again soon because we just got a letter from her saying that she'll be home again next month."

CHAPTER 19

For the next several days, Jack kept busy working around the ranch. At night, he stayed in the bunkhouse, playing cards and talking to Hank and the boys. Rusty's name came up in their conversation quite a bit. Bob said that once he'd seen Rusty in town but didn't even speak to him.

In the months that Jack had been gone, some things had changed, and in some cases, the changes were for the better. For one, since Rusty was not in the picture anymore, things were slower paced both in town and there at the ranch. It was like being in the eye of a storm, and everyone was just waiting for the storm to break. Also, Jack noticed a change in himself. He had matured considerably.

Saturday night rolled around, and Jack decided he needed to go into town. He hadn't seen Shannon since he got back. He asked Hank and some of the guys if they wanted to go along, but they all declined. It seemed that they had gone into town the last Saturday night and got into a poker game and lost all their money.

Jack laughed and offered to stake them some money 'till payday.

"Naw," Hank said. "You go ahead have a good time, and we'll see you in the morning."

When he got into town, he went straight to Murdock's Saloon, tied up at the hitch rail, and went inside to the bar and ordered a whiskey. He downed that and turned around to look for Shannon. Remembering that Frank had said she had taken time off work, he didn't really expect to see her here, but there she was.

She had seen him from across the room and walked over just as he turned. "Looking for someone?" she said.

He grinned and said, "Yes, ma'am. I'm looking for my best girl."

She laughed. "I'll bet you say that to all the girls."

"Nope. I only have one best girl."

"Then come with me, cowboy Jack. I have a room reserved just for you and me."

In that first moment when Jack saw Shannon's face, he was shocked. It was the first time he'd seen her since the beating incident, and the bruises were not completely gone. Now, as he followed her up to her room, he didn't know how to react to her. He didn't want to hurt her feelings, but she looked almost appalling.

Once inside her room, she went to the window and pulled the shade to darken the room. Then she turned around and fell into his arms. "Oh, Jack, I'm so glad you're back. I was so worried about you. And now that I'm in your arms, I realize just how much I missed you."

Jack had truly missed her too, as they had become very good friends. "I missed you too, Shannon," he said.

After a few moments, she pulled away from him. "I'm sorry," she said. "I promised you that I wouldn't cling to you. If there's ever anything between us besides friendship, I want it to be because you truly love me."

She then changed the subject. "Tell me how things went while you were gone. I hear you got all five of those outlaws."

"Yes, I did," he said. "But, Shannon, let's talk about you." As he was speaking, he walked over to the window and opened the shade to get a better look at her.

"No!" she cried out, hugging him tightly, burying her face against his chest. "I don't want you to see my face!" At length, she stepped back, sobbing. "See! I look horrible, don't I?"

Jack looked at her for a full minute. She was still sobbing, ashamed for him to look upon her bruised face. Looking through her tears, he realized that he could look past the black and blue marks that covered her face and see her inner beauty and the true love for him that was in her eyes. "Shannon," he said, "I ... I think you're beautiful."

He pulled her to him and, holding her tightly, began tenderly kissing her bruised face. When his lips finally touched hers, it was like an electric current shot through both of them, binding them together so tightly that they could not pull away from each other. Still kissing her, he eased her down on the bed.

"Shannon, I love you, and I want you."

Shannon could hardly believe what she was hearing. Her head was spinning around so quickly that she thought she might faint. To herself, she was thinking, *This is Jack Montana saying this. This is the man I would die for, and he loves me. He wants to make love to me. Yes! Yes!* Then she realized she could not let this happen. After it was over, he would hate her and himself. There would never be a chance for them to be happy, and marriage would be out of the question.

Suddenly, she said, "No!" and began struggling underneath his body to push him away. "We can't do this. I won't let it happen!"

Stunned, he pulled back and got up off the bed. "Shannon? What's wrong? I ... I thought you loved me? I thought you wanted me?"

She stood up and hugged him. "Oh, Jack, you can never know how much I love you. You can never know how much and how long I've waited and even prayed that you would do and say exactly what you just did."

"But then why?"

"It's *because* I love you so much that I can't *afford* to let that happen. As long as you have Cindy in your head and in your heart, you will never be able to love me completely. You're not just some cowboy that I want to go to bed with. Jack, I love you with all my heart and all my being, and I would rather die than give in to you in this way and have you hate me for it later."

"I guess I understand that. What I don't understand is you've made your living like ... this. So why didn't you just let Rusty have his way with you? Why did you allow him to beat you like that when you could have prevented it by—."

"I'll tell you why, Jack. You see, I fell in love with you the moment I first saw you. And when I saw that you were different than most men and that you really cared for me, I began to fight for you then. You see, I haven't taken anyone to my bed since you and I first made people think that I was *your whore*. It wasn't just Rusty that I wouldn't go to bed with. Jack, I haven't been to bed with anyone."

"But how have you been making a living. How do you earn money?"

Shannon grinned, as she said, "Well, I was pretty popular all those years that I was working, so I had some money saved up. Since then, I've been only hustling drinks. I get paid for that, and you've been paying me for our time together, remember?"

"So Rusty thought you were still taking men to your bed. Why didn't you tell him that you had quit prostituting?"

"He wouldn't have believed me. And I don't think he would have cared either."

Jack was silent for a while, his anger building. Then, through clenched teeth, he said, "He needs to pay for this. Do you know where he is?"

Shannon knew what he was thinking. "No, I don't," she said. "And knowing what you're thinking, I wouldn't tell you even if I did know. Jack, it's over now. Just let it go."

"Okay, Shannon. If that's the way you want it."

They conversed a little while longer until Jack said, "I better go." He walked toward the door, stopped, and turned around. "So you really quit prostituting, huh?"

Shannon's face turned red. "Yes, for you I did! See. You've got me blushing like a school girl."

Jack grinned.

"Stop grinning like you don't believe me, Jack. I really want you to see that I am a God-fearing person and that I can be decent and respectable."

"I've always respected you, Shannon."

"I know that, but I want more from you than respect. If things don't work out for you and Cindy, I'm going after you with everything I got."

"I've already told you that in that case, I'd ask you to marry me in a heartbeat."

"Yes, you did. And I told you that I'd *marry* you ... in a heartbeat."

The next few weeks went well at the Walker Ranch. Jack and the crew rounded up the cattle that the rustlers hadn't gotten away with and branded all the young ones that were not already branded. It turned out that there were more cattle left than they had figured. They hadn't been hit for some time. Hank figured that that was because Jack had recommended that they put an around-the-clock watch on the herd.

In town, things were going well too. No one had seen or heard anything of Rusty for several weeks. It was as if he had just vanished into thin air. "Yeah," Hank said, but he's like a bad penny. Sooner or later, he'll turn up. You can count on it."

On some Saturday nights when Jack would go into town, Hank or one of the other ranch hands would go with him. But it was different now that Shannon wasn't entertaining men in her upstairs room. She would usually serve the drinks and then sit and talk with

Jack. On occasion, instead of going to Murdock's Saloon, Jack would rent a buggy from the livery and he and Shannon would go for a ride outside of town.

One day, a came a letter from Cindy, saying that she would be coming home in three days.

When Jack told Shannon about the letter, she said, "I understand. I'll see you after Cindy leaves again."

He was glad that she did understand, but it made him feel bad, as if he was cheating on both of them.

The day of Cindy's arrival came, and Jack met her at the stagecoach with a buggy. After a very formal hug, he took her luggage from the coach, loaded it in the buggy, and helped her get seated. It was a long drive to the ranch, so both of them had plenty of time to think about what they were going to say.

At length, he heard Cindy say, "I'm glad to be home. I really missed you, Jack."

"I missed you too, Cindy. And I'm glad that you're home again." He wanted to keep the conversation going, and he wanted to tell her about Shannon. He didn't want her to find out about her from some other source because she might get the idea that he was in love with Shannon. Although he was sure that he didn't have a chance with Cindy, he somehow couldn't give up hope. He thought he had better tell her now, but it wasn't coming out right, everything he said made it sound like he had fallen for another woman.

Cindy wasn't taking it well at all. "I really don't want to hear about another woman, Jack! Especially not about some saloon ... whore."

Jack cleared his throat. "Well, Shannon's not a whore! At least not now!"

"You mean she changed her whole life around just for you, Jack?"

"Well, yes! She did quit ... for me! Oh, you think that I'm so funny-looking that no woman, even a *whore*, could change just for me! Is that it?"

Cindy realized that she had now caused Jack to be on the defensive. "Jack, I didn't mean it like that. I don't think you're funny-looking."

"Well, that's what you told me."

They both could see that this was going nowhere, so that was the end of their conversation, and they rode the rest of the way home without so much as a glance towards each other.

When they reached the house, Cindy jumped out of the buggy and began gathering her luggage by herself. "I don't need your help," she said.

"That's good because I didn't intend on helping you anyway," he said and stormed inside the house.

They didn't speak to each other except when at the table, and that was purely out of respect for Dan and Martha. Jack was sure now that he had lost her. But he still loved her, so after a couple of days, he began to speak to her. He just wouldn't converse for very long with her. Dan and Martha was confused at their behavior but decided not to interfere.

One Saturday night, Jack rode into town. He was frustrated and felt like getting drunk. He dismounted in front of Murdock's and was tying the appaloosa up at the hitch rail when Frank Morgan met him on the street. "Follow me to my office. We got to talk!"

Puzzled, he said, "Okay. Lead the way." When they stepped into the sheriff's office, Jack said, "Frank, the last time you said, 'We got to talk,' it turned out that I was in a heap of trouble."

The sheriff shrugged his shoulders. "You know what they say. When it rains, it pours."

Frank sat down behind his desk, and Jack slumped down in a chair, after which he asked, "What's on your mind, Sheriff?"

Frank looked at Jack for a moment and asked, "Do you know where Powell, Wyoming is?"

"Yes. Actually, I went through Powell on the way to Fort Washakie. Why?"

"Well, I received a wire from the sheriff there. He sends a warning that some gunmen are coming here looking for trouble. Jack, they aim to kill you."

"They must be friends of those five outlaws that I was sent after. I wonder if they really intend on coming here or if they're just idle threats. You know, sometimes people say one thing but never follow through with it."

"Well, I thought that at first, so I wasn't going to tell you about it. Then, yesterday, I received another wire from another sheriff in Greybull, Wyoming saying the same thing. Now that's got me worried." Frank handed the two wires to Jack. "Here. Read them."

Jack took his time reading the two wires and handed them back to Frank. "I guess you were right to figure they mean to do what they say. It seems that one of these gunmen was a brother to one of the outlaws that I killed. That would have to be either Jess Barker or Ralph Simmons because Hal Colby, Art Cummings, and Bill Taggard are locked up in the stockade at Fort Washakie, unless they've been transported somewhere else."

"Did you notice who was named among the gunmen that are coming here?"

Jack shook his head. "Yes. My old friend, Rusty Warren."

"Does that really surprise you?" Frank asked.

"No... Yes, it does! In spite of all the rotten things he's done, I wouldn't have ever thought he'd want to bring harm to me."

"It don't surprise me a damn bit!" Frank replied angrily.

"So I guess I'm always going to be in trouble regardless of what I do?"

"Sometimes the chips just fall that way, Jack. But you've got a lot of savvy about you, and you have a lot of folks that have faith in you. I, among many, am confident that you will overcome all of this and will make something of yourself."

"Well, thanks for your vote of confidence, Frank. But what about now? Have you thought of a plan yet?"

"Yep. The wheels in this old noggin started spinning as soon as I received the first wire about this. And I figure I'll make you my deputy until this is over with."

"Well, I was your deputy once before, but I thought you said you couldn't use me in that capacity anymore since my first run-in with the law?"

"That's right, but you cleared yourself of that. Now, do you want to be my deputy or not?"

It didn't take but a minute for Jack to make up his mind. "Okay, Frank. You going to swear me in now?"

Frank let out a breath of relief, and Jack laughed.

"You didn't think I would say yes, did you?"

"Naw," Frank said. "I figured you'd say yes. The only thing that made me doubt it was the fact that Rusty Warren was named in the pack of gunmen."

Jack hesitated and said, "At one time, Rusty and I were an inseparable pair, but now there's nothing left of our friendship."

"Jack, if you're sure that you won't allow your past friendship get in the way when and if you have to draw against Rusty, then I'll swear you in." Frank hesitated to let Jack think about what he said, but then he continued. "Rusty is fast as a striking snake when it comes to gunplay. You know that, Jack. When you were kids practicing quick draw, it was always debatable as to who was the faster. So you have to be sure."

"I said the friendship has ended, didn't I?"

Frank readily agreed but thought he detected a slight hint of doubt in Jack's answer. "Okay. Raise your right hand."

Jack raised his right hand, and Frank swore him in as deputy sheriff.

"Now," Frank said, "let's put our heads together and figure out how to deal with this threat. Remember back when we had to deal with the Dalton gang? I figure we done great then. We wiped the whole gang out and never lost a man. I figure it worked once, so it ought to work again. Right?"

"Right," Jack said, "and I remember what we did to get the town prepared for them. We posted guards around town to warn us when the gang was approaching. And when the guards sounded the alarm, all of the prearranged riflemen took their posts. When the gang entered town, you and I met them in the middle of the street and gave them the chance to turn around and leave. And when they went for their guns, we finished it right there."

"That's right, Jack, and that's what we'll do this time. We want to keep this quiet as long as possible though, so I'll notify the men that we want for guards and riflemen on the sly."

Billings, Montana, was generally a pretty quiet little place for a cow town. It was small enough that a person knew just about everyone else. Before Jack had that run-in with the law over the Dalton gang and became Frank's deputy, most everyone thought well of him. Since then, there were some who said he was a no-account and a troublemaker, but as they say, "Time heals all things."

Now Jack was thinking, *Here comes more trouble to the town, and it's my fault again.*

That was exactly what a lot of people were saying when the word leaked out that more gunmen were threatening their town. When they saw that was Jack wearing a deputy's badge *again*, they knew that it wasn't just gossip. After that, the streets of Billings, Montana became almost devoid of life.

Jack mentioned this to Frank. "What do you think? The town seems deserted."

Frank grinned, "Hell, Jack. That's a good sign. I just hope that those gunmen show up soon or both of us will be out of a job."

Jack gave the sheriff a puzzled look.

"A ghost town don't have a need for a sheriff."

After Jack's discussion with Frank about the threat of Rusty Warren and the outlaws, he hung around town most of the time. He figured that as soon as he left, the gang would show up and by the time someone got word to him and he made the long ride back to town the fight would be over. Not that he considered himself to be a top gun or anything like that, but the truth of the matter was he and Frank were the only ones who had been involved in much gunplay. A lot of these townsfolk had never shot at anything besides a snake or coyote. Other than that, some of the men from the Walker Ranch were the only outside help they could rely on. At one time, Dan Walker himself was a heller with a gun, but since he got busted up in that line shack a few years earlier, he had acquired a bad case of rheumatism and could barely handle a gun at all.

Hank Shaw, Dan's foreman, although a little older now, was still pretty good with a gun. Lucas Duran, Leon Hatfield, and Bob Marshall, Dan's ranch hands, were good. They were in the class of Doc Holiday, Wyatt Earp, Bat Masterson, Wild Bill Hickok, and the rest of them.

They were on the verge of riding the outlaw trail themselves until Dan saw a lot of good in them and hired them on as cowpunchers. Of course, Dan paid them well above the normal cowboy wages. Once they made the change, they were happy about it and stayed with Dan. Jack knew he could count on them to help if needed.

On the Sunday morning after Frank had deputized Jack, one of the lookout guards came galloping into town, yelling, "There's six riders coming and riding fast, and Rusty Warren's leading the pack."

What they didn't know was that there were actually *seven* gunmen. One of them was a brother to Jess Barker, the man Jack had killed while trying to transport him and Hal Colby to Fort Washakie. This seventh man had ridden into town the night before and was right now perched atop of the old water tower, waiting to get a shot at Jack.

It had been their plan to do as before. Jack and Frank would meet the gunmen in the street and try to talk to them into aborting their attack on the town. But the gunmen came in riding fast, guns drawn and blazing away.

However, the outlaws had no idea that they were riding into a trap, so it was like shooting ducks in a row. Rusty's quick actions enabled him to escape. He turned tail and ran. The other five men were shot down in a matter of minutes with the help of the hidden riflemen. When the dust cleared, there were five dead bodies lying in the street. In the midst of the bodies stood Frank Morgan and Jack Montana.

Shannon, being fearful for Jack's safety, had hidden in an alley closeby so she could warn Jack if things went wrong. Seeing the five gunmen lying dead in the street and Rusty gone, she stepped out of the alley to be by Jack's side. As she ran toward him, she caught the reflection of the sun as it glanced off the gunman's rifle barrel.

"Jack!" she shouted.

At that moment, the seventh outlaw that was atop of the water tower took his shot at Jack. Jack heard Shannon's scream and the crack of the rifle. He turned and fired his Colt simultaneously. The gunman tumbled off the tower and fell dead on the ground. At that time, Jack heard Shannon's gasp. She had taken the bullet that was meant for him. He looked down where Shannon lay at his feet, gasping for breath. The front of her dress was wet with her blood, and as she exhaled, little bubbles of red appeared on her lips. Quickly, he knelt by her side and cradled her head in his arms.

"Shannon, what … why did you come out here?"

"Because I love you, Jack. I wanted to be with you."

Cindy had come in fear for Jack's safety too and was standing right beside them. She heard Shannon say the very words that she had always wanted to say but never did.

Jack was desperately searching for the right words to say as Shannon's eyes began to glaze over. He looked up at Cindy with tears in his eyes, eyes that were asking, "What shall I say to her?"

Cindy mouthed the words, "Tell her that you love her, Jack. Tell her whatever she wants to hear you say. She has just given up her life to save you." Then she turned and walked away.

Jack turned his attention back to Shannon. Her breath was labored now, but she managed a crimson smile and said, "Jack, I love you so much."

Jack's tears were mingled with Shannon's as he said, "I love you too, Shannon. Will you marry me?"

With her last breath, she smiled weakly and said, "In a heartbeat."

Jack picked up her limp body and carried her to a nearby wagon and laid her down in the bed gently. Turning to one of the other girls who worked in Murdock's Saloon, he instructed, "Take care of her. I've got a score to settle with someone!"

Jack wasn't thinking of Cindy or himself or anything except settling the score for Shannon. Rusty had beaten her up, and now he had helped murder her. Jack ran and leaped into the saddle of a horse that was nearby and raked his spurs across its flanks. The horse took off, leaving a shower of dirt and rocks three feet in the air.

Rusty only had an hour's head start on him. If Jack kept moving at a brisk pace, it wouldn't take long to catch him. Jack wished he was riding his own horse because the big appaloosa was very fast and had lots of endurance. But the grulla that he had jumped on seemed to be a good choice. You could never go wrong by choosing a mustang. Jack kept hot on Rusty's trail, making good time because the trail was only about an hour old and he didn't have to dismount to examine the trail. However, he couldn't travel as fast as Rusty because he wasn't in Jack's sight and he didn't want to run into an ambush.

For hours, Jack trailed Rusty. Late in the evening, Jack noticed that the trail was getting easier to follow. It seemed as if Rusty wanted him to catch him. If that was true, then Rusty might just be setting up some kind of trap, so Jack slowed down, moving cautiously.

As time wore on, it seemed clear to Jack where Rusty was headed. For the past hour, they had been following a winding trail that led through the woods. This trail crisscrossed a good-sized stream several times. Jack figured that if he was right about where Rusty was headed, the chase would be over soon because just ahead was a large clearing where he and Rusty used to come and spend a lot of time together when they were growing up. They spent many hours there, practicing their quick draw and target shooting. Leave it to Rusty to pick this place to end the chase and the friendship ... and a life.

Ultimately, Jack came to the clearing, and sure enough, there was Rusty, waiting for him. He spotted the horse before he saw Rusty. The horse was on the far side of the clearing, standing sideways with Rusty on the opposite side so that the horse was between Rusty and himself.

"Hi, Jack. Long time no see."

"Yes. It's been a long time, Rusty."

With Rusty positioned on the other side of his horse, only his head and shoulders was visible above the horse's saddle. Jack could see Rusty's legs and boots by glancing underneath the horse.

"You and Frank caught us by surprise by being ready for us like that."

Jack didn't know what was going to happen next, but he knew that this would be the end of the trail for one of them. He kept watching for some sudden movement or something that would alert him to go into action. He knew he couldn't afford to give Rusty any edge. They'd both always wondered who was the fastest. Now they would soon know.

"I heard the shooting stop. Thought it was over, but then I heard another shot. Sounded like a rifle."

"You're right. It was a rifle shot. It came from the water tower. It killed Shannon."

A twinge of regret flashed across Rusty's face. "Sorry about your whore. It must have been an accident. That bullet was meant for you. The rifleman was Tom Barker, brother to Jess Barker. Remember, you killed Jess?"

There was silence for a moment. "Why, Rusty? We were friends all our lives. Dan and Martha took us both in and gave us a home!"

Rusty laughed. "They gave *you* a home. They gave *me* a job."

"So this is all about jealousy, Rusty? Why couldn't you have been appreciative of that much?"

"Aw, Jack, it wasn't just that! I been straddling the fence all my life. I can't really say what made me hit the outlaw trail."

Jack heard a faint sound like something falling in the leaves at Rusty's feet. He glanced down and saw bullet casings falling to the ground. Mentally, he counted them: six. There were six bullet casings that fell. Rusty must not have had time to reload one of his pistols since the shooting in town, and now he's getting ready to make his play. Jack wasn't afraid to shoot it out with Rusty, but he wanted to learn as much as he could about why Rusty, being a longtime friend, would want to hurt him, much less kill him, so he wasn't in any hurry to start the gunplay.

"Why did you get involved with Jess Barker and that gang?"

"I don't know, Jack. I guess I was looking for a change, some excitement."

"Did you really mean to kill me, Rusty?"

"No. I just rode into town with the gang to see what would happen. Otherwise, I wouldn't have left before the shooting was over. But enough questions, Jack. It's time to get the ball rolling."

"One last question."

"Okay. Say on."

"Why did you pick this place to shoot it out? If you had kept going, you might have given me the slip. No telling how long you could have lasted."

Without hesitating, Rusty answered, "I'm already tired of being on the dodge. I hate looking over my shoulder all the time. I ... miss having friends. And I knew that someday someone would put a bullet in my hide or I would stretch a rope. So I decided I'd shoot it out with you. Maybe you'd win and I could die in peace." Rusty grinned and said, "But we both know that I'm faster than you, so that ain't gonna happen."

There was another silence. Then Rusty said, "Enough talk. I'm going to step out from around this horse. Then, anytime you're ready, go for it."

Rusty stepped out from behind the horse, hands down but in the ready position. "Okay, Jack. This time, it's for real, so make your play."

Despite the urge to kill Rusty for Shannon's sake and all the other things he'd done, Jack was hesitant to draw against him. "This is your song, so you start the dance."

Still grinning, Rusty held out his left hand. "When this bullet hits the ground—."

He never finished the sentence. Instead, he opened his fingers and the bullet fell. It seemed like an eternity to Jack before the bullet stopped falling. He saw Rusty's right hand flash down toward his gun and saw the gun come up and his finger tighten on the trigger. Then he was aware of his own Colt in his hand and felt his finger tighten around its trigger. He felt the gun buck in his hand, but he only heard one roar, as only one bullet was fired. Then he watched as Rusty staggered and saw him clutching at his chest. Blood began to ooze out between his fingers as he fell on his knees and then to the ground. Jack holstered his Colt and walked over to where Rusty lay. He was bleeding from the hole in his chest and from the mouth.

Amazingly, Rusty looked up at Jack and said, "I ... beat you to the draw ... I always knew I was faster ... than you."

Despite everything, Jack still had compassion for Rusty. He knelt down beside him. "Is there anything I can do for you?"

"Yes. You can admit that I am faster than you!"

"Rusty, even if your gun hadn't jammed, it would've still ended up like this. I beat *you* to the draw."

"No. My gun ... never jammed. Jack, I love you like the brother I never had. I would never draw against you ... to kill you."

"That's absurd, Rusty. I saw you draw as fast as you could. And I saw you pull the trigger."

"No, Jack. My gun is empty. I wouldn't … shoot you."

Jack couldn't believe what he was hearing. "I don't believe it!"

Rusty managed a weak grin. "Check my … gun."

Jack picked up Rusty's gun and spun the cylinder. Then he whispered, "Six empty chambers." Then a picture flashed back in his mind. In the picture, he saw Rusty reloading his gun. No. He wasn't *reloading*. He was *unloading* it.

"Why would you draw down on me with an unloaded gun?"

"I already told you, Jack. I was tired of running, tired of … living. I'd rather die by your gun than by the gun of an enemy. And I wanted to prove to you that I was faster than you. If my gun would've had a bullet in it, you'd be dead right now."

Jack knew that *he* had been a hair faster, but somehow, it didn't matter now.

"Okay, Rusty. You were faster than me."

Rusty grinned and squeezed Jack's arm. "You're … damned right … I was faster than you." He stiffened and went limp.

Jack put his hand on Rusty's forehead and moved it slowly down across his face, closing his eyelids. Then he said a prayer for his friend.

He didn't want the townspeople pointing their fingers and laughing at Rusty's dead body, so he waited 'till way after dark to take him into town. He rode up to the back of the jail, dismounted, and tied the horses. Then he went around the jail and walked in by the front door. Frank acted as if he was finishing some paperwork, but Jack could tell that he had been waiting for him.

"You got him, huh?"

"Yes. I got him."

"Dead?"

"Yep. No one would ever bring Rusty Warren in alive."

They sat down and had a cup of coffee while Jack told Frank how it all happened. After a minute, he said, "I guess Rusty wasn't *all* bad after all."

Frank shook his head in agreement. "I suppose not." After discussing it, Frank agreed to allow Jack to take Rusty out of town and bury him.

They both agreed that it would have to be tonight.

"That way," Frank said, "he'll be buried before anyone even knows he's dead."

CHAPTER 20

With a heavy heart, Jack rode out of town leading, Rusty's horse. He took his friend back to the place where they had had their shootout, the place where they had spent much time playing as kids. After burying Rusty and marking his grave, Jack said a prayer and spent a few moments just thinking about old times. After that, he decided to go back to town. He had a couple of things to do before he could put all this behind him. He would then go home and tell Dan and Martha what had happened. He was anxious to see Cindy—if she was still at home. However, she too would have to wait.

When Jack got back to town, Frank was still at the jail. They talked again for a few minutes.

Jack yawned while stretching his arms. "I need a few hours sleep. If you don't mind, I'll just sleep here."

The sheriff grinned. "Be my guest."

After Frank left the jail, Jack tossed his war-bag in a corner of a cell, chose a bunk, and stretched out on it. Under different circumstances, it might have been uncomfortable, but he was exhausted and needed rest. Sleep came early, but the morning did too. It seemed to Jack that he only closed his eyes minutes ago.

"Rise and shine!" Frank called. "Coffee's hot, and we got some business to take care of."

Jack sat up and stretched long and hard. "Boy, Frank, you got a damn nice hotel here. Nice, soft beds and coffee served fresh every morning and everything. Next time I'm in town, I'll be sure to stop in. I'm reserving my room right now."

"You're welcome," Frank replied. "Any time you're in town. Just don't expect breakfast in bed or naked ladies."

Jack had slept in his jeans. He pulled on his boots, slipped into his shirt, and buckled his brace of Colts around his waist. He hitched the gun belt up in place, lifted the twin Colts from their holsters, checked them out, and dropped them back in place. The habitual movements were quick and smooth from a lifetime of practice. The Colts slid in and out of the smooth, worn leather with speed and ease like the wink of an eye. The whole ritual took only seconds as Jack moved from his bed and stepped out of the cell where he had been sleeping.

Frank stood and watched in amazement. Then it occurred to him that Jack hadn't even realized what he'd just done. Frank handed him a cup of coffee, "Quite a routine you've got there!"

Taking the coffee, Jack looked at Frank questioningly. "What? Oh, yes. I guess so. But it keeps me alive, Frank! Now what was that business you said that we have to take care of?"

"We need to make out three reports of what happened between you and Rusty. One goes to the city council, one goes in my files, and the third one goes to the *Billings Gazette*."

Jack was surprised. "I thought we were going to keep it quiet for a couple days?"

"We have to make the reports today. If we delay for any length of time, the city council will be all over me like stink on a rotten carcass, and the *Billings Gazette* will make up their version of the story, and you sure don't want that. That's why I gave you the go sign to bury Rusty last night."

"Okay, Frank. You know best. Let's go get it over with."

After writing up the reports, they left Frank's office at the jailhouse and walked over to the *Gazette* newspaper office. The building was small but efficient. The editor-in-chief was a man named William Caldwell. After Frank introduced Jack to Caldwell, he made the announcement.

"Jack here has just reported to me that he has put an end to the five outlaws we've been trying to capture. And while attempting to capture Rusty Warren, our local outlaw, he was forced to shoot him. Rusty is now dead and buried."

William Caldwell was a young but prematurely balding man. He was somewhat paunchy yet still looked to be in fair shape. He appeared to be the typical newsman: white shirt with armbands to keep his sleeves up, a pair of black trousers, and a checkered vest covered with an apron of denim material. He wore spectacles and a visor that partially covered his thinning brown hair.

As he took the papers containing the reports of the six outlaws and Rusty Warren, he raised his left eyebrow at Jack. "So you single-handedly captured Hal Colby, Ralph Simmons, Bill Taggard, Art Cummings, Jess Barker, and Rusty Warren?"

"It's all in the reports," Jack said.

William glanced over the reports quickly. "Yes. I see. Are these reports documented?"

"Yes, sir, by the commanding officer at Fort Washakie, Captain John Goodman. Those papers are in there also."

"And you're Jack Montana, the same man who helped Frank here wipe out those outlaws who claimed to be part of the Dalton gang?"

Jack was getting a little ticked at all the questions. "Yes, I'm Jack Montana, the same Jack Montana!"

Frank could see that Jack didn't like all the questions. "Look, William," he said, "everything's all there. The reports are signed by

Jack and myself, and the captain at Fort Washakie has documented them. If you have further questions after reading this paperwork, feel free to call on me at my office over at the jail."

"Okay, Frank. That's all for now then." William looked at Jack and said, "You are a remarkable man. I admire you, sir."

As they turned to leave William's office, Frank said, "Oh, by the way. I'd appreciate it if you'd wait one day before running this story."

The editor again raised his eyebrow. "I should wait 'till tomorrow because..."

"Because," Frank answered, "I have to go to the town council this afternoon with this."

"Oh. I see. Okay, Frank. I'll hold it until day after tomorrow. Then it hits the street."

Frank thanked William again, and he and Jack left the news office. As they entered the jail again, Frank said, "Well, that does it, Jack. You've fulfilled of your obligation. You can go back to being a cowboy again. Me, I got to get ready for the meeting with the town council."

Jack picked up his war-bag and left the jail. He strolled over to the livery stable to pick up his horses and head out for the Walker Ranch. On the way, he noticed the bank, which caused him to remember the government note for twenty-five hundred dollars that Captain John Goodman had given him. He had packed the note for the reward money in his war-bag, and now he would use that money to pay off the mortgage on the Walker Ranch. He was tempted to go into the bank now and cash in the note, but he was in a hurry to get home, so he abandoned that idea and continued on over to the livery stable.

He paid what he owed for the stabling and feed for the horses, mounted up, and left town. He was riding the appaloosa and leading the roan, and it felt mighty good to be going home. He did a lot of thinking on the long ride. He was thankful for the way things turned out, what with all the fighting and gunplay that he'd been part of during his endeavor to capture the outlaws. He'd come out with hardly a scratch.

Knowing that his obligation was over and done with, Jack felt as if a great weight was lifted off of his shoulders. Rusty had admitted to him that he was the one who had planted Jack's hat in the bank. He'd done it as a joke and thought that if Jack was out of the picture he could have Shannon all to himself. She had become an obsession with him.

Now he was free to go home and try to live a normal life. He didn't know how he would ever manage that without Cindy as his life partner. *Well*, he thought, *a man's got to do the best he can to survive.*

When Jack reached the Walker Ranch and rode up to the corral by the barn, it was noontime. The bunkhouse cook, Ira Hill, had just stepped outside to toss some dishwater out.

When he saw Jack, he stepped back inside the door and yelled, "Hey, look who's here! It's Jack Montana!"

Within five minutes, Hank, Lucas, Leon, and Bob, followed by the rest of the ranch hands, came piling out of the bunkhouse, shaking hands and asking Jack questions.

Then Hank said, "Jack, you better get inside before Martha sees you standing out here jawing with us and comes out here and grabs you by the ear."

Lucas laughed. "She'll do it too, you know!"

"Yeah. You're right," Jack agreed. Then, heading for the house, he said, "I'll see you later, boys."

Jack had been away from home so long that he almost felt like a stranger who should knock on the door before entering. However, he didn't, and as he turned the doorknob and pushed the door open, his heart started pounding, hoping that Cindy would be there.

Cindy was there. She and Dan and Martha were at the table, having lunch. At the opening of the door, they all turned and saw Jack. He noticed Cindy's reaction first. She seemed very excited to see him and started to leap up and run to him, but something held her back.

Martha was the first to rise and run to meet him. Hugging him, she began asking so many questions that she left no opportunity for him to respond. "I'm sorry, Jack. Come and sit down with us. We can talk while we're having lunch."

Jack sat down, and Martha quickly set a plate and utensils before him.

They wanted to know everything that happened while he was gone. He told them the whole story, leaving out the more gory details. Cindy had told Martha and Dan about Shannon getting shot and that she probably saved his life. She hadn't told them, though, that Shannon had said that she loved Jack. Martha asked him about her.

"That woman that got shot... Shannon; how is she, Jack?"

He felt a lump in his throat as he said, "She died. I told Sheriff Morgan to take care of her, and I went after Rusty."

They wanted to know how that had ended. He merely told them that when he caught up with him, Rusty forced him into a shootout, and he had to kill him.

"That's a shame," Dan said. "Actually, Rusty was a good cowboy. He just turned wild somewhere down the road."

"But enough about me," Jack said. "I want to know what's happened around here while I was gone."

Dan cleared his throat. "Well, unless I can come up with some money, I just might lose the ranch. There was a lot of cattle rustling going on while you were gone. Hank says we haven't lost any more cows since we've been putting guards out, but we don't have enough cattle left to make the drive this year. So I don't see how I can come up with the money for the mortgage payment."

Jack was thinking that his government note for twenty-five hundred dollars would probably be enough to pay the mortgage off, but he didn't want to say anything about it until he cashed it into money. He figured that if he told them about it and something went wrong, they would be disappointed. So he'd wait 'till he had the money in his hand. Then he'd go pay the mortgage off and surprise them.

"Well," he said, "I'm sure something will turn up that will enable us to pay the mortgage off."

Later that night after Dan and Martha had retired for the night, Jack and Cindy sat up, talking.

"Jack, did you really love her? Shannon, I mean."

"I don't really know, Cindy. I guess I did in a way, but I think it was more like a brotherly love, like I have for you. I just didn't know what to say to her until you told me to say what she wanted to hear." Jack was shocked by what he had just said. He hadn't meant to imply that he loved Cindy like a sister.

Cindy was completely shaken by what he said too because there was no interpretation necessary. Her role in Jack's life was solely that of a sister. She was shocked and hurt, but she tried to hide it from him. "Well, she deserved to hear you say that you loved her. That was all that was important at the time."

They sat in silence for a while, both feeling a little hurt and saddened because now there was no alternative for them other than to remain in a relationship as brother and sister.

At length, Cindy said, "I guess I'd better get to bed. I have to be in town early in the morning."

"Oh? Why is that?"

"Oh. I thought you knew. I'm going back to Boston tomorrow. I can't do any good here. I'd just be an added burden." She didn't want to go away again. She didn't want to be away from Jack ever, but she didn't know what else to do.

Jack watched her get up and leave the room. He knew what he wanted to say, what he should say, but the words wouldn't come out. Then she was gone.

A melancholy feeling overwhelmed Jack. After a few minutes, he left the house and went to the bunkhouse. He talked to Hank and the men, and then they started a card game. After losing three or four hands straight, he turned in for the night. Maybe things would be better in the morning. Jack lay awake a long time, thinking about Cindy.

Things between them seemed irreparable, but he refused to just give up. *I love her, so I have to find a way.* After a while, he went to sleep.

When Cindy had gotten up to leave the room, she had hesitated at the door, waiting for Jack to say something that would at least give her some hope. When she heard nothing, she went to her room and prepared for bed. A few minutes later, she heard Jack leave the house. Then her mind began to think all kinds of things. *Where did he go? Did he go to the bunkhouse as he usually does, or did he go into town? Why would he be going to town this late at night? The only thing that would be open would be Murdock's Saloon. That was where Shannon used to work. Why would he go there? Was there another woman there who he liked?* Ultimately, still thinking all sorts of negative notions, she drifted off to sleep.

She awoke a few hours later and looked out her bedroom window. A hint of daylight was illuminating the horizon. At first, she thought, *Why don't I hear Mother out there in the kitchen?* Then she remembered that her father wasn't able to get around very well lately, so they sometimes slept late. "Well," she said aloud, "I'll get breakfast this morning. And if Jack comes to the house for breakfast, maybe we'll have another chance to talk before Mother and Father get up to eat and I have to leave for town. Maybe Jack will even drive me."

She had just finished cooking up a skillet of ham and eggs when Jack came into the kitchen. "Good morning, Cindy. Breakfast sure smells good!"

"Sit down and join me, Jack. I cooked enough for all of us."

Jack sat down, and she fixed him a plate and poured them some coffee.

"I'm in kind of a hurry this morning. I have to saddle up and ride into town and then put my horse up at the livery stable. Would you go pick him up for me sometime today?"

"Sure, Cindy, but I'll be glad to hitch up the surrey and drive you into town."

"That would be great. That way I won't have any trouble taking my suitcase."

About that time, Dan and Martha came into the kitchen.

"Sit down," Cindy said cheerfully. "Breakfast is being served."

They sat down, and Cindy fixed a plate for each of them.

Jack could tell by the way that Dan was acting that he was worried, and he knew it was because of the mortgage. He wanted to tell Dan not to worry because he had or was going to have the money to pay off the mortgage. But he held off saying anything because he needed to cash that government note first to make sure nothing could go wrong. He figured the note was good and all that, but he didn't want anything to be made worse by talking about the money and then finding out that, for some reason, he couldn't cash it.

Then Cindy said, "Jack, I have to leave pretty soon now."

Jack scooted his chair back from the table and stood up. "Okay. I'll go get the surrey ready."

Twenty minutes later, they were on their way to town. They rode in silence for a while, and then Jack said, "Damn it Cindy, why are you leaving like this?"

"Because I have commitments in Boston. I have to go."

"Your commitments are here with your parents! They're not only getting old, but also, they're going through a very tough time right now."

Cindy was silent for a while before saying, "Jack, I don't want to leave, but if I go back to my job in Boston, I can help pay the mortgage on the ranch."

"Well," Jack said, "I'm sorry I shouted at you. I didn't think of that. But Dan says the time for payment has run out. The mortgage has to be paid in full within two months."

Neither of them spoke again 'till they got into town. Jack drove to the livery stable and stopped where the stagecoach loaded and unloaded passengers. He got out and helped Cindy out and then got her suitcase for her.

"I guess we're a little early," Jack remarked. "The coach isn't here yet."

"Yes. I suppose so," Cindy answered.

"Well, I have some business to take care of," Jack said. He gave her a hug and said, "Good-bye, Cindy."

Nearly weeping, she managed a weak, "Good-bye."

Reluctantly, he left her there, waiting for the stagecoach, and drove on over to the bank. He had put the government note in his vest pocket earlier this morning. Now he walked into the bank, went up to the teller, and produced the note.

"I'd like to cash this government note," he said.

The teller told him to wait a minute. He had to ask the bank manager about it. Jack became nervous, but he refused to let negative thoughts overwhelm him. After a few minutes, the teller came back with the bank manager.

Jack's heart sank. *What could be wrong?* he thought.

"Ha. Yes, Mister Montana," he said as he looked at the note. "We don't get many of these around here, especially for this amount of money. Do you have identification?"

Jack produced the correct identification, and the bank manager told the teller to give him the twenty-five hundred dollars. He then asked Jack to sign the note. He signed it, and the teller counted out twenty-five hundred dollars.

Not liking to see that much money leave his bank, the manager said, "Mister Montana, we have some very good investment programs here if you would be interested."

Jack smiled, "As a matter of fact, I already have an *investment* in mind."

"Oh? What might that be?" The bank manager asked.

"I aim to pay off the mortgage for the Walker Ranch completely. I believe it's eighteen hundred dollars."

Jack knew that that was the correct amount because Sheriff Morgan had told him so.

"Why, yes, I remember Mister Walker making that loan, and you're right about the amount. Except for the interest, of course. If you want, I can have the papers ready for you to sign in a couple of hours."

"Good," Jack said. "I'll be back in a couple of hours."

Jack walked out of the bank a happy man. Now he would be able to repay Dan and Martha for all that they had done for him. He could pay off the mortgage on the ranch and have money left over. He could invest in more cattle to build the ranch back up.

As he stood on the sidewalk in front of the bank, he was thinking, *There is only one thing that could make me happier.* He looked over at the livery stable. The stagecoach had not arrived yet. Suddenly, he knew what to do to make him the happiest man in the world. He got into the surrey and drove over to the livery stable. He stopped the horses right in front of Cindy, jumped out and grabbed her suitcase, and threw it in the back of the buggy. He walked back over to her, picked her up, and set her on the seat in the vehicle. He climbed in next to her, took up the reigns, and clucked to the team.

The touch of his hand sent shivers of emotion through her. It didn't matter if he was crazy or not. If he wanted her to go with him, she would go. By the time she got settled in the seat, he was slapping the horses with the reins. He turned the surrey around so fast that it almost turned over.

"What are you doing? And where are we going?" she demanded.

Jack wasn't sure if this was going to work or not, but he knew he would go crazy if he didn't do something about their relationship. "We're going to get married. Oh. By the way, will you marry me?"

Laughing and crying at the same time, she threw her arms around him. "Yes! Yes, I will marry you!"

Jack dropped the reins, and they began to kiss and hug each other. The horses were running at a fast gallop, and before they knew it, they were out of town. Soon, the horses slowed down and then stopped.

Cindy was excited, but she said, "I'll marry you, Jack Montana, even if we're dirt poor and we have to live out in the woods."

"We don't have to worry about where we're going to live, Cindy, because we're going to pay off the mortgage on the ranch and build us a brand new home right there on your Dad's range."

Between breaths, Cindy added, "Remember, Jack, it's our land too."

Jack turned the team around and headed back for town. "Yes. I remember about it being our land too, Cindy." Jack grinned and said, "Right now, I'm thinking about the fine Christian home I'm going to build for us and how my son isn't going to live by no gun. No, sir. He is going to be a preacher."